EX-LAWMAN

Could tell Carlton was getting hotter by the second when he said, "No point talkin' 'bout this . . . Gotta come on back to Fort Smith with us."

John Henry shook his shaggy, unkempt head. A sharp edge crept into his voice. "Ain't gonna happen, boys. Might as well make up your minds to it. Y'all made the trip down here to Texas for nothin'. Ain't goin' back to sit in the dungeon under Fort Smith's courthouse, then get my neck snapped by one of Maledon's pieces of oiled Kentucky hemp."

"Put your weapons aside, John, and come along with us," I said. "God as my witness, I'll personally go to Judge Parker and plead for your life. All of us will. Guarantee it."

Tinge of deadly finality in his voice when our previous friend said, "Not today, Tilden . . ."

Praise for
J. LEE BUTTS

"A writer who can tell a great adventure story with authority and wit."
—John S. McCord, author of the Baynes Clan novels

"*Lawdog* should assume its rightful place beside other Western classics."
—Peter Brandvold, author of *Rogue Lawman*

"*Lawdog* has it all. I couldn't put it down."
—Jack Ballas, author of *A Town Afraid*

"J. Lee Butts is one fine Western writer whose stories have a patina of humor, nonstop action . . . and a strong sense of place."
—*Roundup Magazine*

D1012143

Berkley titles by J. Lee Butts

WRITTEN IN BLOOD
NATE COFFIN'S REVENGE
AMBUSHED
BAD BLOOD
A BAD DAY TO DIE
BROTHERHOOD OF BLOOD
HELL IN THE NATIONS
LAWDOG

WRITTEN IN BLOOD

THE FURTHER EXPLOITS OF HAYDEN TILDEN

J. LEE BUTTS

BERKLEY BOOKS, NEW YORK

THE BERKLEY PUBLISHING GROUP
Published by the Penguin Group
Penguin Group (USA) Inc.
375 Hudson Street, New York, New York 10014, USA
Penguin Group (Canada), 90 Eglinton Avenue East, Suite 700, Toronto, Ontario M4P 2Y3, Canada
(a division of Pearson Penguin Canada Inc.)
Penguin Books Ltd., 80 Strand, London WC2R 0RL, England
Penguin Group Ireland, 25 St. Stephen's Green, Dublin 2, Ireland (a division of Penguin Books Ltd.)
Penguin Group (Australia), 250 Camberwell Road, Camberwell, Victoria 3124, Australia
(a division of Pearson Australia Group Pty. Ltd.)
Penguin Books India Pvt. Ltd., 11 Community Centre, Panchsheel Park, New Delhi—110 017, India
Penguin Group (NZ), 67 Apollo Drive, Rosedale, North Shore 0632, New Zealand
(a division of Pearson New Zealand Ltd.)
Penguin Books (South Africa) (Pty.) Ltd., 24 Sturdee Avenue, Rosebank, Johannesburg 2196,
South Africa

Penguin Books Ltd., Registered Offices: 80 Strand, London WC2R 0RL, England

This is a work of fiction. Names, characters, places, and incidents either are the product of the author's imagination or are used fictitiously, and any resemblance to actual persons, living or dead, business establishments, events, or locales is entirely coincidental.

WRITTEN IN BLOOD

A Berkley Book / published by arrangement with the author

PRINTING HISTORY
Berkley edition / February 2009

ISBN: 978-0-425-22630-8

PRINTED IN THE UNITED STATES OF AMERICA

10   9   8   7   6   5   4   3   2   1

For my dear wife Carol:
She's still on the horse with me;

and

Red Shuttleworth,
my good friend and self-professed biggest fan.

ACKNOWLEDGMENTS

Should I live to be a hundred, I'll never be able to thank Kimberly Lionetti enough for her untiring efforts on my behalf. Every writer needs someone like her on their side. Special thanks, once again, to Linda McKinley. Don't know what I'd do without her advice, friendship, and wondrous skills as a reader and editor. And a special bow to my buddy Red Shuttleworth for providing me with the idea for this tale.

"It is a good thing to escape from death, but it is not great pleasure to bring death to a friend."

—Sophocles, *Antigone*

". . . the death of a dear friend, would go near to make a man look sad."

—Shakespeare, *A Midsummer Night's Dream*

"A friend is long sought, hardly found, and with difficulty kept."

—St. Jerome, Letter 1

PROLOGUE

MIDDLE OF LAST week, spring finally arrived at the Rolling Hills Home for the Aged here in Little Rock. Season came in real wet this time around. When the sun managed to slice through rain-saturated clouds and show its fiery face, my Lord, but the result was something glorious to behold. Turned every growing thing available for view so green, came nigh on to bringing pain to a body's eyes just to take a squint-eyed peek.

Big ole bush of pink azaleas bloomed right under the window of my room. Flowers smell mighty good on a cool night breeze. Put me in mind of a patch of the shrubs my wife Elizabeth once planted all around the front porch of our place on the bluff overlooking the Arkansas River north of Fort Smith. Beautiful gal of mine sure worked hard keeping those flowers alive.

Rolling Hills' chief nurse, the redoubtable Leona Wild-bank, loves this time a year almost as much as all the ole broke-down folks living here. Hell, she's happier than a two-tailed puppy to see winter take a hike. Strapping female likes to count the noses of all us shambling old geezers what made it through the icy fingers of winter one more time.

Big ole raw-boned gal just can't wait to have the other staff members under her iron-fisted command sock all the aged gomers as can't perambulate any longer into a wheelchair and roll them out onto the sunporch. Ceiling fans and potted plants make the spot a right pleasant place to hang out, leastways until full-bore, blazing summertime comes along. July in this part of the country gets hotter than a jug full of red ants. Blistering heat has an inclination to send everybody back inside on the prowl for a shadier, cooler spot.

'Course I don't need no wheelchair yet. Still shuffle around pretty good for a man that's damn near ninety years old. Most folks my age, and loads a lot younger, are already in the ground, or slumped in a chair somewhere slobbering on themselves and pissing their pants.

Somehow the Good Lord helps keep me cranking along. And since I'm gifted with something akin to reasonable health and mobility, me and my twenty-five-pound, yellow-striped tomcat, General Black Jack Pershing, make it a point to get ourselves out of bed bright and early. That way we can beat all the other old farts to our preferred corner spot in the solarium. Have our lunch out there amongst the plants. Sometimes we even dawdle around till the sun starts going down.

My very own personal caretaker, little gal named Heddy McDonald, came cruising by looking for us late one afternoon of recent. She works the second shift. Girl bears a striking resemblance to that astonishingly beautiful movie star of a similar name—Hedy Lamarr. And she looks damned fine in one a them white nurse's getups. Swear 'fore Jesus, she's got a caboose that I could spend days just a-watchin' move away from me. Gal stirs feelings in my pants young folks claim us old men ain't supposed to even have. Sweet mother of pearl, but that's a bunch a bilious hooey. Shit, might be older'n rocks layin' on the bottom of the Red River, but I ain't dead—leastways not yet, by God.

Anyhow, Heddy found me and the cat in our favorite, overstuffed, corner chair trying to sneak a smoke after all the other old codgers give it up and got their leathery old asses wheeled back to their individual cells. Hell, they'd already damn near ruined the day with their endless coughing, hacking, wheezing, farting, bellyaching, and complaining anyway. Truth be told, me and Black Jack weren't all that pained to see the whole bunch of them vacate the premises.

My friend Franklin J. Lightfoot Jr., staff writer at the *Arkansas Gazette*, who went and made me semifamous with his article named *LAWDOG*, had recently passed through for a visit. Brought me a Cuban cigar called a *corona gorda*. Big sucker looked like a stick of honest-to-God, country-stuffed bologna—kind you can't even buy anymore.

Took a spell of huffing and puffing to get the beast lit, but damn that big booger sure tasted good. Was right in the middle of enjoying the hell out of Lightfoot's gift when Heddy breezed up.

'Course she went and did her indignant nurse's dance soon as she spotted the stogie. Hovered over me, shook a scarlet-nailed finger in my face, and hissed, "Mr. Tilden, you know full well that if Mrs. Wildbank catches you with that awful, stinky thing hangin' out of your mouth, she'll have a blue-eyed hissy fit right here. Put a mound of bumps on your head and probably mine as well."

Black Jack rolled over in my lap and showed me his furry belly. Scratched him while I took another satisfying drag on my see-gar. Blew out a blue-gray ring the size of a wagon wheel, then said, "Come on now, Heddy, you know damn well that a good see-gar's the only vice I'm still able to indulge in. Poor older-than-dirt women in this asylum for the decrepit won't have nothin' to do with a man. Sure as hell cain't interest none of the gals your age in a little of the old slap and tickle."

Rared back on her heels and squinted at me like she might slap my face. "Your opinions on *see-gars* and Rolling Hills' female residents just don't matter one whit," she snapped, and then snatched that sweet-smelling, half-finished stogie out of my mouth. Damn near cried when she stubbed it out in the damp soil of a potted palm I'd tried my best to hide behind.

"Aw, jeeze, girl, now why'd you go and do that?" I groaned. "That was an honest-to-God Cuban see-gar, for cryin' out loud. You got any idea how good Cuban see-gars are? They're rolled on the sweaty, silken thighs of beautiful Cuban senoritas. Makes my mouth water just thinking about how one a them beauties comes to life."

Made a hurried attempt to fish whatever remained of the stogie from the soggy dirt. Figured I might be able to indulge some other time, but she placed an authoritative hand on my shoulder, squeezed, and said, "Stop worrying about that stinky thing and listen, please."

Leaned back in my chair, but kept a covetous eye on the plant. Said, "I'm listenin'. Honest."

"I'm going out of town for a few days and won't be back until next Monday at the very earliest."

Glanced up at the raven-haired beauty. Really touched my shriveled-up, leathery ole heart when I realized she truly looked a mite concerned. "Now why would you want to go and do a thing like that?" I asked. "Much as decrepit ole fogies like me need your God-given talents and kind attention. Bet the ranch they's gonna be a lot a whinin' and bitchin' while you're gone."

She gave her neck a coquettish twist and gifted me with an appreciative smile. "Most kind of you, Mr. Tilden. But, truth be told, my husband's mother passed away yesterday.

4

We've got to drive over to Hot Springs for the funeral to-morrow. Visit with the bereaved family for a day or two. Not exactly the way I'd like to spend time in Hot Springs, but the trip can't be avoided."

Reached out and took her beautiful little hand in mine. Girl's paw was like a block of ice. "Oh. Well, I'm right sorry to hear the sad news, darlin'. Right sorry indeed."

Odd thing happened to her smile. Corners of her ruby-colored lips kind of twisted down at the corners and she stared off into the distance as though distracted for a moment. "Well, no need to get yourself all that concerned. Couldn't stand the hateful ole bat myself. Just being in the same room with her was usually more than I could take. She had a way of setting my teeth on edge every time we got within a hundred feet of one another."

"Uh-huh," I grunted, then let go of the cute little gal's paw and went back to scratching the cat. "Mothers-in-law can sometimes have that effect. 'Course I never had to suffer with the problem myself. But, if my former law-dog memory serves, it's still against the law to kill 'em, I suspect."

She jammed her fists against a pair of shapely hips. "Yes, still can't kill 'em. And yes, they can be a royal pain in the rump. But I didn't hunt you up this afternoon to talk about my recently departed mother-in-law."

"Well, ain't no point tellin' me 'bout Jo Ellen House neither, if that's what you ferreted me out for, girl. Hell, I heard them snake-bellied, body-stealin' sons a bitches come gather her poor, ole, limp corpse up last night."

"Oh, Jesus."

"Yeah. Uh-huh. Know you caretakin'-type folks try and hustle all the dead ones out late of a night so as no one gets upset 'bout their passin' and all. But, Hell's bells, Heddy, I don't sleep well, and you know better'n anybody around this haven for used-up, antique people that my hearing is sharper now than it was sixty year ago."

She patted my arm. "You heard everything, I take it?"

"Why, hell, yes. Jo Ellen was serving out her final days in the room right next to mine. Just biding her time and waitin' for God to show up. Always been real quiet over in her direction. 'Sides, ever time that pair of four-eyed trolls in the squeaky white shoes show up, I know some poor soul's done gone to meet his or her Maker. Them body-snatchin' hobgoblins try to be quiet, but I can always hear 'em scurryin' around like sneaky cockroaches when some-one passes on to their long-awaited, heavenly re-ward."

"You didn't get out of the bed and look, did you?"

"'Course I did. I'm a former lawman. My life's always been lookin'. Sniffin' out whatever'n hell's goin' on. What'd you expect? Ghoulish, dead-eyed bastards had Jo Ellen on one a them wobble-wheeled gurneys what makes a helluva racket. Damned thing sounds like somebody's beatin' hell outta the floor with the big end of a snooker stick."

"God Almighty. I had hoped you'd be asleep."

"Yeah, well, just keep on hoping. Jo Ellen 'uz all wrapped up in a sheet like one of them Egyptian mummies. Only thing I could see when I took a peek through a crack in my partially open door was the poor woman's wrinkled, bloodless face. But I have to admit, she looked right peace-ful. Pale, but peaceful. Had a smile on her lips. Almost like she'd been kissed by an angel or somethin'."

Heddy smiled. Reached down and patted the back of my hand. "How poetic, Mr. Tilden. Kissed by an angel. Quite accurate actually."

"Yeah. But after I dropped off to sleep and woke up a time or two, went to thinkin' as how maybe I'd gone and dreamed it all. Us old buggers have strange dreams, you know, girl."

"I've heard as much from you on a number of occasions before, Mr. Tilden."

"Yeah, well, some of us even see ghosts now and

again—more and more often for me lately. I've had visits recently from folks been dead nigh on fifty year. Got to figurin' as how maybe what I'd seen was just a buncha ghosts messin' around in the hall. But when I walked by Jo Ellen's empty room this mornin', knew for certain as how what I'd observed weren't no nighttime vision of unearthly doin's. No, sir. Poor ole gal had died sure 'nuff."

"Dear God. Well, I'm truly sorry you had to see Mrs. House taken away like that. Even so, informing you about the poor lady's passing is not what I came for either."

She turned and made a come-on-over-here motion with one hand. Young feller dressed in one a them baggy, puke-green, hospital worker's outfits strolled up. He nodded and flashed a mouth crammed full of the finest-looking teeth I'd ever seen. God as my witness, that boy had the kind of choppers made it look like he could bite a chunk out of a blacksmith's favorite anvil and spit horseshoe nails.

But, Lord, Lord, Lord, that wasn't the half of it. Sweet bleeding Jesus, damned near fell outta my chair when I gave him a second eyeballin'. Kid looked so much like John Henry Slate, I could barely catch my breath for what seemed like a dragging eternity. For several seconds there, that fresh-faced youngster actually scared the bejabberous hell out of me.

Honest to God, that boy stirred me up to the point where I went to grabbing at my hip for one of the Colt pistols I hadn't carried in more than twenty year. Way I figure it, if'n I'd a had a gun at that exact moment, would've drilled him right on the spot sure as little white mushrooms grow on big steaming piles of horse manure. Good thing Heddy'd gone and confiscated my cigar, too, or I'd a probably choked slap to death on the ax-handle-sized son of a bitch.

Heddy, being a perceptive young woman, quickly detected the stricken, somewhat panicked look on my face.

She bent over, patted my wrist again, slapped me on the back a time or two like she thought maybe I might be choking, and then said, "You okay, Mr. Tilden?"

Nodded, then kinda grunted, "Yeah. Yeah, darlin'. I guess so. Just got somethin' of a surprise when this young feller showed up. Bears a right striking resemblance to a man I knew back when I 'uz chasin' thieves and killers out in the Indian country for Hanging Judge Isaac Parker."

She waved at the boy as though presenting something akin to royalty and said, "Well, Mr. Tilden, this is Royce Turberville. Royce is a recent honor graduate from the University of Arkansas Nursing School in Fayetteville. The Rolling Hills family of caregivers considers itself most fortunate to have acquired his educated, professional, and very knowledgeable services. He'll attend to all my patients while I'm gone for the next few days." She shook her finger at me again. "Want you to be a good boy while I'm gone. If you're not, I'll certainly hear about it."

Pinched the bridge of my nose, clenched my eyes shut, and groaned. "Heddy," I said, "this is still the year of Our Lord 1948, ain't it?"

Of a sudden, seemed like she'd somehow moved way off and was hovering over me like one of them eggbeater flying machines that can go straight up. But I heard her say, "Why, yes, Hayden, and Mr. Truman is still President of the United States."

Snuck a corner-of-the-eye glance at the handsome, grinning Turberville kid again. Same rugged, broad-shouldered, narrow-hipped shape. Same square-jawed, open, friendly face. Same mane of long, fine, wavy black hair. Something distinctly Indian 'bout the boy. Swear 'fore Jesus, smoldering hazel eyes blinked at me just like John Henry's had back in 1882, or '83, maybe '84, or whenever in the hell it was we first met. Memory ain't worth spit sometimes when it comes to details of the long ago and far away.

Anyhow, in spite of the sunporch's natural warmth, just

snatching a sidewise gander at the kid now and again made a cold, creepy river of chicken flesh run up and down my sweaty back. Ocean of long-smothered memories flooded back into my near calcified brain—memories of blood, betrayal, and death.

Finally, I kind of wiggled a finger at Turberville and said, "You got any relatives from over 'round Fort Smith, son?"

Kid shook his head and looked puzzled. "Not that I'm aware of, Mr. Tilden. Nope. Can't think of any."

"Maybe some folks who settled over 'round Vinita, Oklahoma, 'fore it became a state, or maybe down 'round Fort Worth, Texas?" Had suddenly remembered as how John Henry was rumored to have kept time with an Indian gal before he went and got involved with that witchy woman from Fort Smith. Same one as caused all of us so much heartbreak and death.

Turberville rubbed his neck, shook a shaggy head like a big ole dog with a flea in its ear, then said, "No, sir. Don't think so."

"Ain't got no kin with the last name of Slate, or maybe Henry, by any chance?"

"No, sir. That's all new to me. You think I might look like someone by that name, huh?"

Stared at the boy like one of them biology fellers what studies bugs they've pinned to a piece of cork in the bottom of a glass-topped box. Discombobulated me so much I hopped up—quick as a man of my advanced age can hop—and dumped Black Jack onto the floor. He yowled his displeasure at being so rudely treated, then reached over and swatted my leg to let me know he didn't like it one little bit. Started shuffling toward the hallway and the hoped-for safety of my room. Cat scampered along behind.

Heard Turberville call out, "What's your hurry, Mr. Tilden? Nurse McDonald mentioned as how you were once some kinda famous lawman who worked for that judge that hanged so many men up in Fort Smith—think his name was Parker."

Glanced back his way and muttered, "Yeah, Judge Isaac C. Parker. Helluva man."

Damn near yelling when he continued with, "Heddy says somebody's written articles 'bout you that appeared in the *Arkansas Gazette,* and maybe even a book or two. Thought you might regale an interested party with some of your old horse-manure-and-gun-smoke stories 'bout huntin' for badmen over in the Nations. Bet you could tell some mighty tall tales. Come on back."

Threw a wave over my shoulder and muttered, "Maybe later, sonny. Got somethin' I've gotta do right now. Catch me some other time." Under my breath I added, "Maybe in a year or two, you spooky sonuvabitch."

Trundled on down past the nurses' station, along the hallway of the building's north wing, and finally made it to my room. Pushed my door open so Black Jack could get in ahead of me. Shot a suspicious glance back down the hallway toward the sunporch just to make sure no one had followed. Slipped inside. 'Course I couldn't lock my door. Ain't no damned locks on the doors of this depot for used-up people.

Flopped into the overstuffed, tack-decorated, Moroccan leather recliner I have setting next to my window. Fell into those welcoming cushions like a man on his last, trembling leg. Have a right nice view out that window—better than the one from the sunporch.

See for miles in either direction along the Arkansas River. Sunsets are damned glorious most evenings. Settled my gaze on the spot where I'd cruised out on a paddle wheeler and tossed Carl's ashes to God when he passed away couple a years ago.

Pisses me off no end that I can't smoke in my room. Chief Nurse Leona Wildbank's always prowling around looking for some reason to pounce on rule-breaking ole

scoundrels like me. Sneaky moose of a woman likes to con-
fiscate our cigars, cigarettes, cut-plug tobacco, and such.
Make us toe the line like a bunch of antique criminals, wet-
nosed little kids, or something worse.

She'll take a man's liquor, too, if she can sniff it out.
Well, by God, that's just intolerable. Can't be having such
impertinence from a meddling female. So, I figured out
how to keep a half-pint bottle of bonded jig juice hid 'neath
the padding in the leg rest that pops up when you pull on
the little wooden lever on the side of my recliner.

Got another beaker hid in the base of a big ole lamp
atop my chest of drawers. Then there's a third bottle—the
one stashed up behind a loose ceiling panel. Kinda dangerous trying to stand on the bed to retrieve that particular
jug, but, hell, a man's gotta do what a man's gotta do. And,
oh, yeah, there's a twenty-year-old treasure taped to the
back of the mirror on my dresser. Figure if I've got three or
four different spares squirreled away here and there, meddling woman surely won't be able to find all of them at the
same time.

Even if by some oddity of chance she does, I can always
sneak out to the front desk and dial up Lightfoot. Put in a
request for whatever brand of coffin paint he can get his
hooks on.

May take a day or two, but my scribbling buddy can
slide by on the pretext of another interview, first chance he
gets, and slip me a fresh flask. Hell, a man needs a nip now
and again. Opens up your brain cells and helps a feller ru-
minate. Good for a body's constitution, too. No doubt
about it, pays to have friends on the outside when you need
them.

Sure as hell, and for damned certain, needed a healthy
snort after I met Royce Turberville. Sends a man into a
bunch of deep pondering once he's seen a living, breathing, walking, talking phantom from his past in the flesh.

Guess I'd been nipping at the bottle, napping off now

and again, and thinking the whole dance over for about an hour, maybe more. Sun had dropped low on the horizon, like it was perched on the edge of the world somewhere way off to the west. Happened to glance over in the corner and spot the ghostly presence of Carlton J. Cecil perched on top of my favorite chest of drawers grinning back at me.

Swear 'fore Jesus, that redheaded scamp's misty spirit hadn't aged a day past twenty-five. Flaming shock of stringy, shoulder-length hair jutted from beneath his sweat-stained Stetson. Sporting that droopy moustache he favored back when we chased criminals all over Hell and half of the Indian country for the judge. Grinned at me and went to picking at his fingernails with a big ole bowie knife.

Shook my bottle at the vaporous spirit and said, "Jesus, Carl, done seen what I thought for sure was one unearthly specter today. Now you go and show up. Seems like none a you folks what've done passed over to the other side wanna leave me be more'n a day or two at a stretch."

"Just checkin' in, Hayden. Got somethin' of a shock with that Turberville kid showin' up and all, I 'spect. Amazin' resemblance to John Henry Slate, don't you think? Could be ole John Henry's twin brother, couldn't he? Bet as soon as the kid popped up you had a flood of more'n vivid memories come raging to the surface."

Took another nibbling peck at the bottle. Stared at the liver-spotted backs of my hands for a second, then mumbled, "Sure 'nuff. That he could, Carl. That he could. 'Course you could be Satan in the form of an old friend, too."

The ghost chuckled, then said, "Aw, hell, you know that ain't true. Ever notice how the older you get the more it seems as how everyone you meet reminds you of someone you've already known? And it's usually somebody that's been amongst the dearly departed for nigh on fifty year. Right curious, ain't it?"

"Yeah, Carl, I've noticed. Couple a weeks ago Leona

Wildbank hired a feller to come in and mop the floors. Be damned if he don't look enough like Handsome Harry Tate to be his long-lost great-grandson or something. 'Tween him and the kid who bears such a striking resemblance to John Henry, the whole dance is beginning to make me feel like maybe God just might be a-tryin' to send me a rather pointed message of some kind."

Then, God as my witness, must've dozed off. Snapped awake like a Texas teamster had cracked a whip at the foot of my bed. Carl's smiling ghost had vacated the premises. Suppose his ethereal departure might have been what caused the air to snap, sizzle, smell like burning rope, and ensure my leap back into living consciousness. Then again, maybe my return to pained awareness didn't amount to anything more than the fevered memories of John Henry Slate. Recollections brought on the undeniable realization that my short, brutal acquaintance with John Henry still burdens my soul and remains written in blood across my barely beating heart, even after the passage of so many years.

Whatever the cause, I went back to staring out my window, along the slowly drifting waters of the Arkansas, and finally let my gaze settle on a bank of puffy, white clouds hovering over the whole scene. Not sure whether it was real, or maybe just the mental gyrations caused by the liquor, but those clouds started to move and take on shapes. As God is my witness, the whole bloody tale came back to life right before my unbelieving eyes. Gore-saturated saga spooled out in front of me like the flickering frames of those old moving picture shows they play for us every Wednesday night down in the recreation room. Except this particular stereoscopic lamp show was all too murderously real.

Haunting images in my restless brain told a tale of ghastly slaughter, and of friendship brought on by the vagaries of time and circumstance. They whispered of betrayal and danced like hellish demons across a brain that hurt and made my fingers itch for the comforting feel of easily accessible, walnut-gripped, case-hardened steel tucked in a greased leather holster and strapped high on my hip—always ready for instant, deadly use.

1

"... Shot Deader'n a Petrified Hoe Handle ..."

HERE OF LATE, I've been spending an inordinate amount of my dwindling time on this earth trying to pull the fuzzy curtain draped over my aging brain away from the events of the distant past. As a consequence, I've discovered there are big, honking gaps in the entire fabric of my recollections of everything imaginable.

Even stranger still, for reasons way beyond my less-than-educated understanding, the exact opposite is also true. Seems certain smells now have the uncanny ability to bring on instantaneous and crystal-clear remembrances of events that occurred nearly seventy years ago. Events I'd not so much as thought of, or even tried to think of, in that entire passage of time.

At breakfast the other day, the aroma of fresh-fried bacon took me back to the time me and Carlton J. Cecil and Billy Bird came together as the Brotherhood of Blood and ran them murderous Crooke boys to ground. Thought for the most fleeting of seconds I was back out in the Nations sitting beside a campfire while Carl whipped up a pan of victuals to get us going on our quest to rid the earth of those lethal sons of bitches' infernal shadows.

Thanks to the appearance of Royce Turberville, I can still gaze into my turbulent former life and summon up with unerring precision exactly how John Henry Slate and I came to be acquainted. Our history remains as indelible and as clear as a cut-crystal goblet filled with fresh, icy-cold springwater. Not sure why such a thing can occur, but there it is. On top of all that, I can positively recollect—in detail—the dreadful and unfortunate circumstances that brought our brief, violent friendship to its ultimate, blood-soaked, tragic demise.

See, the whole, heartrending dance started when, a couple of weeks after his twentieth birthday, a benighted half-breed Kiowa feller name of Zeke Blackheart led a gang of other desperadoes that stormed into the Missouri Pacific Railroad's depot at Claremore out in the Indian country. That murderous bunch of whiskey-dipped idiots robbed hell out of the station agent, then pistol-whipped the defenseless man to the floor. Came nigh on to killing him when one of the licks from a gun barrel punched a hole in his skull the size of a nickel just behind his right ear.

My friend Carlton J. Cecil, that red-haired demon with a pistol, slapped his leg with a thick sheaf of telegraph messages as he went over the whole violent tale for anyone within earshot who cared to turn an ear and listen. Nothing like mindless criminal activity to get Carl all hopped up like a banty rooster. And when Carl got the spirit, my God, but it was a sight to behold. Damn near like watching a fire-and-brimstone-breathing preacher at a traveling tent revival. Took everything I could do not to laugh when he went on one of those rips because, hell, that just made him madder.

He got to jumping around, waving his arms and such,

before he yelped, "Well, accordin' to what I've read here, once them gutless bastards finished taking everything the railroad man could offer 'em, Blackheart and his thuggish bunch turned their savage attention on eight or ten blameless citizens awaiting arrival of the next passenger train going south."

"Smells to me like there's a killin' comin'," I said.

"One man, a well-liked local grocer, vociferously objected to having his pockets riffled. And, sure by-God enough, he got his sad self shot deader'n a petrified hoe handle right on the spot for his efforts."

'Course I couldn't do much of anything but shake my head in the face of such barbarity and mutter, "Sweet merciful Father."

"Oh, hell, Hayden, that's only the beginning of this Shakespearean tragedy." He held the papers up, pointed at the top sheet as though reading from it, squinted, then said, "Says here as how several of the traumatized bystanders who witnessed the heartless murder of that grocer feller said Zeke Blackheart was the man who should be held accountable for a cold-blooded deed of pitiless butchery. Others claimed one of his henchmen, a sweet-natured soul identified as Jackson Bowlegs, bore responsibility for the reprehensible act of gratuitous slaughter. Still others maintained that both men took a hand in the witless carnage."

"I remember Bowlegs," I offered. "Got a warrant for his worthless self in my pocket this very instant. He's wanted for a terrible murder down in the Choctaw Nation. White feller, I think. Seems he went and married an Indian gal so he could live out here in the Nations legally. But he got drunk and beat the poor woman to death with an ax handle, if memory serves."

Carl stared at the fistful of telegraph messages again, shook his head like a tired dog, then said, "Whatever the actual truth of the matter might finally prove out to be, Hayden, the killing of that grocer's gonna stick to Blackheart

like a fresh gob of manure sticks to a horse blanket. Soon
as that poor, unarmed gent hit the floor dead, ole Zeke's
appointment with the hangman, or bony-fingered death at
our hands, was a lock-nutted cinch, by God. Unfortunately,
the pickle-brained skunk's descent into murder and mayhem had only just begun."

"Just begun? Jesus, how much worse is this lunacy
gonna get?"

Carl rolled his eyes, then held the wad of papers up like
a lantern used against the dark forces of evil. "Oh, trust me,
Hayden, it's gonna get a lot worse 'fore I finish with tellin'
this yarn of epic outlawry. These ole boys have been on a
crime spree unparalleled in the annals of the U.S. Marshals
Service."

"Well, get on with your tale of criminal madness then.
Might as well hear it all."

No smile on his face when he went back to hacking at
the story like a man possessed. "In a matter of seconds, after the brutality and bloodshed inside the depot, Blackheart
led his yelping gang of thieves and killers out into the
street where they set to indiscriminately firing their pistols
at everything and sundry. That's when our good friend
Deputy Marshal Rogers Kelso just happened onto the scene
of the rampage by accident."

"Kelso? Don't tell me they killed him, too?"

He shook the papers in my face again. "Way I read it
from these here messages, Hayden, Kelso pulled his pistol,
held his badge up so everyone within a hundred yards
could see it, then called for those desperadoes to drop their
weapons and throw up their hands. Poor man fell dead
beneath a hailstorm of hot lead fired into his body by
Blackheart and his entire crew of iniquitous, addlepated dis-
ciples."

"Damnation. Sure as hell didn't need another dead deputy
U.S. marshal. How many does that make this month, four?"

For a second, Carl looked puzzled. Scratched his ear,

then said, "Can't recall the exact figure. One's enough. But you know, just sure as they ain't no icicles hangin' from Hell's front porch, Kelso's bullet-riddled body had scarcely dropped facedown into the dust when Blackheart's entire band of desperadoes jumped on their animals and fogged away from the scene of their crimes, headed southwest. Residents of Claremore said the killers hooted and laughed like a gang of red-eyed, horned imps straight from the bowels of the sulfurous, burning pit as they departed the scene of their nefarious misdeeds."

"Well, by God, that really cuts it, Carl. Rogers Kelso was as fine a member of Judge Parker's cadre of stalwart lawmen as ever took up the badge of a deputy U.S. marshal. People responsible for his death damned sure need to pay heavy for the crime."

"True. Shameful part is, he might still be alive if he'd a got some help. Unfortunately, that first-rate gentleman lay on the depot loading dock and leaked a rudely abbreviated life into a growing pool of hot blood beneath his crumpled body. Poor soul bled out long before anything like serious medical help could arrive on the scene and come to his aid and assistance. As anyone with a brain well knows, a hatful of 255-grain, .45-caliber slugs will do that for a body when they slice through muscle and bone. And especially if one of 'em punches a thumb-sized hole in a person's heart."

"Shot through the heart. Damnation."

"And get this. Barely three hours later, barely twenty miles from their initial foray into violent criminal activity and slaughter, the same band of drunken brigands once again applied the old five-fingered withdrawal slip in an effort to lighten the till of the station agent for the Missouri, Kansas & Texas line in Choteau."

"Blessed Christ on a crutch, Carl, that ain't the end of it?"

"Not even by a damned sight. 'Pears as how Claremore was only the beginning."

"This gets crazier by the minute. Them boys must have something against railroads in general, from the sound of it."

"Yeah. This here wire tells as how under some fearsome duress, a few nervous, reluctant witnesses told the local Light Horse police that none other than Zeke Blackheart himself had personally shot the railroad's representative for no apparent reason whatsoever—other than pure-dee, low-down, scurrilous, evil meanness. A blue whistler from the bandit's Remington .44–40 pistol hit the agent just above the right eye. Splashed all manner of brain, bone, and gore over most of hell and yonder."

"My God."

"Several of them as beheld the unspeakable act claimed that the heavy aroma of bust-head whiskey could be easily detected on every member of that bunch of cold-blooded bastards. One God-fearing Choteau lady loudly proclaimed to investigators as how those thugs who got within ten feet of the group of terrified travelers smelled like they'd been saturated in the kind of giggle juice that would make a jackrabbit rear back on its hind legs and spit in a rattlesnake's eyes."

"If this bunch is loaded up on bust head, ain't no limit to what they might be capable of doing, Carl."

"Well, by God, you oughta have one a those multi-colored, A-rab tents and be readin' palms in a travelin' carnival, Hayden."

"Get on with it, for the love of Pete. Tell it all. Ain't no point holdin' back. Gimme the whole weasel, hair, toenails, and all."

Carl flashed a toothy smile and jumped in with both feet. "'Pears as how two days after murderin' the M.K. & T. station agent and Rogers Kelso, that selfsame pack of slavering, yellow-toothed dogs threw the switch on the Missouri Pacific Flyer about five miles outside Wagoner. Sent the hurtling engine and following cars onto a blind siding and directly into a chain of empty boxcars parked there."

"Sweet merciful Father. Goes a long way to provin' that Blackheart must, beyond any doubt, have a thing about railroads, if you ask me."

"Fortunately, a quick-thinking engineer name of Beauchamp kept the train from derailing, but the wreck still made a hell of a mess. Some folks claimed they heard the thunderous crash two miles away. True or not, the collision turned three of the idle boxcars on the siding into an enormous pile of splintered kindling."

"Can tell from the way your eyes are shining, Carl, that what I've heard so far ain't nowheres near the end of this saga of murder and madness."

"This here might well be studied at some time in the future as the damnedest crime spree I've ever heard tell of, Hayden. See, engineer Beauchamp fell under a heavy curtain of gunfire just as his train slammed into the first of the stationary cars. Once everything had settled out a bit, the robbers jumped on board and snatched the wounded Beauchamp and his fireman out of the bullet-riddled engine cab. Hustled both men down the track to the express car, where they were forced, under threat of death and at gunpoint, to try and talk the messenger into opening the heavily barred doors."

"Be willing to bet everything I own they didn't have any luck with that trick."

"'Course not. And when the railroad's distressed employees' pleading efforts failed, Blackheart, with the assistance of two of his compatriots, set to blasting away at the immobilized express car. Dismayed messenger, a feller named Rufus Smoot, finally opened up for 'em. Ole Zeke hopped into the car, shoved his pistol barrel into Mr. Smoot's ear, and forced the terrified man to give up the contents of the only safe aboard. At the exact same time, a pair of the other thieves strolled though the passenger car, smoker, and sleeper, taking everything they could lay wicked hands on of any value. Beat several of the guiltless travelers insensible with their pistol barrels as well."

"Did the thieves get much?"

"Couple a thousand dollars, near as could be determined."

"That the end of it?"

"Oh, hell, no. Once those evil bastards had possession of all that could be stolen, they rode up and down the tracks firin' their weapons at the still-occupied cars with no regard as to who or what they might hit. Unfortunately for a good woman name of Mrs. Leotis Crump, one of those promiscuously fired bullets caught her in the spine. By the time the badly damaged, shot-to-pieces engine had backed up the bullet-riddled train all the way to Wagoner, Mrs. Crump had slipped over to the other side."

"God almighty. Another viciously murdered innocent whose life was snatched away by the carelessness of men too crazed on cheap panther piss to care. Can't remember a time in my tenure when the Indian Nations have seen such an orgy of criminal mischief. That is the whole animal, ain't it?"

Carl whipped out tobacco and papers and set to rollin' himself a smoke. "Yep. Leastways, far as anyone's able to tell—right now. But, hell, Hayden, you know as well as me that there could be bodies all over the country between each of their bigger crimes. Once a bunch like this gets goin', ain't no tellin' how many good and decent folks might end up dyin'."

2

"... Murderous Doin's Afoot, Ain't They, Marshal Tilden?"

CARL, NATE SWORDS, and I had happened on the complete skinny about the Blackheart gang's mind-boggling spurt of brutal murder and mayhem kinda by accident. We'd stopped over at the Cherokee Nation's damned fine, brick courthouse and jail in Tahlequah. Figured on leavin' a fugitive we'd chanced on, name of Luther Blind Wolf, in the care and custody of the Cherokee Light Horse police.

Luther raped and murdered a kindhearted woman who lived on her own farm over near the tiny community of Ten Killer in the Brushy Mountains. She'd fed the evil sack of scum, given him a job, a place to sleep, and treated him well for the damned little work he did while in her employ. He repaid that good soul's kindness by delivering several crushing blows to her skull with a double-bit ax.

When we caught Blind Wolf, in a thick stand of cane along Ironwood Creek just off the Verdigris River, he still had possession of the dead woman's distinctive palomino pony. Animal had been described to us in the minutest detail by a number of her distraught neighbors.

Well, we dragged the murdering skunk in so the Cherokee courts could decide his fate. Carlton figured as how the rape would probably get ole Luther fifty to a hundred lashes with an iron rod while tied to a tree. He had no doubt the murder would result in his brutal departure from this life at the hands of an Indian executioner. Hard to argue with the simple rightness of my good friend's reasoning.

As dredged up from the foggy bottoms of my swampy brain—way I remember it all—we'd just stepped through the front door of the courthouse, on our way to the hitch rack, with every intent of heading our posse on back to Fort Smith. A Cherokee policeman of our acquaintance caught us about the time we made it to our animals. Chewy Birdsong handed Carl all those copies of the telegraph messages that graphically described the Blackheart band's lethal binge of slaughter, carnage, abuse, and strong-armed robbery. Carl read them silently, then gave me his detailed rendition of the bad news.

Officer Birdsong stood nearby, shook his head, then said, "That M.K. & T. robbery and killing happened 'bout six hours ago, less'n twenty-five miles from where we're a-standin' at this very moment. God-awful, murderous doin's afoot, ain't they, Marshal Tilden?"

Handed the various messages concerning the Blackheart gang's brutish acts back to Chewy after I'd scanned them just to make sure Carl hadn't left anything out. Swept my hat off and wiped a sweaty forehead on my sleeve. "Indeed, Chewy. Yes, indeed. Murderous doin's, for sure. Kind of vile wickedness that's powerful enough to take a decent man's breath away. Bet when this entire bloody tale hits the front pages of all the newspapers here in the Nations and those over in Fort Smith, there's gonna be a serious public outcry for some kind of immediate, and lethal, retribution."

Nate had listened in on the whole story, too. He'd looked over my shoulder and read along to get the official gist of what had occurred. "We goin' after 'em boys, Hayden?" he said. "Just askin' is all. Bein' as how we've already been out in the briars and brambles, and a-livin' by a campfire for nigh on three weeks, I'd just kinda like to get my head right if we ain't gonna point ourselves on back toward Fort Smith."

Motioned in the direction of a slat-seated wooden bench in a shady spot on the boardwalk right next to the courthouse's front door. Said, "Carl, why don't you boys have a seat over yonder. I'm gonna wire Mr. Wilton and Marshal Dell. See what those gents and Judge Parker think of this dance. Might take a spell to get an answer. Y'all take a load off. Roll yourselves a smoke. Take it easy till I have a definitive reply on this one."

Birdsong shoved his hat off and let it dangle down his back on a silver-tipped, leather thong. Shook his head as though he bordered on being too weary to carry on with life, then followed me back inside the courthouse.

Didn't take anywhere near as long as I first expected to get a sharply worded directive on how to handle that particular assignment. My company of lawdogs hadn't even had time to finish their original smokes when I came back out with Mr. Wilton's instructions. Handed his response to Carlton, propped my foot on the arm of the bench, then pulled a panatela from my jacket pocket. Fired a lucifer and stoked the tobacco to life.

By the time I'd inhaled my first puff of the sweet, heavy smoke, Carl passed our most recent communication from Fort Smith back to me, then said, "From what Judge Parker's bailiff says in there, Hayden, 'pears to me like we've been approved for another job."

Nate sat with his elbows on his knees. He picked the

smoking cigarette off his lip, then shot me a scrunch-faced look. "Well, damn," he said, and snatched a stick off the ground at his feet. He scratched around in the dust and said, "Lookin' more'n more like MaryLou West's gonna have to suffer without the pleasure of my company for a spell longer."

Carl poked my knee with his elbow, then slanted a conspiratorial, corner-of-the-eye glance over at Nate. "Suffer? Poor gal ill, Nate? She real sick or somethin'? Undertaker gonna have to warm up his hearse?"

Swords took a puff off his stubby smoke and looked thoughtful. "Well, naw, nothin' like that. Jus', you see, fellers, that affectionate little filly does have a tendency to pine away, not eat, lose weight, and such when she cain't see me on a fairly regular basis. Kinda like a pet dog'll do. Sad. I'm tellin' you, boys, it's really a sad thing to witness."

"Well, now, she wouldn't get so lovesick as to pass away from lack of your frequent company and affection, would she, Nate?"

"Hard to say, Carl. Surely you remember that last time we went out for almost two months a-huntin' for Thurgood Blodgett, don't you?"

"Feller what beat his wife to death with a brand-new bucket a lard 'cause she used too much flour in his biscuits?"

"Yeah, he's the one."

"Hard to be a woman in the Nations, that's for damned sure," I offered.

"Well, when we got back from that rump-burnin' chase, I swear the poor gal had damn near wasted away to a frazzle from lack of my lovin'. Sweet-natured little thang was to the point where I feared she just might blow away with any little half-assed breeze comin' outta the west. Got me to thinkin' as how I just might have to take off and spend some time over in Tennessee or Mississippi somewheres, a-searchin' for her once I got back from our next raid into the Nations."

"Sweet merciful heavens," Carl grunted, then hopped off the bench. "Swear 'fore Jesus, Swords, you're a bigger bullshitter than William Tecumseh Bird ever thought about bein'. And that's sayin' a mouthful. God Almighty, but sweet William could sure 'nuff stack the stuff deep, but he couldn't hold a candle to you. You get to tellin' these tales and I swear me'n Hayden would have a tough time gettin' a notary to certify anything as came outta your mouth."

Pulled a ten-dollar gold piece from my vest pocket. Handed it to Nate, then said, "Take our packhorse and go on over to the mercantile, across the street yonder, and buy us enough in the way of provisions for at least ten more days out on the trail. You know the drill. Me and Carl will wait right here for you."

He hauled his long, stringy-muscled self off the bench, resettled those bone-gripped Colt pistols he wore backward in the Wild Bill fashion, then flipped the ragged butt of his still smoldering cigarette into the dusty street. "Should I get some lemon drops for you, Carl? Know how much you like 'em. Think you're very possibly the only man I've ever met what could live on nothin' but hard candy, bad coffee, and fatback bacon."

"Have the clerk throw some in with whatever else you buy," I said. "Maybe a few sticks of peppermint, too. Never know if we might need it. Now get along with you, Nate. We've got badmen to catch."

He snatched the lead for our pack animal loose and ambled away. Carl waited till he was out of earshot, then said, "We ever gonna tell him about the Brotherhood of Blood, Hayden? Boy's been with us on some pretty hairy cases over the past few months. 'Pears to me it's time we brought him in on what we're actually all about. That is, if the instructions you got back from Mr. Wilton are anything like I expect."

Eased a second telegram out of my pocket and handed it to Carl. He glanced over the sheet and handed it back.

"Well," he said, "anyone who didn't know 'bout the Brotherhood wouldn't come away from reading that and suspect a blessed thing. But it seems damned clear to me. Murder of another one of our comrades in arms musta sure as hell lit a fire under somebody up in Fort Smith. Seems plain as the nose on my face that not a single living soul back there cares whether we bring Blackheart and his bunch in alive or not."

"Been losing one or two deputy marshals a month lately. And that mess with Pink Butcher is still pretty fresh on everyone's mind. Ain't often one man manages to kill a deputy U.S. marshal, three of his posse, put bullets in five other men, and escape. But Butcher sure as hell managed to do it."

"Yeah, and the stalwart Heck Thomas tracked that snake down and killed him deader'n Hell in a Baptist preacher's front parlor."

"Well, we'll put on a show of making a concentrated attempt to bring the Blackheart gang in alive for suitable trial and hanging. If they choose not to come along, then we'll damn sure kill 'em all. Now let's get on over to the mercantile, then hit the trail quick as we can."

Midway of the dusty street, Carl said, "Still didn't answer my question. Gonna bring Nate into the Brotherhood?"

"Let's wait and see how this chase shakes out. No doubt he's a good man to have beside you in a pinch. Almost as good as Billy Bird. And in some ways he's even better. Proved that during our raid down to Fort Worth when we dispatched Maynard Dawson, Charlie Storms, and the Doome brothers. We get done with Blackheart, promise I'll figure out which way to go."

Carl nodded, then said, "Sounds like a good enough plan. But think as how I'll go on ahead and cast my vote right now. I say we tell 'im 'fore we have to get serious with Blackheart and his crew. Just knowin' what we're really a-doin' might make a big difference. 'Course the fact that you'd be payin' him some more wouldn't hurt the man's feelings none either."

"Your vote is duly noted, Carl. But I think I'll wait till the right moment to broach the subject just the same. Brotherhood of Blood ain't the kinda thing you'd want to just mention in passing. Have to look for the right opportunity to bring such a subject up for consideration. Explain just exactly how you and I actually work. Maybe he won't particularly care to hire on as a paid assassin."

"Well, you could be right as rain about that, but I personally doubt it. See the same attributes in Nate I saw in Billy Bird. But however you wanna handle this hair ball suits me right down to the ground, Hayden."

3

"Buster Perkins Shot Him in the Back..."

THE BLACKHEART BUNCH headed south from the scene of their robbery and slaughter near Wagoner. They'd been on the scout for about a day and a half, past that particular foray into heinous wrongdoing, by the time we could pick their tracks out of all the other confused sign working to keep their location a mystery. But once a tracker of Carlton J. Cecil's skill nailed them down, their trail proved more'n easy to follow.

Recall watching Carlton as he squatted over a confused set of tracks along the banks of the Arkansas. Glanced up at me and said, "Sure as hell ain't makin' no real effort to cover the direction they've picked to travel. Stupid buncha idgets might as well be pullin' a grasshopper plow behind 'em." He pointed toward the west side of the river. "'Pears as how they swam across down yonder, Hayden. Bet whatever we can make in re-wards on this raid, they're headed for that den of vipers over at Beehive Creek. More liquor, and maybe even a willing woman waitin' for 'em, if they can get there alive, I'd wager."

Nate Swords grinned and said, "Beehive Creek? That a town, fellers?"

"Not really," Carl said as he climbed back on his mount. "Not even sure you could seriously refer to the spot as a crude settlement. More like a campsite that comes and goes with the phases of the moon. Just a spot for outlaws, gun-runners, and whiskey peddlers to lay their weary heads for the night."

"Place's rougher'n a cobb, Nate," I said.

"Yeah," Carl continued. "And when it's active, a body can gamble, buy the company of a willing woman, and maybe get a bottle of bust-head liquor. That is, if you don't mind gettin' your throat cut whilst you're conductin' your business, doin' the big wiggle, gettin' drunk, or sleepin' the whole dance off."

Sat my big sorrel gelding, Gunpowder, and gazed at the sluggish, muddy river as it churned its relentless way south. No one had seen a drop of rain in that part of Indian country in weeks. Water level of the Arkansas had fallen by several feet. Hadn't been for the recent drought, crossing behind those outlaws might have proven a sight more than a bit problematic. As it stood, though, I figured we'd be on 'em again, like ugly on a caged gorilla, soon as we hit the west bank.

Slapped the reins against Gunpowder's rump, headed him down the rugged slope of the weed-choked bank. Over my shoulder, I said, "Well, boys, let's get on across so we can hurry up and dry out a bit. Make certain our weapons are dry, loaded, and working on the other side. Sure as hell wouldn't wanna show up in a rat's nest like Beehive Creek unprepared."

Took nigh on half a day of rough travel over grassy, scrub-covered country to close in on our objective. The coarse camp's crude hodgepodge of tents and temporary structures squatted along a rutted, dirt track that couldn't be described as a street in the most liberal interpretation of the word. Rough-and-tumble conglomeration of rickety, tin-roofed, board-and-batten, clapboard shacks raggedy tents, false-fronted buildings, and even an actual house or two appeared somewhat less transitory than I could recall from past visits.

The fleeting nature of the rugged village just seemed to me as fairly typical of such quickly established hangouts catering almost exclusively to bandits, card-bending gamblers, rustlers, killers, pickpockets, footpads, and other desperate men on the run from society's hard-handed reach. Any concentration of such stellar citizens also just naturally attracted its share of gunmen, pimps, whores, strong-arm robbers, bootleggers, and other such parasites.

The undeniable fact that liquor sales were strictly prohibited in the Indian Nations didn't prevent anyone who wanted a nip from finding exactly what they desired. Half a dozen or so dance halls and gambling joints haphazardly erected here and there along the dirt track catered to those who *supposedly* brought along their own bottle, jug, or other container of alcoholic brew.

While everyone, including and especially, Judge Isaac C. Parker, decried the act of "introducing spirits" to the Indians, the sad truth remained that catching the scum responsible for the unconscionable act of selling or transporting scamper juice of any kind bordered on the well-nigh impossible. Overlapping jurisdictions between the U.S. Marshals Service and the various law enforcement arms of the Indian Nations tended to water down our effectiveness in such efforts. Even so, nothing stopped us from fining the hell out of violators, or arresting them if the opportunity arose.

We stepped off our animals beneath a gigantic pecan tree on the woodsy fringes of the lethargic rivulet that provided the rough collection of shelters with its colorful name.

Carlton immediately pulled his short-barreled shotgun from its bindings.

"Ain't gonna take no chances, fellers," he said. "I'm loadin' this big-bored blaster up with the heaviest shot I've got. Get into a spittin' contest in this hellhole, I intend on cuttin' through all the horseshit like a hot sickle through dry grass."

Reached back and dragged my scattergun down as well. "I'm with you, Carl. Mighty dangerous territory we've stepped into here. Place just about like this one down in the Kiamichi Mountains, twenty or so miles from La Flore, is where Deputy Marshal Quincy Broadhurst got caught short and ended up dead."

Nate looked surprised. "Damn. Hadn't heard that one. What the hell happened?"

"Buster Perkins shot him in the back when Quincy attempted to cuff Buster's amigo Jefferson Krum. Quincy was trying to get Krum ready for the trip back to Fort Smith and a guaranteed date with hangman George Maledon, a length of oiled Kentucky hemp, and the Gates of Hell gallows."

"Guess a man just cain't be too careful," Nate muttered.

"Ain't that the truth," Carlton said. "Quincy evidently didn't think Buster had murderous intent in him. 'Course his judgment proved a mite faulty. That single lapse of common sense got the man killed deader'n a rotten fence post."

Nate took the hint. Pretty quick, all three of us had a big boomer draped across one of our arms. 'Course we checked over all our various hip pistols and hideout guns as well. As Handsome Harry Tate always liked to say, "A body can never be too careful when you're about to walk into an undeniably dangerous place."

Led our horses along the makeshift thoroughfare toward the largest and busiest-looking establishment we could see. Sign hanging over the bright red swinging doors, which

looked as though someone who'd just put an opium pipe
aside had painted it, proclaimed the joint as the Enterprise
Social Club. Single-pane, double-hung windows decorated
the walls on either side of the batwing doors. Neither window appeared to be level or plumb. Came nigh on to making
a body walk funny just to look at them.

Surprised me that not many of the local riffraff appeared
in evidence at the time. But those soiled doves, cardsharps,
dice-shaving craps-shooting gamblers, gun hounds, and just
plain no-accounts who did happen to be on the street as we
passed turned and stared as though they'd spotted a trio of
walking carriers of some deadly disease.

Typical of the reception us men who rode for Parker
had grown to expect and accept, several gawkers shook
bottles of bootleg scamper juice our direction. Let us know
exactly where we could go and what we could jam up our
backsides as we picked our way toward the Enterprise's
front entrance. To our complete surprise, though, some of
those folks actually seemed glad to see us.

Guess Carlton didn't evaluate the situation the same way
I did. Out of the corner of his mouth, he snarled, "Keep an
unblinkin' eye on 'em, fellers. Ain't a damned one of these
wicked bitches, or sons a bitches, who wouldn't give everthang they've got to see some of us badge-totin' boys cut
down like rabid dogs."

We draped our animals' reins over a rickety hitch rail
out front of a rough-looking tent café right next to the Enterprise. Smell of frying beef, baking biscuits, and cooked
potatoes wafted from the joint's wide-open flap. Didn't
seem to be anyone inside eating.

No alleyways between the buildings or tents. Every
business was pressed cheek by jowl to the next one on both
sides of the near nonexistent street. Some of the concerns
in evidence, other than dance halls and gambling joints, included a barbershop, a small grocery and mercantile, and a
traveling blacksmith operation.

Glanced over at Nate as we stepped onto the Enterprise Social Club's covered veranda. Porch had a crazy lean to it. Whole shebang was constructed of rough-cut pine boards. Timber still leaked gooey, fragrant sap. Most all of the poorly put-up buildings had only been in place a short time. Got me to thinking as how Beehive Creek might be in the midst of a half-assed attempt to go from a coarse, temporary camp devoted to loose women, gambling, and illegal liquor to something along the lines of a semipermanent settlement.

Said, "Watch our backs, Nate. Carl and I'll stroll inside first. See what we can find out. You hear anything as sounds uncommon, come a-runnin'."

To say the Enterprise Social Club didn't amount to much would be giving the place a good bit more in the way of praise than it deserved. Step or two inside the fancy set of swinging doors exposed the iniquitous hangout's true identity. Appearance of permanence proved little more than four inches thick. Back side of the recently constructed front facade amounted to nothing more than a flapping, flimsy, roof-and-wall affair made of canvas.

Pair of two-by-twelve boards atop some empty whiskey barrels on the right side served as something roughly akin to a bar. No liquor in evidence, though. Several battered, circular tables, each surrounded by four or five empty kegs used as chairs, were scattered around the open floor. An ancient upright piano, peppered with numerous bullet holes, stood forlornly abandoned in one corner. Appeared as how someone might have attacked the instrument with an ax as well. Here and yonder, brass spittoons sprouted from the floor like tarnished, blossoming mushrooms.

Only nod toward anything like decorative embellishment amounted to a single framed painting of a nude woman on the back wall. Her ruby-lipped smile invited the passing viewer to crawl onto the couch where she reclined in a most sexually fetching, come-hither manner.

Wizened, stoop-shouldered, sweaty feller wearing a greasy, off-white shirt, faded red garters on his arms, and a bowler hat hopped up from the only occupied table. He sidled over to the far end of the makeshift bar and, right careful-like, placed both hands in front of him as though to indicate he was unarmed. One of his eyes was swelled shut. His lower lip sported a deep, scabbed-over crease that a nervous tongue kept going at.

The three other men at the table turned their cards down, then shifted around on their rough seats as if to get a better view of us. Couple of those boys looked like someone might've thumped them pretty good, too. Tension in the room shot up to a lethal level—leastways on mine and Carl's part.

Caught sight of Carl from the corner of my eye as he moved to a spot along the canvas wall on my left. Jingle of his spurs was the only sound I could hear in a place that seemed to be holding its collective breath. Once he'd got himself settled, Carl nodded to let me know he was ready for just about anything without having to look back my way for directions or approval.

Turned back to the feller in the bowler hat, but before I had a chance to get a word out, he said, "Surprised us, gents. Usually get at least a few minutes' warning when you Fort Smith lawdogs are about to pay us a visit. Got a fair chain of folks for miles around who usually set up the alarm 'fore your kind can go more'n a few feet. Surprised you managed to get in here without everyone in Beehive Creek knowin' you 'uz a-comin'."

"Sorry, but we didn't feel the need to announce our arrival," I said. "You own this establishment, mister?"

For about a second he looked confused. "Why, no. No, I don't. The Enterprise belongs to Mr. Harold McCormick. And to tell the absolute truth, I'm pert sure he'd be damned glad to see you boys if'n he had the wherewithal to be glad about much of anything right now. All I can say personally is thank God you're here. Have to admit I didn't believe I'd ever find myself sayin' such a thing to any lawdog, but there she is."

To say I was stunned doesn't come close to how much he'd flabbergasted me.

Fellers at the poker table all nodded. Then one of them smiled and said, "Yep. We're all damned glad to see you law-bringin' boys."

4

"... Screamin' Like a Gut-Shot Panther..."

SHOT A PUZZLED, suspicious, sidelong glance over at Carlton. He appeared about as shocked as me. Given the circumstances of our being where we found ourselves, and the fact that most of the riffraff who haunt places like Beehive Creek had no use for any lawman—Indian or white—I found myself at a complete loss for words for damn near half a minute.

Mr. Bowler Hat must've perceived my confusion. He bobbled his head up and down. Thought for a second he might break into some kind of demented dance. He gestured toward his friends at the poker table. "My friend's right, fellers. Just ask anyone in the Enterprise. Hell, yes. Tellin' the absolute truth. We're all gladder'n hell you boys showed up. 'Specially after last night's dose of unbridled savagery. Swear 'fore bleedin' Jesus, previous evenin's doin's set a whole new standard of violence—even for a place as lawless as Beehive Creek."

"Well, what the hell happened? Might as well spit it all out, mister. 'Pears you just might be wearin' some of the aftereffects of whatever you're alluding to—what with that damned fine shiner and busted lip you're a-sportin' and all," Carl said.

Feller slipped his bowler hat off to reveal a gashed bump the size of a goose egg on the side of his head that had obviously not scabbed over very well. Looked to me like someone had hit him in the head with a horseshoe hammer, then sliced the bump open with a razor.

He gingerly fingered the bump, then looked at me and said, "'Bout three yesterday afternoon ever one a the businesses you seen when you rode in here was doin' a thrivin' trade. Beehive Creek was a-blowin' and a-goin'. Then a buncha fellers rode up a-shootin' at anythang movin' and raisin' almighty hell. They stormed into the Enterprise. Went to beatin' the stuffin's outta anyone they could lay a fist on. Mr. McCormick tried to stop 'em. Hell, he's a rough ole bird. Tougher'n a sow's snout. Well, two of 'em jumped on 'im. He held his own, till the third one stepped in. 'Tween the three of 'em, they beat hell out of the poor man. Once they got 'im down, one of 'em shot 'im."

Felt like somebody'd slapped me in the face. Spite of that feeling, I relaxed a bit and leaned against the makeshift bar. "You know any of the men who attacked your boss?"

"Oh, I'd seen a couple of 'em in here a time or two. Didn't know but one by name. Big ole boy who answered to the handle of One Cut Petey Mason. I heard him call the jackass what seemed to be their leader Zeke. Leastways, that's what it sounded like. But hell, that didn't occur until several hours after they arrived. By then, they'd beat the bejabberous hell outta me and boxed my ears till they rang like church bells. My hearin' warn't workin' so well after they done that."

He jabbed a finger into one ear and kind of jiggled it around, then added, "Still ringing some."

Feller at the poker table, the one who sported a handle-bar moustache that drooped down onto his shirtfront, perked up and said, "Oscar's right. I knew that 'un named Zeke Blackheart. Kiowa breed. Angriest, most dangerous son of a bitch on the planet when he's drinkin', and mean as a teased diamondback. That gang a his 'un was the drunkest buncha bastards I ever seen. Damned wonder Blackheart didn't let them boys a his do fer us all. But, thank God, guess they took what they wanted. Headed on out. Damned good thing, too. Personally, I was glad to see 'em go 'fore somebody else got shot."

"You say they took something and left. What'd they take?" Carl said.

Mr. Handlebar Moustache shook his head. Tapped a nervous finger on the table. "Took Rachael. That's what they took. Snatched the poor girl up and left."

For a second or so, my trail-weary brain didn't quite grasp what he'd said. "Rachael? They took Rachael. That what you said, mister?"

Moustache, whose position at the card table had kept me from seeing anything but his profile, turned just enough to reveal an ugly, scabbed-over gash down the side of his face. Could tell right then he was having trouble talking. "Yeah. Five of 'em gathered up all the liquor McCormick had on the shelves. Every bottle he owned. Then they grabbed Rachael and stormed outta here. Rachael Little Feather's the gal Mack had workin' the tables. 'Course, she did a bit of business on the side as well—if you get my drift. We all got to thinkin' as how she and McCormick mighta been married so's he could claim to be in the Nations all legal-like. She'd only been around for a short time. They never said for sure one way or t'other, but that's what we all got to figurin'."

"When? What time was it when the Blackheart bunch thundered out of here?" I said.

Feller with the slashed face scratched his stubble-covered

chin. "Oh, musta been sometime 'tween ten and eleven last night. Ain't that about right, Oscar?"

Mr. Bowler Hat bobbled his head in agreement. "Yep. Think McCormick mighta died right then and there if'n them boys hadn't vacated the premises when they did. He'd been laid out in the floor a-bleedin' like a stuck pig for nigh on three hours when Blackheart and One Cut Petey herded Rachael and the rest of that buncha cutthroats back out into the street."

"Didn't leave quiet, I'd bet," Carl said.

"Oh, hell, no. They went to firin' off their pistols at every-thang and sundry again. People was a-squealin'. Runnin' in ever direction tryin' to find someplace safe to hunker down. Heard Rachael a-screamin' like a gut-shot panther, too. Feel right bad 'bout it, but warn't nothing any of us could do for her."

Moustache said, "Once them bastards got mounted, they hoo-rahed the camp pretty good. Look close, Marshals, and you can probably find bullet holes in every wall facing the street. Tell you what, I've been all over the West. Mining camps, railroad camps, cattle towns, railheads, worst of 'em a body can imagine. Ain't never seen nothin' like what happened here last night. Surprisin' to me as how them boys didn't manage to kill nobody 'cause they sure 'nuff gave it one helluva try."

Laid the shotgun over my arm in an effort to let all the cardplaying deacons in the Enterprise know I figured they were telling me the truth. Said, "Where's the McCormick feller you boys keep talkin' 'bout?"

Oscar hooked a thumb toward a slit in the back wall of canvas, then said, "He lives back yonder. Has a bed and stuff. We laid 'im out on his cot as best we could. Been checkin' on him ever since Doc patched him up. Ain't lookin' good, I can tell you that for damned sure. Man makes it through the night, he'll be luckier'n the guy who got gold in change ever time he spent Confederate money."

Carlton let out a snort of disbelief. "Sounds mighty cosmopolitan, by God. Mean to tell us that Beehive Creek has an honest-to-God, for-real sawbones in residence? Find that right hard to believe myself."

Oscar toed at the dust-covered plank floor. He acted like an embarrassed kid who'd been caught taking a peek down his sister's cotton knickers. "Well, he ain't exactly a fer-real medical doctor or nothin'. Leastways, I don't think he is. Served the South right well as a battlefield stretcher bearer, from what I understand. Were a damned fine vet once, too. Then the drink got 'im. Fell on hard times. Ended up in Beehive Creek. Actually, fixed Mr. McCormick up pretty good. Better'n anybody else 'round here coulda done."

Flicked the barrel of my shotgun at Oscar, then said, "Show me." Shot my partner a quick glance. "Keep your eyes open, Carl. Gonna check on the McCormick feller. See how he's doin'."

Followed Oscar through the flapped opening in the back corner of the tent. Rough-cut doorway in the cloth led to a freestanding, makeshift shacklike affair—a single room of about ten by ten. No windows at all. Plank door hung from leather hinges. Damn near passed out when Oscar jerked the complaining door open. Smell of festering, puss-oozing flesh and imminent death was enough to take paint off a New Hampshire barn.

Jerked a faded blue bandanna out of my pocket. Held it over my nose and mouth, then stepped into the dark, dank, foul-smelling room. Nothing much there but an empty, up-turned shipping crate with an idle kerosene lamp atop it. Nearby, a sagging military-surplus cot took up most of the tiny space. A battered steamer trunk occupied a spot of honor at the foot of the folding bed.

McCormick lay draped over the cot like a human blanket. His bootless feet dangled off one end. Would've touched the filthy floor had it not been for the trunk.

Dying man groaned when he heard the noise we made

on entering. His head swiveled our direction. Swollen, bloodshot eyes blinked as he tried mightily to discern who had entered his hellish digs.

I stepped up close enough to the stinking bed to see that the unfortunate, badly wounded man appeared to have been shot at least twice. Either wound had the potential for threatening the poor man's dwindling life. Worst of it was a hole in the chest just under his heart. Amazed me all to hell and gone that the poor goober had managed to stay alive.

McCormick tried to say something, but didn't do any good at it. Couldn't seem to get his mouth around the right words. Made a come-to-me motion with the fingers of a hand he obviously couldn't move.

Oscar hustled forward. Pulled a bucket of water from under the cot. Dipped his employer out some of the liquid, and held it to the fading man's cracked lips. "This feller's a deputy U.S. marshal, Mack," he said. "Been tellin' him all 'bout what happened here last night. Done tole him as how you got shot."

Watched as Oscar leaned closer to McCormick, nodded, then glanced back at me. "He says you gotta go after Rachael." McCormick kept whispering. Oscar leaned down. Listened again. Unintelligible words came between gurgling, blood-soaked breaths. "Says the girl don't deserve misuse by a gang of cutthroats like them as took her." Oscar shook his head, then stood.

"That it?" I said from behind my bandanna.

He pitched the dipper back into the bucket, then snatched his hat off. "Guess it'll have to be. He's deader'n Andy by-God Jackson. Last little bit of talkin' musta took everthang he had left."

Flicked one more quick glance at the dead man, then hustled on back to the somewhat more fragrant climes of the Enterprise's open barroom. Stopped just long enough to ask Oscar, "What's the girl look like? Can you describe her for me?"

He held the bowler hat up and scratched his head with the same hand. Shrugged as though I'd asked him to tell me the distance to the moon—in inches.

"Come on, Oscar. The girl worked here. Might've been McCormick's wife, according to what you boys said earlier. She's only been gone since last night. Surely you remember what she looked like."

"Naw. Not really. Kinda commonplace, if you know what I mean. McCormick took pity on the pathetic creature. Hell, she was just kinda like a stray cat, Deputy."

"Had pointy ears and a long tail?"

"Oh, hell, no. That's not what I meant. Gal just warn't very memorable. Mousy. All-over mousy. Mousy brown hair. Dull mousy eyes. Virtually no figure as I could detect. Besides, all them Indian gals look the same. Can't for the life a me understand what that gang a idgets wanted with 'er. Mean, hell, they's lot better-lookin' whores a-hangin' 'round in every crack and cranny of this place."

Wanted to slap all his teeth out, but restrained myself. Said, "Did anyone bother to notice which way Blackheart and his boys went when they left?"

"Oh, hell, yeah. Headed due west, sure as shootin'. Ridin' fast as good horses could run. But I'd bet they won't get real far."

"Why's that?"

"Carried off every bottle a nose paint McCormick had in stock. Hell, you can see we ain't got nothin' left on our shelves. Sons a bitches took every drop of ours and all they could carry from everyone else in town what had any. Bet by now they're so drunk cain't none of 'em get it up enough to pump poor, mousy little Rachael—even if'n they might want to get a little."

Well, that was enough for me. Had heard all I ever wanted to from Oscar and his bowler hat. Stomped toward the door and motioned for Carl to follow. We made it out to the boardwalk and gathered up Nate.

"What happened, Hayden?" Nate said as he trailed us to our mounts.

"We're headin' west. We'll get as far away from here as we can before dark. Then find us a safe place to bed down. Gotta make sure we're forted up good just in case any of these skunks decide to track us down in the dark and cut our throats."

"We find out which way the Blackheart bunch went?"

"West. Went west, Nate. And from what I've just heard, should be real easy to cut their trail. They're draggin' a woman along with 'em now. I'm hopin' maybe she'll slow 'em down some. Figure they'll be stoppin' every so often to take turns havin' a go at her. That is, if they aren't all too drunk to perform."

Got mounted as quick as we could. In less than an hour, we'd urged our mounts far enough into the rolling, grass-and-scrub-brush-covered countryside that we didn't have to keep looking back to see whether anyone had followed. Didn't take long to realize our quarry had turned south and appeared to be headed in the general direction of Dripping Springs.

Nate took the point. Hour or so before dark, he came hightailing it back up to me and Carl. Snatched his animal to a hopping stop right beside me. Jerked his hat off, then rubbed a sweat-drenched face on the sleeve of his shirt. He shook his head, fixed me with a piercing stare, then said, "Not gonna believe what I found 'bout a mile up ahead."

Felt like God had my heart in a tight-fisted grip when I said, "The girl? They killed the girl and left her somewhere up ahead on the trail?"

Swords grimaced, then slapped his hat back on. "Nope, but this might qualify as something worse."

Carl said. "Worse. How could killin' an innocent woman not be any worse than what you found?"

Nate raised one arm and pointed down the gentle slope of a grass-covered hill we'd figured would lead us to a convenient creek and campsite. Could see the tops of several cottonwoods in the deep cut where we'd planned on spending the night.

"Just follow me, boys. And get yourselves prepared. What's a-waitin' for us down there is a real stomach churner. So to speak." He threw a tight-lipped, ironic grin my direction, then muttered, "Yeah, so to speak."

5

"Gutted Me Like a Beached Sunfish..."

COULD HEAR SOMEONE crying and moaning near a hundred feet before we got down to the creek bank. Sounded almost like a hurt dog. We headed our animals down through the tall grass, into a jagged cut in the earth created by a nameless, shallow stream that rippled over a bed of water-polished rocks.

Carl spotted the damaged boy first. He pointed along a meandering trail of blood and drag marks in the sand to the kid's nest, then shook his head in disbelief. God Almighty, but there just ain't much in this world that can prepare a human being for what we found. Worst days of Mr. Lincoln's War of Yankee Aggression against the South might qualify, I suppose. But being as how I was too young to fight at Gettysburg, or any of them other unearthly hell-holes, what we found on that unnamed brook in the Nations appeared about as awful as anything I could have ever imagined. Hated to admit it, but Nate was right. Scene was enough to turn a body's stomach. Immediate taste of coppery flavored bile crept up on the back of my throat.

Fine-looking young feller had settled into a crumpled, sitting position. Could barely make him out, semi-hidden inside a sheltering cavity formed by the massive ground-surface roots of a cottonwood tree hugging the rugged creek bank just a few feet from the undulating water. So quiet you could hear dried leaves clinging to the branches overhead as they whispered their love for the sky on a slight, sultry breeze.

Bed of crackling, wind-desiccated foliage beneath the youngster was drenched in gouts of thick, dried gore. He'd smeared blood on his face as he'd swiped at bugs, or tried to wipe sweat away from his eyes. His appearance would've led even the most inexperienced observer to think someone had attacked the kid with a well-honed bowie knife the size of a Kansas City butcher's meat cleaver. No way to determine, from a distance, where he'd actually been cut first, but sweet, merciful Jesus, that didn't matter.

We drew our animals to a halt some distance from the boy's sheltering tree. The wide, flat, sandy spot appeared to have been used as a campsite by passing travelers for eons. From all outward evidence, the Blackheart gang had camped there for at least a few hours at some point before we showed up. But they'd deserted the camp in a mighty big hurry. Left the poor gutted boy to the whims of nature, or perhaps the kindness of any shocked passerby who happened to have the piss-poor luck to chance his way.

Far as Carl or I could determine, from undisturbed sign left in the soft soil and sand by Blackheart and his bunch, the feller denned up next to the tree had received a mortal wound near the abandoned camp's ancient fire site. Then he'd stumbled, dropped to his knees, and somehow dragged his pitiable, dying ass to the place where he'd finally snuggled down between the tree's roots.

Stepped off my mount and strolled up for a closer look. Maybe three or four feet away, I squatted, picked up a twig, and scratched around in the sand. Poor little feller, who couldn't have yet seen sixteen years, still struggled with both blood-saturated hands to stop his oozing innards from dribbling out onto his lap and thence onto the ground. Took everything I could do to keep what I'd eaten that day tamped down so it wouldn't come up in a gush of odiferous puke.

Trickling rivulets of bright red, along with bubble-shaped lumps of grayish purple gut, oozed from between his grasping fingers. The blood had quickly coagulated into a thick, gooey, blackish brown coating on everything from his breastbone to his knees. The barely stanched flow of his leaking life had already soaked the front of a black, frayed, hand-me-down suit jacket, the tail of a chambray shirt that'd pretty much been rendered to shreds, and a pair of oft-patched sailcloth pants. Whole damnable mess crawled and seethed with a living carpet of bluebottle flies, shiny black beetles of various sorts, and other bugs I couldn't begin to name.

Obvious to me that the butchered-up feller'd bought the ranch. He just hadn't realized his chips had already been cashed in, or given up on his young life yet. Nothing short of amazing to me that he'd lived long enough for us to find him still amongst the living. Always did surpass all my imaginings, and surprised hell out me, when it came to realizing how long people could cling to a rapidly dwindling hold on this world despite wounds that would normally kill a full-grown buffalo.

Hard to look at him, but I locked my gaze on him and said, "What's your name, son?"

Spasm of terrified agony pulled his cracked lips away from gritted teeth. Kid had a damned fine-looking set of choppers. Red-flecked steam of liquid leaked from one corner of his mouth, along with a froth of thick, yellow spittle.

He blinked coal-black, swollen, bloodshot eyes at me, and attempted to bury himself deeper into the perceived safety of his hidey-hole. A flash of face-twisting, lip-biting pain caused a sharp, ragged intake of air.

Not even sure he could see me when, in a terror-laced, agony-thickened voice, the unfortunate boy gasped, "Glass. Name's Milt Glass."

"Cherokee?"

"Yeah." He grimaced, turned his head away, and coughed. His grasp on the gob of exposed, seeping innards tightened. "Aw, God. It hurts . . . Really hurts. Not . . . sure I can . . . stand it much longer, mister. Tryin' to decide . . . to die or not for hours." An enormous tear formed in the corner of one eye, ran down a filth-spattered cheek, and dropped onto his nasty shoulder.

Carl quietly eased up on one side of me, Nate on the other. Nate couldn't even talk. He took one fleeting glance, made a gagging noise, then couldn't do anything but shake his head between the times he stared at the tree tops or toed at the dirt beneath his feet.

Heard Carl mutter, "Jesus," under his breath. Then, to take his mind off the horror of it all, I suppose, he scratched a lucifer to life on the buckle of his pistol belt. Fired up a hand-rolled cigarette, then flicked the smoking match toward the creek.

Coffin nail dangled from Carl's lips when he squinted and said, "What in the blue-eyed hell happened to you, Milt?"

Kid tried to look up, find whoever had made the inquiry, but couldn't get his head back far enough to see Carl's face. "One Cut Petey Mason. That's . . . what happened to me, mister."

"One Cut Petey sliced your belly open?" I said.

"Yeah. Gutted me . . . like a . . . beached sunfish from outta that creek yonder."

Carl was talking to the ground when he muttered, "Reckon that's why they call him One Cut Petey?"

"Took three . . . four swipes . . . to put me down," Glass said, a tinge of bold and angry pride in his shaky voice. "Carved . . . me up pretty good. Doncha think?"

Turned to Swords. Figured if he had something to occupy his mind, maybe the situation wouldn't be so hard to handle. Said, "Do me a favor, Nate. Get your notebook and a pencil. Think we should record everything this youngster says. If he lives long enough, we'll have him sign it. Even if he don't, a written account of a man's deathbed testimony will prove mighty powerful evidence in court. 'Specially when three deputy U.S. marshals can swear to its authenticity."

Heard Carl mumble, "That is, if we ever get any of 'em whiskey-vicious sons a bitches to court alive."

Nate disappeared for maybe a minute 'fore he came running back. He kneeled down in the sand, licked the tip of his stubby piece of pencil, then said, "Okay, Hayden. Guess I'm as ready as I'm likely to get."

"Write down as much as you can remember of what you heard earlier," I said. "Then we'll get on with some more questions."

Carl leaned over, tapped me on the shoulder, and whispered, "Think we should give this kid some water? Ain't exactly a penetratin' stomach wound. Looks to me like One Cut Petey sliced him across the belly several times with somethin' razor sharp. Opened the kid up like pullin' on a loose thread."

"Can't see any reason why we shouldn't give the boy a drink," I offered under my breath. "Doubt he's gonna last a whole lot longer anyhow. Ain't gonna matter much if he has a bit of liquid in him or not. Could well ease the pain of his passing a mite. If such a thing is even possible."

Carlton retrieved a full canteen from our pack animal. He knelt down beside the slashed-open boy. Dribbled some of the fluid onto the youngster's swollen lips. Barely heard it when the mortally wounded youth said, "Good. Oh, that's . . . really . . . good."

Nate went back to staring at the treetops when he said, "One Cut Petey a friend of yours, Milt?"

Glass coughed. Jerky, convulsive motion of his body caused the kid to cry out as though he'd been cut open a second or third time. He was steadily losing the battle to hold his guts behind the open wound. Looked to me like having one finger out of place would sure enough lead to all his intestines flopping out into his lap.

Beads of sweat popped up on Milt Glass's dirt-smeared brow. They melded together, formed a tiny brook, then coursed down his fuzz-covered cheek and dripped from a tremulous chin. In spite of all his concentrated efforts, couple of chunks of gut the size of doughnuts popped from between twitching fingers.

Nate abandoned his scribbling long enough to cover his mouth with a bandanna and make a half-assed retching sound. Then he turned completely around and squatted with his back to the bloody scene. Must admit I couldn't blame him much for not wanting to look at what One Cut Petey had left of Milt Glass.

Finally, the butchered boy managed to say, "Never . . . even met . . . Petey . . . till I fell in with Zeke, Jackson, and Crawford Starr. They 'uz all friends. Hell, 'uz only a week ago. Didn't . . . know any of 'em . . .'fore then." Burst of talk appeared to take everything out of the boy. His head lolled to one side. Thought for a second he'd gone and passed to the other side right before my eyes.

Whacked him on the foot with my tree twig. Have to admit it surprised me some when he came back around. Thought for sure he'd already woke up shoveling coal in the furnaces of Hell. Anyhow, got him blinking at me and I said, "One Cut. You were tellin' me about One Cut Petey Mason."

Glass groaned. Cast a baleful look down at his leaking

guts. "Petey joined up a few hours . . . after I threw in with 'em. Zeke brought him . . . into camp over on the Verdi-gris . . . week or so ago. Never found . . . how . . . they knew each other."

Nate stayed in place, but still tried his level best to avoid looking at the outlaw's exposed bowels. Over his shoulder, he said, "What'd you two get to fightin' over that he done all this damage to you?"

"That Indian gal. Took from . . . saloon keeper . . . down on Beehive Creek."

Carl perked up when he heard about the girl. "He try to kill her or something, Glass?"

"Or something . . . guess you could say. Humped her ever hour or so. Went to carvin' on her . . . with that big ole bowie knife he carries." The lethally wounded boy coughed. "Water . . . more water. Please."

Carl trickled a few more drops onto Glass's swollen tongue and bruised lips. Boy turned his head away. For almost a minute didn't utter another word. Then, as though he'd simply rested up for a final run at life, he said, "Tried to stop him. Hell, he and them others . . . had already had their way with her . . . till it was makin' me sick. Shit. Didn't feel what he'd . . . done to me at first." Of a sudden, he stopped. His eyes rolled into the back of his head. "Damn . . . sure 'nuff cold today," he mumbled. "Freezin'. Slap freezin'." He groaned, let out a long, sad breath. His eyes snapped wide open like a paper window shade. Relaxed all over. Just went slap limper than a wrung-out bar towel.

Blood-encrusted hands dropped away from the massive wound across his belly. All the viscera he'd been trying to hold back came flooding out like those from a freshly slaughtered steer. Nate must've seen what happened out of the corner of one eye. He gagged, and jumped away from the horrific scene. Staggered to a spot behind a sizable stand of huckleberry bushes. Could hear him retch like there wasn't nothing left to puke up.

Few minutes later, Nate sucked a swallow or two of water from his canteen while we all stood in a circle under a spot of shade offered by the tree. He said, "You know, I've butchered hogs. Cattle. Animals of all sorts for something to eat. Kilt my share of men, too. But boys, there's just something 'bout seein' a human being sliced open like that sets my stomach to churnin' like the wheel on a Mississippi riverboat. Don't think I coulda kept an anvil down—even if I coulda swallowed one."

Carl took a swig from his canteen, spat it out, then wiped damp lips on the sleeve of his shirt. "Know what you mean, Nate. I 'uz havin' lunch in a restaurant a block off the railroad tracks in little Arkansas town of Pine Bluff few years back. Finished my meal. Headed outside to pick my teeth. Standin' there rubbin' my belly and feelin' mighty good 'bout everthang. Noticed the switch engine a-creepin' through town off to my left. Then, as though time somehow slowed down to a crawl, seen this old man comin' my way on t'other side of the tracks. Heard the whistle on the engine blast four, five, maybe six times. Engineer sure set the thing to hootin'."

"Aw, Jesus," Nate groaned. He toed at the ground, then wagged his head back and forth. "Aw, shit, think I see where this tale's a-goin' already."

"Yeah. Poor, old coot musta been deafer'n a rotten hoe handle. People yelled and hollered at him. Whistle kept screechin'. He never even so much as looked up. Stumbled onto the tracks just in time to get hit by the switch. Damned engine was barely moving. 'Course it knocked him down. Engineer got the thing stopped 'fore it rolled completely over the ole feller. Kinda got halfway on top of him."

Nate stared at the treetops again. Shook his head and mumbled, "God Almighty."

Carl was locked into this tale. Wouldn't have quit if a cyclone had blown over, sucked all of us up into the heavens, and dumped us somewhere in Kansas. "Crowd stood around for near an hour. Cussed and discussed what to do 'bout the whole situation. Engine sat there on top a the dead man. Finally, somebody went and made a decision."

"What the hell was there to decide?" Nate grumped.

"Guess they figured it'd take too long to get a crane on site to lift the load off the poor dead bastard. So they just backed 'er up. Big ole cast-iron wheel rolled off his belly. Guts went everwheres. Made a helluva mess." He turned, cast a sad-eyed gaze over at Milt Glass again, then added, "But, shit, bad as that death was, it weren't nothin' compared to this boogered-up glance into the fiery pit."

Only had one shovel between us, so we took turns digging a grave for Milt Glass. Figured we'd put him under the cottonwood tree. Soft soil of the creek bank made the job fairly easy, but it was hotter'n a fresh-forged horseshoe. Helped some that he'd passed so late in the day. Got downright dark 'fore we finally got him under the dirt. Piled as many big rocks on his poor dead ass as we could so the coyotes and such wouldn't dig him up.

Then we all stripped off and sat in the creek. Passed a cake of lye soap around for nigh on to an hour. Soaked ourselves till we'd got all pucker-skinned like we were a thousand years old. Slept like a dead man that night.

Woke up to the aroma of Carl's damned fine cooking. He'd fried up some fatback bacon and half a dozen hen apples. Even had Dutch oven biscuits goin'. Don't, to this very moment, know where those eggs came from. Man did have the talents of a superior scavenger, though. When Nate and I couldn't have found food of any kind in a fully stocked emporium, Carl had the ability to cadge vitals in places that hadn't seen a living human being since the beginnings of time. Amazing and incredibly important talent.

Time the sun got up good, we were running hot on the Blackheart gang's trail again. Whippin' along pretty good till we ran across an affront against nature of such unmitigated evil none of us could believe what we'd laid eyes on.

In truth, though, we smelled the poor bastard 'fore we actually caught sight of him.

Swear 'fore Jesus, just ain't nothing in all of nature like the repellent fragrance of burnt hair and blistered-to-a-state-of-crackling human skin. Whiff of that particular bouquet has the uncommon power to send any feeling man's stomach into churning flip-flops. Bring up a good breakfast faster than bad news travels at a church picnic.

Drew our tired animals up in a grassy, pastoral field near a stand of trees nestled down at the bottom of a shallow ravine. Spot was typical of the wind-and-water-eroded, rolling, scrub-covered landscape for miles in any direction, not far from a branch of the Deep Fork of the Canadian River.

Stood on the edge of a charred, circular site the size of two, maybe three, Concord coaches. Slapped Gunpowder's reins against my leather-gloved palm. Blackened grass no longer smoldered. Concentrated flames appeared to have burned themselves out some hours before we arrived. Hushed, smoky haze had settled over the entire area. Made the centermost section of the spot somewhat difficult to see.

Nate pointed toward the dead center of the ring of burnt grass. Odd, flame-blackened lump moved. Limblike appendage appeared to wave at us. "Sweet, merciful Jesus, Hayden," he said. "I do believe that's a man."

Carlton shook his head, then covered the bottom half of his face with one hand. "Sure as hell don't smell like a man," he said, and blinked back tears.

6

"PLEASE, JUST PULL YOUR PISTOL AND SHOOT ME."

CARL AND I dismounted out along the edge of the flame-blistered patch of what had once been knee-deep big bluestem grass. Held our reins out for Nate, but had to wait for him to take them. He'd fished a bandanna from his pocket, and was tying it over a flushed face. Once he'd finished, the boy looked like a Texas brush popper riding drag on a cattle drive to one of the Kansas railheads, or a Cherokee Outlet stickup artist.

"Ain't no smell on earth as bad as burnt people," he said through the cloth. "Only ten years old when I helped bury six of my cousins what perished in a house fire. Near as could be determined, one a them kids got up durin' the night. Dumped kerosene on a dwindlin' fire. Damned stove exploded. Burnt 'em all up just like Satan had decided to cook 'em for breakfast. Smell from those bodies still lingers around inside my nose. Get anywhere close to another burned human being, and the whole horrid mess comes right back to the surface in a rush of pukey bile I have a helluva time holdin' down."

Pulled the canteen loose from my saddle horn, then said, "Try not to think on it. And while you're doin' that, keep a keen eye out. Sons a bitches responsible for this atrocity could still be skulkin' around anywhere. Be mighty easy to hide in that patch of trees yonder. See any movement over there, just go on ahead and start blastin'."

"You know, Hayden, if this is another one of Blackheart's gang we've run across, I think we should just pitch camp somewheres, sit back, and wait," Carl said.

"Wait for what?" I said.

"Wait for 'em to kill each other off to the point where there ain't but one of 'em left. Then we can scoop him up. Take 'im back to Fort Smith and let Maledon hang 'im."

Nate kept pawing at his nose. Looked like he might be about to heave his socks up. He coughed, then slipped his Winchester from its boot. Hung back with the animals as Carl and I turned and headed for the poor burnt-crisp feller stretched out dead center of the scorched spot. Black clouds of ash puffed up around our feet as we trudged toward the still-waving body.

Incredible stench of flame-broiled flesh got worse as we got closer. By the time we'd stepped right up next to the poor soul, I had to pull my own bandanna out. Carl took one glance, then turned away. Acted like he was checking the toes of his own boots, the backs of his hands, or the surrounding area for anyone who might have laid in wait to ambush us.

Knelt down beside the flame-charred feller. Not much in the way of clothing left. Most of the unfortunate soul's garments had completely burned away. Fire left little more than flaked scraps of ashy material here and there, the remnants of a set of leather suspenders, and the cooked vestiges of a pistol belt along with an empty holster. Every exposed area of skin had coiled into flaky curlicues of brittle, crispy flesh—almost like deep-fried pork skins. Appeared someone had most likely taken his boots before they set him ablaze.

At first I felt sure the ill-fated man had probably died before we got to him. But as I gazed at the body in absolute revulsion, a shallow, ragged gasp escaped what little was left of a set of swollen, blistered-black lips. Held my canteen over the charred face and dribbled water into his open mouth. Few drops at a time. Took a while before the barbecued man finally responded to the moisture.

Of a sudden, eyes missing brows and lashes popped open; then he shuddered all over as though freezing to death. An agonized, tortured, soul-rending moan, unlike anything I'd ever heard before, rumbled up from inside his charred chest. Made sharp-pointed chill bumps run from my neck all the way down my sweaty back.

"Can you speak, mister?" I said.

Ragged, muffled, and strained but still intelligible, he said, "Please. Kill me, friend. Use your pistol. Get me over to the other side."

His request stunned me. Fact that he could even speak stunned me. Took a second to collect my thoughts before I said, "My partner and I are deputy U.S. marshals, mister. Sure you'll want us to notify family members of your misfortune. Can you tell us your name?"

Even though his face was cooked beyond anything like recognition—all the hair had burned away along with most of his ears and nose and lips—I could tell how hard he strained to speak. Have to say, it proved nothing short of amazing that what he had to tell me came out so clear and strong from such a badly devastated body.

Man croaked some, as though recovering from a severe cold. But the voice was friendly, like we'd met at church of a Sunday morning and decided to stand beneath the oak tree outside the front door and exchange our feelings about local politics, crop futures, our kids, our wives, or our faith in a forgiving God.

"Name's Bosephus Harvey," he gasped. "Own a small horse ranch, seven, eight miles . . . north. Hundred yards or so off the Deep Fork of the Canadian."

Trickled more water across nonexistent lips. So much of his face had vaporized that the lack of lips, nose, and ears gave him a flame-kissed, monstrously grinning, skull-like appearance.

"What were you doin' out here, Mr. Harvey?"

Without moving his head, he cut murky gray, unseeing eyes in the direction of my voice. "On my way to a settlement named Boggs, 'bout thirty miles south of here on the Deep Fork."

"Ah. We're familiar with the place."

"Thought to check on any strays as I rode along. Ran across a group of men camped on this very spot. Yesterday— I think—late yesterday. Been layin' here all night." He stopped speaking. Those milky, clouded eyes shifted in their fire-blasted sockets. "Right sure I'm blind, Deputy. Can't see nothin' much now but some hazy movement. Bastards poured so much bonded-in-the-barn jig juice on my head the blaze burnt my eyes away."

"Want us to prop you up?"

"No. No. Sweet Jesus, don't touch me. Please, don't touch me. Pain's already unbearable. Touch me and I might not be able to finish what I must tell you."

"You know any of the men who did this to you by any chance, Mr. Harvey?"

He made an attempt to swallow, but couldn't. Went to gagging. I dripped more liquid into his opened mouth. A tongue, swollen to the size of a housewife's pot-holding rag, swabbed its way across his exposed upper teeth.

He gasped, then said, "Never seen any of 'em before. Stumbled over their campfire purely by accident. Tried my best to be neighborly and back away, till I noticed a couple of 'em goin' at some poor, hysterical woman. She started screamin' bloody murder . . .'bout a minute after I drew up."

"You should've run right that instant."

"Know that now. Can't call time back. Whole crew drunk and belligerent. God couldn'ta made friends with 'em boys. Shoot any one of 'em in the head and he'd have to sober up 'fore he could die." Man went to puffin' like he was drownin', let out a wheezin', crouping, blood-soaked cough.

Hoped to get his mind off his situation and back on the Blackheart bunch when I said, "Did the men you met up with do this to you for no reason?"

Finally got his coughing spell under control, then growled, "No reason. None as I can figure. One they called Zeke jerked me off my horse. Hit me with his pistol barrel. Riffled through my pockets. Found a couple a dollars and my tobacco pouch. Made 'im madder'n a rained-on rooster. Doused me in whiskey. Set me aflame. Rest of 'em laughed the whole time I burned."

Carl muttered, "Jesus."

"Kept sloshing more liquor on me. Oddest thing, even while I was blazin', couldn't do nothin' but stumble around grabbin' at 'em. But they wouldn't stop. Never quit their insane hootin' and hollerin'. Not till I fell down and couldn't move no more." Harvey choked, gagged, then went silent.

For some seconds, he didn't say anything more. Then I realized he appeared as though locked in a desperate attempt to close his eyes. Quick as I could, pulled my own bandanna. Saturated the cloth with water, wrung the chunk of rag out, then carefully laid it over his flame-blasted face.

Through the material, he said, "Thank you, sir. The sunlight hurts my eyes. Can't see mucha nothin', but it still hurts."

Figured no reason existed to dance around the truth any longer. Said, "Don't appear as how you're gonna last too much longer, Mr. Harvey."

"Believe you're right, Deputy. Sincerely hope not. You just can't imagine the pain."

"No, sir. No, I'm absolutely certain I can't. Not sure anyone could."

Carl turned his back, kicked at the dirt, refused to look at the man any longer.

"You know, Deputy, something I heard many a dyin' man say durin' the war's turned out to be true," Harvey added, then groaned. "God puts enough hurt on a body and you start to ignore it like a dyin' dog. All I want right now is to pass on to my final, heavenly reward. Want all my trials, all my sufferin' to end, this very minute if possible. You can help me along that path, Deputy. Please, just pull your pistol and shoot me."

"Sorry, but I can't be responsible for your death. None of us can help you onto the final path to God's glorious presence by such an act. Gonna be ruthlessly blunt and truthful with you, sir. From all outward appearances, only the Lord God Almighty can help you now."

A tired, ragged, gurgling breath surged through the bandanna at a spot where the holes that had once been his nose and mouth were located. "Well, then," he gasped. "You must take my body home to my family, sir. Not much out of your way. Just follow the river north. Can't miss the place. My wife, Millicent Yellow Hawk, please tell her that my final thoughts were of her and the children. Promise a dying man you'll do that for me, Deputy."

Found it difficult to speak for several seconds. Finally managed to force out, "We'll see to your family, sir. You have my oath on it."

Heard Carl stir behind me. Sounded almost as though he'd let a stifled sob get loose. Understood exactly how he felt. My good and faithful friend was tougher than the calluses on a barfly's elbows. We'd seen a boatload of dead or dying folks in just as bad, or worse, condition, but Bosephus Harvey was the first we'd ever come across who'd been burned alive and could still speak with such clarity and authority. Man's calm, reasoned acceptance of his plight had a powerful effect. Had it not been for his appalling appearance, a person wouldn't have known how bad off he really was—leastways, not by the sound of his voice.

The damp bandanna puffed up and down over the gaping wound that was now his mouth as he said, "Please, leave me alone for a few minutes. When you come back I'll have made my peace with God." After a long pause he added, "And won't be here any longer."

"You sure about that, Mr. Harvey? My friend and I can stay here with you. A man should have someone by his side when he goes out. Assure you it won't be a problem."

"No. No. Leave me with my God. Just a few minutes, I beg you. When you return, I'll be gone. Just make sure my body gets back to my family."

Trickled some more water on the piece of rag over his face. "Thank you, sir. And I'll thank you for seeing to my family ahead of time. Now leave me, please."

Touched the back of his cooked hand with one finger, then stood and strode away without looking back. Carl ran a shirtsleeve under his nose as he trudged along beside me.

Nate stepped off his horse as we marched up. "Even from over here," he said, "that feller's plight don't look good a'tall."

Carl looked away, then stared at his feet. "Ain't nowheres near *good*, that's for damned certain. Poor man sent us away so he could get right with God and die. 'Pears he's made up his mind not to live any longer. Can't blame him much, though. Don't know 'bout anyone else, but I'd sure 'nuff hate to live another thirty years after bein' burnt up like that."

A confused look flashed across Nate Swords' face. He flicked a glance in the direction of Harvey's resting place. "Man just decided not to live no more? That what I just heard you boys say?"

"Sure appears so," I said. "I've heard of such before.

Just ain't never seen it happen. Thought dyin' whenever you wanted was just an old wives' tale. Still don't believe in it myself. But we'll give him the time he asked for anyway, then see to his comfort once he realizes the end ain't comin'."

"What about Blackheart and his bunch?" Nate said.

"Yeah, what about 'em?" Carl said. "Hell, Hayden, you and I've seen the most awful kinda evil shit men can do. Waded through a river of blood chasin' them Crooke boys along a trail of astonishing insanity and murder. Swear 'fore Jesus, I thought that was as bad as men could get. Couldn't see how we'd ever be faced with anything worse. Then came Charlie Storms and the Doome brothers. Now this. Christ, still find it hard to believe men can do such things, but it looks like the name Blackheart is destined for a level of infamy impossible for most sane folks to conjure up in a nightmare."

"Well, I personally thought them Doome boys were the perpetrators of the most horrible kind of vicious behavior I'd ever come across," Nate said as he danced from foot to foot. He looked mighty anxious when he added, "And now you boys feel like what the Blackheart bunch did to this feller is even more awful than that?"

Pulled my hat off a sweat-drenched head and used it as a fan. "Settin' fire to a livin' man is about as evil as it gets, far as I'm concerned. Leastways, the Crooke brothers killed most of the folks they burned 'fore they set 'em ablaze."

Carl snatched his own hat off, wiped a pinched face on his shirtsleeve again, then used the hat to point off to the north. "Well, Blackheart and his bunch went thataway. Damned near due north along the river. Accordin' to what that roasted-up Harvey feller just told us, they're headed right straight for his ranch. 'S almost like he told 'em which way to go. Or like they could read his mind. All I gotta say is Lord help the man's wife and family if them killers run across those folks."

Took a swallow from my canteen, then spat. Said, "Well, shit. This really cuts it."

Carl hooked a thumb in the direction of the Blackheart bunch's probable trail. "Bet he's got a pretty little Injun wife, couple a beautiful, big-eyed, half-breed kids about five miles over thataway. And I'll go even further and say I'd be willin' to bet, right this minute, the whole hapless family's deader'n a buncha them yellow-winged, spring-time butterflies drowned in a pitcher fulla sweet cream."

Prospect of Carl's horrific prediction being true threw a hush of shocked revulsion over the three of us. Nate cast a baleful glance off to the north, then said, "Reckon there's any chance we could get to this feller's unsuspecting family quick enough to keep such a horror from taking place? Mean, hell, if we ride hard, really put the spurs to our animals, there's a chance, ain't there, boys?"

Of a sudden, a light, imperceptible breeze swept through our midst. Soft, cool, sweet-smelling puff of air hit the patch of flame-seared grass, cut a soot-raising path to where Harvey lay, hovered over the body, then swirled upward like a tiny, heaven-bound cyclone. In spite of the blistering heat, an icy shiver ran up my spine.

"Damned if that ain't a wonderment. Think God just came and got 'im," Carl muttered.

All three of us hurried back to the fallen man's side. I stooped over. Checked the body for any signs of life. Sure enough, Bosephus Harvey had departed this world.

"Seen a lot of men go out," I said, and stood. Gazed toward heaven and watched the twisting, fragrant cloud dissipate, fly into vaporous fragments, then disappear. "First time in memory that I've known a body that predicted his own departure from this life with such amazing accuracy. 'Nuff to give a body the cold shivers."

Nate gazed at the corpse, a look of inquisitive confusion etched onto his handsome face. "For sure? He actually did what you boys said? Hell, I thought you were just foolin'. Kiddin' with the new guy in the group, you know. Never figured either of you actually meant it."

We wrapped Harvey's body in a blanket. Placed him over the back of our pack animal. Never did find any trace of his own ride. Figured Blackheart and his boys must've taken the bangtail when they left.

Nate led the overburdened beast carrying Harvey's charred body. Headed north as fast as we could urge our own knotheads along.

By the time we finally got to the ill-fated dead man's ranch, Carl and I'd left Nate at least half a mile behind. We reined up on a grass-covered hillock several hundred yards from the main house.

Sat our animals and waited for Nate to catch up. Pulled our long glasses out and surveyed the scene at the same time. What we saw didn't appear to bode well for Harvey's wife or children. Nothing moved. No chickens in the yard. Couldn't see any dogs, cats, or other such pets. Place proved eerily still, silent, even sinister. Looked to me as if death had already been there and gone.

7

"... MIGHTY HARD TO TELL WHICH IS WHICH."

BOSEPHUS HARVEY'S MAIN house lay nestled on a flattened piece of well-tended, bare earth surrounded on three sides by rolling hills. The breeze that swept through the water-starved, waist-high grass covering those sheltering hills gave his prairie home the appearance of floating just below a yellowish brown ocean of slowly heaving waves.

A deep, inviting veranda covered the entire front of the spacious-looking building. Cane-bottom rocking chairs appeared to openly invite visitors to stop over and sit a spell. Board-and-batten walls had recently been painted and the shingle roof repaired. The bright, fresh coat of whitewash caused the house to cast a shimmering glow in the afternoon's diminishing sunlight. Splash of colorful wildflowers planted all around the porch gave evidence of a woman's touch.

From our vantage point atop the highest of the surrounding hills, some 150 yards to the south, Carlton and I sat our horses and continued to scan the dwelling through collapsible, army-surplus spyglasses. Carl threw a leg over his saddle horn and leaned against it on one elbow. Said the tactic helped steady his telescope. Made it easier for him to pick out small, sometimes important, clues from a distance.

Hadn't inspected the spot for any more than five minutes or so when Nate rode up pulling the weighted-down packhorse. He dropped the reins of both animals, stepped down, stretched his back, then rubbed his right shoulder.

"See anything?" he asked as he leaned against my blue roan and set to rolling a smoke.

"Nothin' so far," Carl replied. "And, to me, that's the horror of the thing. Can't see any of them kids that Harvey claimed to have, or his wife. Not even a dog or two. Corral, over on the east side between the house and barn, appears empty, 'cept for what looks like a dead mule. No activity around the outhouse behind that big ole sycamore tree. Place looks deserted. But, hell, there could be twenty people inside the house, or the barn for that matter. And all of 'em could be lining us up in their gun sights for some long-distance killin' as we speak. 'Course, that's doubtful, given as how there ain't no horses in the corral."

"Front door's standin' open," I added. "So are all the windows I can see from here." Closed my glass with a series of loud clicks. Slipped it back into the case, then said, "Might be a good idea for one of us to slip around back just to make sure this ain't some well-planned trap. Been ambushed a time or two before. Wouldn't want it to happen again."

Carl pushed his glass into its near worn-out leather case, dropped his foot back into a stirrup, then said, "I'll ease on around to the west. Come up from behind that hill over yonder on the backside of the place, where all them cotton-woods are behind the barn. Bet there's a small creek of some kind 'round that way. Otherwise, there wouldn't be any of them trees a-growin' back there. Soon's I make sure there ain't nobody layin' for us, I'll fire two shots. You boys can come on in soon's you hear 'em."

Before I could say anything, one way or the other, he'd put the spur to his animal. There was no calling him back. Once the little redheaded peckerwood made up his mind, you'd best stand aside 'cause there wasn't any stopping him.

Nate snatched up the reins of our packhorse, and headed for the shade afforded by an umbrella-shaped live oak not far from where Carl and I'd set up. "Gotta get our friend Bosephus Harvey outta the sun, Hayden. Poor feller's a-startin' to ripen up mighty damned fast. Think we need to put 'im in the ground just as soon as we possibly can. Festeratin' corpse is drawin' flies like a stink magnet."

Led Gunpowder over into the shade as well, then went to pulling all the weapons and ammunition I thought I might need. "Figure I'm gonna take this double-barreled blaster and my long gun, Nate," I said. "Along with a bandolier of mixed shells." Threw the canvas ammo belt over my shoulder, then headed off. Dry, waist-high grass swished and cracked around my legs as I plowed my way toward the poor dead feller's neat little ranch house.

"Ain't we gonna wait for Carl to fire off a shot or two?" Nate said as he scurried up beside me, a shotgun in one hand, his rifle in the other.

"Well, figured we could hunker down and creep through all these weeds till we get right up to where Harvey appears to have cut the stuff back to make a kind of yard for his wife. Maybe settle in behind that wagon, just on the other side of his rail fence. Don't think there's anyone here, from all I could see through my long glass. Figure them folks as might still be around here are likely dead."

We'd sneak along for a few steps, drop to our knees, listen for anything that might be out of place, then scramble a few more steps, and repeat the process. Made it to the fence line, crawled between the top and bottom rails, and took shelter behind the remains of an old freight wagon that looked like it hadn't been moved in some time. Wheels had sunk into the dirt nigh on halfway up to the hubs.

At almost that exact instant we heard the sound of two muffled pistol shots. Stood, propped my rifle against the wagon bed, pulled back both hammers on the Greener, then headed across the grassless, dusty yard toward the dwelling's front porch.

Nate fell in on my left and a few steps behind. A peculiar, spine-chilling quiet seemed to envelop everything. Undisturbed stillness made it possible to hear insects that sprang from the ground and fluttered into the air as we crunched along. Swirling breeze tickled the edges of my flared nostrils. Brought the familiar, pungent, coppery scent of blood and death.

Spotted Carl as he made his way around the east side of the main building—between it and the barn. Cocked pistol in each hand, he darted from one cottonwood tree to the next. His nervous glance cut back and forth as he searched for any trouble he might've missed.

The three of us converged on the partly opened front doorway at the same time. Carl had the right side, Nate and me flattened ourselves out against the wall on the left. Nodded at Carl and, honest-to-God, we were less than a breath away from storming into the house and killing everything in sight, when a child of about four or five wandered out onto the porch with her little brother in tow. Kids didn't even notice us pressed up against the wall, armed to the teeth, with blood in our eyes. They quietly toddled out to the edge of the veranda's raised, wooden deck, stopped, and kind of squatted down. Appeared they were looking for something.

Glanced around the doorframe and stared into the interior darkness, but couldn't really see much of anything, then stepped over to a spot beside the youngsters. Both kids looked up at the same time. Their faces were smudged with dirt. Boy's dy-dees hadn't been changed in some time past. You could smell him from several feet away. Aroma was enough to make a body's eyes tear up.

Little gal flashed a sweet, coquettish smile at me, then said, "Have you seen my mommy, mister?"

Waved at Carl and Nate. They darted through the open door. Disappeared inside. Kinda hunkered on the porch next to the kids. Let the hammers down and laid the shotgun across my legs, then said, "No, darlin', haven't seen your mommy. Do you know when she left?"

The child stood and fiddled with the hem of her flour-sack dress. Swayed back and forth as though thinking, then flicked another brown-eyed glance at the empty yard. "With some men."

"No, sweetie, when did your . . . never mind. Your mommy left with some men?"

She moved closer, placed a sweaty, unwashed hand on my shoulder, and leaned against me. "Yes."

"Do you remember when your mommy left, darlin'?"

Tiny, inquisitive fingers picked at the badge pinned to my bib-front shirt. "No."

"Did Mommy leave yesterday?"

"Don't know. She didn't come back last night. We were scared."

Placed my hand on her shoulder. "What's your name, sweetie?"

She chewed on a filthy fingernail, inspected the damage she'd done, rubbed the finger on her dress, then said, "Matilda."

"Have you had anything to eat, Matilda?"

"Not today. Mommy will fix us something when she gets back home."

"Did your mommy say where she was going when she left?"

Before the child could answer, Carl and Nate strode back out onto the porch. Nate propped his sawed-off next to a pole holding the veranda's roof up, leaned against it, then started rolling a smoke. He puffed the cigarette to life, then flicked the smoldering match into the grassless yard.

"Find anything inside?" I asked.

"Place is a mess, Hayden. Hardly a stick of furniture left in there what ain't busted all to kindling. Spots and pools of blood splattered around here and there, but these young'uns' momma ain't nowhere to be found. Blackheart bunch either took her away, or . . ." Carl hesitated, then cast a squint-eyed, worried glance toward the barn before he almost whispered, "Maybe she's somewheres else."

"I'll go," Nate said, then flicked his cigarette away and hustled off toward the barn.

Fresh breeze brought me a new whiff of the boy's nasty behind. Said, "Go back inside, Carl, and see if you can ferret out a clean dy-dee for this kid, or at least something we can use for one. Poor little whippersnapper stinks to high heaven. Gonna have a helluva rash on his skinny butt if we don't get 'im cleaned up."

Matilda leaned against my knee as though she wanted to crawl up into my lap. "His name's Beaver."

"Ah. Beaver, huh? Well, Matilda, we need to get Beaver outta all that stink. Maybe wash him up a mite."

She did a cute, childish point of her finger toward the side of the house. "There's a pump around back."

"That's good. I'll send Mr. Cecil for some water soon as we can find something clean for Beaver to wear."

Patted her on the head about the same time I happened to cast a glance toward the barn. Nate stumbled back into the sunlight. He leaned against one of the double doors like a man who'd just run a footrace all the way from Fort Smith. Boy snatched his hat off, buried his face in the crook of one arm. Then he leaned over and puked. Looked to me like everything he'd eaten in a week came up, including one of Carl's damned fine breakfasts from earlier that morning.

Slowly rose to my feet. "Stay here with your brother, Matilda. I'll be right back." Stepped over to the front door and, without taking my eyes off Nate, called out, "Carl, get back outside. Come on out right now."

I'd already made my way to the eastern end of the veranda when Carl stormed through the doorway and grabbed up Nate's shotgun. "What goin' on, Hayden?"

Kind of gestured toward the barn with my own big-barreled blaster. Before I could stop him, Carl darted around me, legged it for our friend. I stayed right on his heels till we got to Nate. Do believe the boy looked more shaken than I'd seen him in almost a year of chasing killers and badmen together. Came as something of a shock when I realized that, in addition to being a shade of ghastly white just this side of dead grass, he appeared on the verge of tears.

Carl grabbed him by the elbow, then leaned over to get a better look into the boy's ashen face. "Look at me, Nate. Tell me, what the hell's the matter?"

Nate raised his arm. Shook the hat in the general direction of the barn's partially opened double door. "Woman didn't leave with anybody," he said, then stuffed his hat back on. He gulped hard, then scratched his throat as though a fragment of something he'd upchucked mighta stuck somewhere. "Damnedest carnage inside there I've ever seen, Hayden. Think maybe it's both of 'em. Poor gal from Beehive Creek and that Harvey feller's wife. But, Hell's eternal fire and damnation, it's mighty hard to tell which is which."

Under his breath to the point where I barely heard him, Carl said, "Sweet Jesus have mercy."

8

"How We Gonna Clean This Bloody Hair Ball Up?"

PUSHED PAST BOTH my friends and stepped into the shadowy, dim, somewhat cooler interior of Harvey's barn. Snapped the hammers back on both barrels of the shotgun. Readied myself for the worst.

Carl came in behind me. Waited until my eyes had adjusted to the inner gloom before I took one more step. Stopped again. Ran a quick glance around the barn's shadowy core. On the surface, couldn't detect much that appeared out of place.

Typical of most such crude structures, the rough-cut wall boards had shrunk under the unrelenting assault of ruthless summer sunshine. Resulting contraction left spaces that allowed knifelike shafts of sunlight to cut their way inside and slice through billowing clouds of the drifting dust we'd stirred up. Here and there, a variety of harnesses, trace chains, leather straps, singletrees, and tools of every sort imaginable hung from thick wooden pegs.

Three stalls stood on either side of an open, dirt-floor common area, most of which had been covered with an ankle-deep layer of straw. Pair of decrepit McClellan cavalry saddles sat on the top rails of one of the animal pens.

At first glance, it appeared that all the cubicles were stone-cold empty. Then Carl elbowed me and pointed at the dirt floor. Series of drag marks in the hay-littered dirt led to two of the open-fronted enclosures—one on either side of the building.

Raised the shotgun to my shoulder and headed for the nearest of the corrals. Didn't even get inside. Stench was enough to curl your nose hairs. Hit me in the face like somebody had slapped me across the mouth with a sock full of rancid manure with a hole in the toe.

Scene of murderous depravity I beheld in that blood-soaked, three-sided compartment stopped me dead in my tracks. Had to cover my nose with a bandanna tied over my face. Little doubt in my mind that One Cut Petey Mason had once again worked his diabolical magic with a bowie, or perhaps an ax. Maybe it'd been a group effort. Just couldn't imagine one man doing that much damage to a human body. Either way, Nate had hit the nail right on its square-cut head. Blackheart and his bunch had left one hellacious mess.

Now, I'll freely admit that a considerate, well-brought-up Southern man wouldn't have dared stare at that poor woman's completely nude remains the way I did. But, hell, my job required me to examine the scene in the minutest detail just in case we caught the monster responsible for such a sickening act.

There was every possibility Carl, Nate, and me might find it necessary to testify at the bloodthirsty fiend's trial so Judge Parker could condemn him to death after a fair and speedy trial. Then he could assign George Maledon the responsibility of stringing the murderer's sorry ass up to the cross member on the Gates of Hell gallows in the little hollow down the hill from the courthouse in Fort Smith.

So even though I felt pretty sure One Cut Petey would never make it back to civilization alive, if either me or Carl had anything to do with it, I went ahead and rested the shotgun across my arm, then pulled my notepad out of my pocket. Started jotting down my observations. Just reading the things I had to write in that notebook had the power to make any normal, caring person sick as a slobbering, hydrophobic dog.

Truth be told, Nate was as right as spring rain. It proved damned hard to determine which of the women I'd had the misfortune to find first. Everything you'd normally expect to be inside a body was outside, strewn around the stall, even hanging from the walls like Christmas tree decorations. Perhaps even worse, she appeared to have been skinned. One particularly grisly trick involved intestines and the handles of a sodbuster plow. But I can't go into that, or, to be more precise, I won't go into it. Some things are just better left unsaid.

Felt Carl ease up beside me. Could hear his breathing coming in short, strangled gasps. "God Almighty, Hayden. Can this be real? Sweet merciful Father." Then he made a gagging sound and staggered back outside.

All told, spent maybe another minute in there myself, then stumbled for the open air. Had to bend over, catch my breath 'fore I came damned near heaving up my own spurs. Just isn't any point going into an overly detailed accounting of what we'd stumbled upon inside Harvey's barn. Suffice it to say, the dead man's unfortunate wife and, as nearly as we could determine, the girl from Beehive Creek both died in ways that defied the ability of sane people to understand or even find the proper words to describe.

Hour or so later, with a bloodred sun dipping low on the horizon, we dragged several of the rocking chairs down off the porch, built a campfire on the ground, and cooked some coffee. By then we'd cleaned the kids up. Seen to it they were fed. Both of them got drowsy and fell asleep just as soon as we'd filled their grumbling bellies with some food. We put 'em down on pallets made of a pile of patchwork blankets Nate dragged from the house and laid out on the porch. Figured we could keep a closer eye on the pullets that way, while we talked the dreadful situation over.

Lounged in the somewhat cooler shade of the sycamore tree growing near the west side of the home's covered veranda—as far away from the barn as we could get. Tried to collect our thoughts but, you know, it's hard to think on the kind of savagery that confronted us.

Carl held a two-foot piece of tree limb in one hand. He leaned over with his elbows on his knees and scratched in the dirt. "How we gonna clean this bloody hair ball up? Don't know 'bout either of you, but I ain't sure I can go back in that barn again. Given how long I've been working this job, thought sure I'd seen about all the hellish evil men could do. But I have to admit, this beats all I ever saw, or even heard tell of."

"Aïn't no doubt in my mind how I feel about it," Nate snapped. "I'd rather clean all the outhouses and slit trenches from here to Tucumcari—with a teacup and a spoon—than go back in there."

After a second or two of silence, Nate added, "'Sides, how would we get 'em picked up? Mean, Jesus, they're strung out all over hell and yonder. Organs and innards pretty much everwheres. Have to use a pitchfork, a garden rake, and a shovel to get those poor butchered women into a sack, or box, or whatever'n the hell we might decide to bury 'em in."

Of a sudden, I noticed that Carl's attention had shifted toward something on the eastern edge of Bosephus Harvey's property. Without speaking, he stood. Had a look of concern on his face when he cast a squint-eyed gaze at a patch of cottonwood trees that grew on the banks of the shallow creek trickling along the base of the low, rolling hills that surrounded the house.

Carl whacked his leg with the stick, then used it to point in the direction he gazed. "Somebody's comin', Hayden. Heavily armed. Lookin' damned mean."

Three of us huddled up and watched as a lone rider eased from the leafy cover provided by the swaying trees. He reined up and sat a long-legged calico horse as though leisurely trying to decide whether to approach. Nervy son of a bitch eyeballed us for a spell, lit a cheroot, took a couple of puffs, then nudged his gaudy animal our direction at a slow, deliberate walk.

Something about the man seemed more than a little familiar. Tall, lean as chewed rawhide, decked out in a fringed leather shirt and huge palm-leaf hat, with twinkling flashes from Mexican spurs and three silver-washed pistols that highlighted his long-legged, muscular appearance. Man and animal were loaded down with multiple forms of death-dealing iron that included the pistols, a Winchester rifle, shotgun, and a massive bowie knife. Took me ten, fifteen seconds before I realized that, from a distance, the stranger could have easily passed for my Texas Ranger friend Lucius Dodge's twin brother.

Nate grunted, lowered the barrel of his weapon, then said, "I know him, Carlton. Hired on as a deputy marshal several months ago. Name's John Henry Slate. Think we met the day he signed up. Dangerous man if there ever was one, but seems friendly enough. Know one thing for certain, sure as hell wouldn't want him on my trail."

"Oh, I've heard the name," Carl said. "Hear tell he's sure 'nuff hell on wheels, Hayden. Texas boy. Tougher'n the back wall of a shootin' gallery. He'n Bucky Starns was the ones who ran that murderin' bastard Freeman Chillingsworthy to ground up on Talimena Mountain. Brought ole Freeman in a week or so ago. Judge Parker'll hang him sure as death, taxes, and Texas."

"Helluva catch. Way I hear it, Chillingsworthy would've murdered half a dozen people by now if'n he was still loose," I said.

About then, Slate reined his colorful ride to a stop not twenty feet away. Reached up and thumped the brim of his hat in greeting. "Gents. Name's John Henry Slate. I'm a deputy U.S. marshal out of Fort Smith. Trackin' some damned evil men. Sign led me right to this very spot. Didn't realize till I seen your badges that we might all be in the same kinda business."

Nate heeled it to Slate's side, held his hand up, and said, "Good to see you, John Henry. Might not recognize me. Nate Swords. We met in the courthouse the day the U.S. marshal swore you in."

"Just be damned," Slate said as he bent over and shook Nate's extended hand.

Soon as they had exchanged a few ice-breaking pleasantries, Slate swung down in a single, fluid, athletic move. While he put on a good show of having relaxed, a practiced eye could easily tell John Henry Slate didn't trust any of us any farther than he could throw his pinto horse. Man moved like one of those fancy-assed, New York ballet dancers, or maybe a big, dangerous, and extremely deadly cat.

He nodded toward our fire, then said, "That coffee I smell? Sure could use a decent cup of belly-wash. Have to admit I cain't cook the stuff worth a damn. Feller I knew back in Texas stopped drinkin' anything I brewed up. Got some of my coffee on one of his shirts. Damned stuff ate a big hole in it. Said I was the only man he'd ever known what could brew coffee strong enough to float one of those old five-pound Walker Colts."

Well, his affable manner soon put us all at our ease. Got the impression Slate was one of those men who never really met a stranger. In no time at all, he struck me as being the sort who'd have just about anybody feeling like they'd known him all their lives in a matter of minutes after meeting him.

Dragged another of the rockers off the porch. Pretty quicklike, the four of us had told a few jokes, exchanged a number of tall tales, and, in Carl's case, told plenty of downright lies. About an hour into our get-to-know-each-other session, the sun went completely down. Carl fished a bottle of tonsil paint out of his possibles bag and juiced our coffee up a bit.

Slate doctored his own cup, took a sip, started flapping one arm like a big ole rooster, then made a series of comical sounds like *"Clickety, click, click."*

"'S damned powerful stuff," Carl offered.

Slate grinned, leaned over, and added some to my cup. "Genuine, hunnert'n-fifty-proof, stump-holler, jig juice, I'd wager."

Nate grinned. "We took that stuff off'n a feller we caught introducin' illegal liquor into the Nations down 'round Atoka. 'Member that 'un, Hayden?"

I nodded, then said, "That the crazy sunuvabitch we caught mixin' snake heads in with his brew?"

Carl nodded. "Yeah, but that was another batch. This stuff here's pretty good for bust head. Clean as a whistle. You can drink a tubful. Won't even make your head hurt the next day. Plus, you can rub it on sore, achin' muscles. Works like a charm. Been known to cure the festerin' toe rot, too."

John Henry Slate let out a snort. "Just be damned if'n I'm gonna rub anything on my achin' ass that I can drink." Set us all to laughing.

Sipped at my cup for a while, then turned to Slate and said, "When you first rode up, mentioned as how you'd tracked somebody all the way out here, didn't you, John Henry?"

He swirled some of the coffee around in his mouth, then spat into the fire. "I did. Yes, indeed. Arvil Boston and his worthless brother Delbert. Followed 'em all the way up from Lone Oak over in the Winding Stair Mountains. Robbed a combination bank and mercantile operation down that way. Managed to kill hell outta the gent who owned the place in the process. Dead gent's name was Marcus Flint. Either of you fellers know him?"

Carlton made a noise like a cornered bear. "Didn't know Flint personal. But I've had dealin's with both 'em Boston boys before. Pair of 'em's lower'n a couple of rattlesnakes' belt buckles."

"All the sign got so confused once we arrived this afternoon, I couldn't tell whether anyone else had thrown in with Blackheart and his bunch or not, Hayden," Nate said. "Most likely wouldn't have realized they had acquired new blood till we got back on their trail again."

"Damned wonder we couldn't smell 'em," Carl said. "Sons a bitches ain't had a bath since '65. Last time we had 'em in Judge Parker's jail, they stunk so bad it caused a riot. And hell, you know how bad the dungeon smells, but them boys stunk the place up so bad hardened criminals tried to kill 'em."

We laughed at that one for a spell, but then the conversation turned serious when Slate said, "Speakin' of smellin' bad, does kinda reek a bit of death 'round these parts, fellers."

Took all three of us to get the whole story out to the newest member of our posse about Blackheart, Harvey, and the dead women, and completely explain the problem of what we were going to do about the bodies. Once more, Nate and Carl both swore as how they'd never go back in the barn again.

Blanket of silence fell over the conversation for a spell. Surprised the hell out of me when John Henry said, "You fellers ever heard about how Vikings used to bury their honored dead? They'd put 'em in a boat full of straw and stuff. Some of their belongings, mementos of their lives, that kinda thing. Then set 'em adrift. Shoot fire arrows into the boat. Watch as the burning boat sank."

"Ain't got no boat," Nate offered.

Slate pushed his hat back on his head and grinned. "Nope. Sure don't. And that creek out back's barely ankle deep. But here's what we can do. Think we should carry the Harvey feller into the barn, lay him out beside the lady we think is his wife, then set fire to the whole shebang. Cremate 'em. Barn's big enough the flames should reduce all those poor folks to nothing more'n a pile of ashes. Then we can just scrape 'em all up and bury everything. Even put up some crosses if you want."

Couldn't believe my ears when Carl said, "Well, it's an idea all right. Ain't never done nothin' like that before, but in this particular instance might be something we'd want to consider. Just one question. What the hell's a Viking?"

Thought for a spell we might wake the kids with all our hootin' and hollerin' at that one. Carl got to actin' like a sore tail over the whole thing before we finally explained it all to him.

Could tell he was still kind of sensitive over his ignorance when he said, "Hell, I knew that. Just forgot. Vikings ain't the kinda thing as comes up in everyday conversation, by God."

Well, got pretty quiet after that. Nate doctored everybody's cup at least one more time, maybe twice. After half an hour or so of sitting around the fire and mulling it all over, God help us, we did exactly what John Henry had suggested.

Slate carried a lantern into the barn, checked the remains of both women, and pronounced one of them as most likely being Mrs. Harvey. Said he based his considered opinion on the way the corpse was dressed. Claimed the one he decided on was dressed in a few remaining threads that were closer to what you'd expect an Indian lady who'd married a white feller to wear.

Couldn't argue with such reasoning much, because none of us really wanted to do any of the examining ourselves. Me, Carl, and Nate had already seen all we really wanted of the blood-spattered massacre.

Four of us placed Mr. Harvey's overripe carcass beside what was left of the lady John Henry picked out. Drove a pair of iron stakes into the ground beside the bodies so we could find them after the fire finally played out. Doused the whole barn with a five-gallon can of coal oil Carl found in a corner somewhere.

Watched as Nate pulled a match out of his pocket. Before he could strike it, I said, "Can't anyone know what we're about to do here, fellers. 'Cause no matter what our intentions, this'll never play well back in civilization. Far as anyone other'n us is to ever know, all these folks were found intact. Buried 'em the same way. Want all of you to swear you won't tell."

"No problem for me. Swear I won't tell nobody," Carl said.

Nate and John Henry nodded their agreement, but I said, "That won't do, boys. Gotta say it out loud. Do you fellers swear you won't tell anybody how we disposed of these bodies?"

Nate held his hand up like he was testifying in Judge Parker's court. "I swear, I won't tell a soul."

"Swear I won't tell nobody," Slate added.

Reached over and took the match from between Nate's fingers. Scratched it to life on the butt of my belly gun. Thumped it at a spot I knew we'd doused pretty good with the coal oil. Thought for a second the match had gone out. Then it caught. Flame shot up the side of the barn's dried, warped door, ran into the hayloft, and in a matter of minutes the whole shebang went up in bloodred flames that shot a hundred feet high.

Damned place burned all night long. Good thing we were down in that bowl-shaped spot or everyone within a hundred miles would have seen the fire. All the popping and crackling made so much noise, I wondered at how it didn't wake the kids. Then the walls started to collapse. Ceiling fell in on tons of hay that dropped into the main stable area. Covered the bodies with flame and burning ash for hours. Fire got hotter than the hinges on Hell's front gate.

'Bout the time the walls caved in, Carl slipped up by my side and said, "Damned amazin' this conflagration hasn't set the whole countryside alight, if you ask me. Wouldn't take but one spark in all this grass and we'd have a helluva inferno goin'."

Mountain of ashes stayed so hot we couldn't get to the spot where our iron rods were sticking up out of the ruin until late the following afternoon. Wasn't much left of those bodies. More than I'd expected, but still not much. Must admit it was a lot easier to clean up than what we'd started with.

Kids woke up right in the middle of everything. Nate and John Henry did their best to entertain 'em. Wasn't very hard. Tykes seemed more interested in digging in the dirt with spoons than watching grown folk burn down a barn. Given the situation, wished it were that easy to keep my mind occupied on something other than what we'd just found it necessary to do.

Shoveled everything we could recover into some burlap bags middle of the next morning. Buried those unfortunate folks under the sycamore just a few steps from where we'd cooked coffee the night before.

Made their final resting place look as much as possible like there were actual bodies laid to rest in that spot. Even brought piles of rocks up from the creek. Stacked them around the three-by-six-foot graves. Put up some plank markers. Even went so far as to add names, as best we knew them. 'Course we weren't for certain sure about whether we'd got the right woman with Harvey, but, like Nate said, it didn't really matter much.

Carl patted on the last shovelful of earth with his spade, then stood with his arm resting on the handle. Flicked a big drop of sweat off his nose, then said, "Reckon someone oughta send 'em off with a few good words, don't you think?" Sure as shooting, he was looking right at me when he said it.

Nodded, swept my hat off, and placed it over my heart. Carl, Nate, and John Henry did the same, then bowed their heads. Kids were back to napping again, thank God. Out of nowhere, a right nice breeze came up about then. Set that big ole tree's leaves to rustling. Sounded almost like music— a primitive, natural hymn provided at just the right moment.

"Lord," I said, "must confess I didn't know any of these unfortunate folks. Only met Mr. Bosephus Harvey shortly before he passed into your eternal care. Seemed as though he was as fine a man as you're likely to run across in this wicked part of the world. Wish I could have met his wife. Very likely she was an exceptional woman, given the pair of wonderful children she left behind. Can't say anything much 'bout this unlucky girl from Beehive Creek, other than she didn't deserve to die the way she did. 'Course none of them deserved the horrific deaths that came for them."

Lifted my head and gazed up through the tree boughs toward Heaven and added, "With you as my witness, Father, I do hereby swear that the men responsible for this act of mindless cruelty will pay with their lives."

Bent over, picked up a handful of dirt, and as I dribbled it back onto the graves, said, *"In the midst of all life we are in death. Earth to earth, ashes to ashes, dust to dust; in the sure and certain hope of the Resurrection unto eternal life. May they rest in peace."*

Carl stuffed his hat back on, then said, "Amen, by God. Now, what we gonna do about these kids?"

9

"OH, SWEET JESUS, BABY'S COMIN' RIGHT NOW."

THE DISPOSITION OF Harvey's children had completely escaped my consideration. Made me feel a lot better when John Henry perked up and said, "On my way here, I passed a house not more'n five miles back to the east. Seen smoke comin' outta the chimney, so I figure it'd be safe to assume there's gotta be people livin' there."

"What've you got in mind?" I said.

"Well, there's a good chance those folks might know who these children belong with, now that their parents are no longer amongst the livin'. Figure if we ask the right way, bet they'd be willin' to take the kids in and see to it they get reunited with the families of the poor dead folks we just got though a-plantin' under this big ole sycamore."

After about half a minute's worth of consideration, got me to thinking that I liked John Henry's suggestion and thoughtful reasoning in the matter. Figured as how acting on his advice had the potential for taking the unwanted load of a pair of orphaned towheads off the overburdened plates of us Indian country manhunters.

So I said, "Sounds good, John Henry. Should be able to run the kids over that way, then get back on the trail 'fore Blackheart and his bunch have got too much more of a jump on us."

Carl punched something of a tiny hole in my balloon when he popped up and said, "Done wasted nigh on two days, Hayden. What with disposin' of the bodies like we did and all. Way they were a-blowin' and goin', evil sons a bitches coulda done murdered a dozen other innocent people by now. Need to get ourselves on the trail again right this instant—young'uns or not."

'Course he was right. Thought on that problem about another minute, then said, "Tell you what, Carl, why don't you and Nate head on out after Blackheart and his bunch of thieves and killers. John Henry and I'll run the Harveys' children over to the neighbor place, then hoof it after you boys quick as we can. All you'll have to do is leave plenty of sign for us to follow. Barrin' any kind of unexpected delay, we should catch up with you no later than noon tomorrow."

Nate and Carl glanced at one another, grinned, and headed for their animals. Those boys got saddled up quicker than double-geared lightning. Had kicked away so fast, my head was still spinning as they topped the hills off to the west, waved their hats one last time, then disappeared.

"Damn," John Henry muttered. "You sure didn't get much guff over that assignment."

"Nope," I said. "Ole Carl's not real comfortable around kids. If you'd a-seen him trying to change that little boy's dirtied britches, you'd know what I mean. Man acts like baby shit is something akin to rattlesnake venom. Guess he figured it'd be a lot less trouble to tackle a gang of crazed man killers than have to deal with a four-year-old girl and her infant brother."

Well, with the beautiful Matilda's help, we gathered up everything we thought the kids might need from the ransacked house, stuffed it all in a pasteboard valise salvaged from the wreckage, and headed east. Little girl rode with John Henry. It was my first indication that women, no matter what their age, found the man just downright irresistible. I toted the boy.

Took our time because of the human load we carried and, less than an hour later, we arrived out front of a ramshackle dog-run house that looked about twice the size of Harvey's place. Dwelling appeared to have been built years prior, abandoned at some point, and only recently reinhabited again.

Squawking flock of scrawny chickens scattered as we reined our animals up near the home's set of rickety, warped front steps. Kitchen was on one side of a large open porch–living area. Sleeping quarters on the other. Outbuildings, rail fencing, in fact the entire home place in general sported a tired, disused, neglected appearance. Whole affair was in sore need of attention from a good carpenter.

Appearing somewhat out of place, an inviting, freshly painted, slat-bottomed swing, large enough for two, maybe three, people, dangled from a spanking new set of chains attached to a roof rafter on one side of the spacious veranda. A light breeze had the seat moving back and forth on its own, as though ghosts had taken a seat and watched over our arrival.

Shaggy, mottled-yellow dog, the size of a small pony, lay stretched out in a splotch of creeping shade beneath the swing. Beast raised his massive head, flopped a ragged tail, but made no move to get up, much less bother to announce our arrival.

Didn't matter. Our booted feet had barely touched the

ground when a couple stepped from the kitchen door and eased up to the edge of their ramshackle porch. A bit atypical for the Nations, the man was black, the woman Indian and heavy with child. Poor girl looked like she carried a babe the size of a number-ten washtub. Remember thinking to myself that if it had been me, I wouldn't have left the house without carrying a shotgun along. Just never knew who might ride up on you out in the Nations.

Back in those days, most folks outside the Indian country probably never even realized that there may have been between six and seven thousand freed black slaves living there. Those folks had once been the property of local tribal members, but chose to stay in the Indian country after the Great War. A good many Freedmen were adopted into the tribes at the behest of the federal government. Those not adopted were supposed to be relocated to other areas of the country.

But the mandated removals seldom occurred due to the government's failure to enforce their own rules. As a consequence, the vast majority of Freedmen chose to continue living in the midst of their Indian friends. And some decided to establish their own towns rather than take a chance among whites that they felt might be prone to mistreat, abuse, perhaps murder them and their children. Given many of the events of the dreaded Reconstruction, no one in their right mind should ever blame those good Freedmen for their actions.

Mr. Harvey's closest neighbor obviously chose to stay put, and had even taken an Indian girl as his wife. Strained, anxious-looking gent appeared no older than twenty at the most; his wife was quite a bit younger—perhaps only fifteen or sixteen. Haggard-looking pair brought to mind sorely put-upon folks that hadn't slept for days, or changed their clothing for weeks on end.

Girl had a pinched, deeply pained expression etched into her dark, striking face. She approached the edge of the porch and carried the enormous burden in her belly with both grasping hands.

"Afternoon, folks," I said. "Name's Tilden. Hayden Tilden. Deputy U.S. Marshal out of Fort Smith. This is my friend and fellow deputy, John Henry Slate. Wondered if we might . . ."

Didn't even get a chance to finish what I wanted to say before the girl's worried-looking husband raised both hands as though in supplication, then said, "Either a you . . . gennamens . . . know anythin' 'bout bringin' babies into dis here cruel ole world?" The obvious desperation in his tired, cracking voice was nigh on to heartbreaking.

If God had come down out of Heaven and slapped me nekkid right on the spot, I wouldn't have been any more flabbergasted than I was by that feller's astonishing request. Question came as such a surprise, about all me and John Henry could manage to do was stand there, each of us with a dirty-faced child clutched in our arms, and stare at the poor goober like he'd lost his mind.

Then, as if a scorching blue lightning bolt had forked across the heavens and hit dead center in the middle of the woman's head, she snapped over at the waist like a carpenter's rule that'd just been folded up. Her childlike hand snatched at her panic-stricken husband's muscular arm, and she hissed, "Baby's comin' now, Jonah."

God Almighty, she went to jerking on him so hard, I thought for a second she just might tear her shocked mate's limb right out of its socket.

He cast wide-eyed, beseeching looks toward heaven, raised his free arm as though begging, then zeroed in on me and said, "You've gotta do somethin', please. My wife's 'bout to birth our child right this minute. And, Lord help me, I don't know shit from scrambled eggs 'bout this kinda thang."

"Well, what'd you have in mind?" I asked.

"Come on inside and he'p me. This is our first chile. I

ain't got the slightest damned idea what I'm 'sposed to do. Had in mind to send over to the Harvey place for help but, as you can readily see, ain't got no one around as I could send."

Shook my head in disbelief, then said, "You didn't have any prior plans for this event, friend?"

"Yessir. Did indeed. Uh-huh. My very own mama had agreed to make the journey over from Okmulgee for the birthin'. But this chile's decided to march his little ole self out about a month early. Don't have no way to get in touch with her."

Turned to hand Matilda's brother off to John Henry. About that time the poor, heifer-sized girl squealed like a gut-shot panther. Scared hell out of the horses. They pawed at the dirt. Shook their heads for a spell. Then, when she kept screaming like a lunch whistle at a sawmill, they humped up and went to crow-hopping around the yard. Kids set to bawling like somebody had gone and pinched the tar out of them.

Racket that pregnant gal let loose made the hair on my arms stand up on top of rippling waves of crawling chicken flesh. Dog yelped like he'd been kicked, then jumped to his fist-sized feet and headed for the comforting shelter of parts unknown out in the tall grass.

Of a sudden, the poor shrieking woman dipped over like she might topple off the porch headfirst into the chicken-manure-covered yard. Just in the nick of time, she grabbed a support pillar from the porch's overhang. Between that and the flusterated aid of her shocked mate, she finally got herself about halfway erect again.

Wild-eyed, she shot a strangled gaze in my direction and nailed me to the spot, as sure as if I'd been driven into the ground like a tent peg. "My water broke 'bout half hour ago, Mr. Marshal. Baby's been a-tryin' to come out ever since. Think maybe his time's now. He's comin' sure as summertime follows the spring."

As John Henry took the Harveys' youngest child from me, he eyeballed the poor girl and said, "Cain't it wait till we could maybe fetch a doctor, ma'am? Hell, Okmulgee's only twenty-five miles or so over yonder way. Maybe I could get on over there and find a . . ."

Woman let out another unearthly screech that I swear could've blistered paint off a St. Louis bank's fireproof vault door. She stood spraddle-legged and hugged her sagging middle. Through gritted teeth, she growled, "Don't you understand what I'm sayin'? After ten years in missionary schools, my English is about as good as you're likely to find out here in this wilderness. Ain't no waitin' left. Baby's done made up his mind. He's comin' out. Anyone gonna help me, or do you all intend to just stand there lookin' stupid?"

Guess we let our stunned faces hang out for a bit too long. She grimaced, turned, and waddled toward the side of the house where I figured the beds were most likely located. Grabbed at the doorframe, then disappeared into the interior darkness on the other side of the open doorway.

We could hear her ricocheting off furniture and glass breaking as she continued to yell for her bewildered husband. Then there was a resounding thump when she must've gone down hard, and of course that set her to screeching even louder.

"You're gonna have to watch the Harveys' whippersnappers for a spell, John Henry," I said. "I'll see if I can't help these folks out."

Slate flopped down into the swing with a young'un under each arm. Tried not to, but I had to smile. He looked like a confused farmer on his way to town for market day with a squealing shoat under each arm.

Shucked my pistol belt. Dropped it in the swing seat right next to him. Was rolling up one sleeve when he flashed a weak smile and said, "You be a-knowin' anythin' 'bout 'bringin' babies into this cold, cruel world there, Mistah Tilden?"

Still working on one of my uncooperative arm covers when I glanced down at him again. Smile had turned into a big, toothy grin, as if he was really enjoying the fact that I'd stumbled my way into an unexpected form of hellish discomfort.

"Not a damned thing, as a matter of pure fact," I muttered. "My wife, Elizabeth, has delivered two of 'em so far. But I 'uz out here in the wild places both times. Have to reckon as how this is just God's way of forcin' me to catch up on my absences. But, hell, John, how difficult can birthin' babies be? Little children gettin' born happens every day. Most natural thing in the world. Leastways, that's what I keep hearin'."

He threw his head back, and I thought he was about to bust out laughing, but he only snickered a bit. "Yeah, that's what I've heard, too. Soon as you've seen to it that this lady's child gets into the world safe and sound, well, then you can come on back outside. Tell me how *easy* it all was. Cain't wait to hear the whole tale. And, oh, yeah, glad it's you and not me."

Woman's disconcerted husband and I found her down on hands and knees crawling toward a sagging bed in the corner of the home's farthest room. Cramped, stifling, eight-by-ten-foot cubicle sported a much-abused oak chest of drawers, bedside table, rocker, and a single, closed window. We helped her to her feet. A body could barely turn around in there. Three people had trouble breathing the muggy, unmoving, oppressive air.

As though touched by an invisible hand from the past, and as clear as a bucket of ice-cold, fresh-fallen rainwater pitched across my naked back, the realization of what had to be done suddenly came to me in a flash of understanding. The long-forgotten memory of my younger sister

Rachael's birth sliced its way across my fevered brain. Out of nowhere, I recalled hiding behind a door and watching my father as he prepared for the delivery.

Jesus, I thought, we're in for a rough night and then some.

10

"... HE'S ALL GRAY LIKE HE'S BEEN DEAD FOR A WEEK."

GRABBED THE STRUGGLING, near-hysterical girl by the elbow and helped her back to her feet. Turned to her husband and snapped, "Get that window opened, Jonah. Throw a clean blanket over this bed, then boil up as much water as you can."

The clearly perturbed man floundered around like a chicken with its head wrung off. Looked like he was in the midst of some kind of palsied seizure as he jerked the window open, then pulled what looked like an unused wedding quilt from the bottom drawer of their oak chest. He gingerly spread the coverlet over the rumpled bedding, and finally thundered his way toward the kitchen without so much as looking back. Could hear him banging pots and pans around as I helped ease the girl into a more comfortable, reclining positon.

She flopped onto her back hard, then, with trembling fingers, made a grab for the wooden rails that held a corn-shuck mattress in place. Immediately drew her knees up, grunted, and set to trying to force the baby out. Rivulets of steaming sweat beaded up on her pain-twisted face and forehead. Ropy veins popped out along either side of her neck.

Soon as she relaxed for a bit, I patted her on the arm and said, "Gotta get you outta this dress, ma'am."

With eyes so brown they were almost black, she stared at me like I'd surely gone slap crazy. For several seconds her breathing came in short, labored bursts.

In an effort to put her more at ease, I said, "What's your name, missus?"

Could see the terrified confusion etched into her bewildered face. Finally, she gasped, "Mary. Mary Two Wolves. Mary Two Wolves Matthews."

"Good. Now, can you tell me where there's another blanket, Mary? I'll cover you over as best I can."

She gritted her teeth as another wave of pain racked her overtaxed body. Sweat and tears mingled and ran onto the pillow beneath her mass of already drenched hair.

"Under the bed," she grunted, "but hurry. Please. You gotta hurry, mister."

Dropped to my knees and rooted one arm around beneath her bed, then yanked out a coarse, threadbare cavalry blanket. Pushed Mary Two Wolves' skirt up above trembling knees, and spread the blanket gentlelike over her parted thighs.

Stepped outside the door of the stifling room for a second and started to fire up a panatela while she disrobed. Got the stogie to my lips. Got a good clinch on it with my teeth. Scratched the match to life on the doorframe, then bit clean through that stick of tobacco when Mary Two Wolves let out a shriek that sounded like something you'd expect to hear from afflicted souls being tortured in Satan's fiery, smoldering pit.

Yelled for her husband to bring me a pan of hot water and some soap damned quick. Pitched my stogie away and headed back into the bedroom to try and do what I could for the tormented girl. Plain, cotton dress she'd been wearing a few minutes earlier was clutched to her chest. Ragged, rapid-fire breathing sounded like a Gatling gun going off. I rolled up my shirtsleeves, eased down on the foot of the bed, and, as tenderly as I could, placed a hand on one of her trembling knees.

She kinda jerked like I'd surprised her, but relaxed a bit when, in as soothing a voice as I could muster, I said, "Promise I won't look 'less I find the need, Mary. Please forgive the intrusion, but I'm gonna have to reach under the blanket and feel around some to see if I can tell how things are goin'. That okay with you?"

With dark eyes scrunched closed, she jerked her head up a time or two. "Yes. Yes. I understand. Go on ahead. Do whatever you have to."

About then, her jittery husband showed up carrying a pan of steaming water and a bar of lye soap. He held the pan while I washed off, quick as I could. Offered me a towel but, to be totally truthful, the tattered piece of rag didn't look all that clean.

Waved him aside and said, "Get on back to the stove. Keep the water goin', Jonah. Probably gonna need all of it later." Thank God the man wasn't inclined to argue. He vanished like a puff of befuddled smoke, and I turned my attention back to his struggling wife.

Now, there's no way I'm going to claim talents I didn't possess. Did what I could think of to do, based solely on experiences so far back in my past I could barely remember them. And I managed it all under something less than ideal circumstances.

Slid a damp hand under the blanket and felt around between Mary Two Wolves' legs—not knowing exactly what I expected to find, or even much of exactly what I was *supposed* to find.

Twitching girl helped me a bunch when she said, "That's the baby's head. Think he's in the right position, but it seems like maybe he's stuck, or hung up, or somethin'."

Well, now, that came as one hell of a surprise to an ignorant man like me. "Stuck? Hung up? How can he be stuck?"

She let out an agonized groan that sounded like it came from the tips of her toes, twisted the dress into a lumpy knot, then placed both hands on her mountainous belly and pushed. "Arggggh, God, I don't know," she spat. "Just doesn't feel right. Nothin' feels right. Might not ever feel right again till I die. Merciful heavens, it hurts."

Ran shaky fingers around the exposed portion of the baby's hairy noggin. "Near as I can tell, seems like he's facin' down. Is facedown the proper way?"

She wiped at her sweat-covered face with the dress, then pitched the garment onto the floor. "Guess so. Not sure," she grunted. "Tell the truth, mister, this child's been a problem ever since the night he was conceived. Once he got big enough, papoose's fought me like a wildcat. Come nigh on to kickin' me to death over the past few weeks."

Tried my best to put a positive face on the situation when I offered, "Well, that's a good thing, don't you think?"

A tortured moan escaped her lips. "Woulda seemed so, but I ain't so sure now. Thought he was ready to pop out when you and your friend rode up." She groaned and clawed at the blanket beneath her sweat-soaked body. "Now it feels like he's got his fingers buried in my womb and is clawin' like a wildcat to stay inside. Wish to Jesus he'd make up his mind."

Of a sudden, Mary Two Wolves went to huffing and puffing like one of those Missouri, Kansas and Texas Railroad line Baldwin locomotives sitting on the track next to a depot. She grabbed her knees, grunted, strained so hard finger-sized veins popped out along the temples on either side of her head, then set to squealing so loud the noise level almost made my eyes glaze over. She reached up and latched onto the hand I had resting on her knee and, I swear 'fore God, thought for a spell there she was about to reduce my knuckles to nothing more than a pile of powder.

Poor girl went through a hellish form of torment no man could conceive of on the worst day he ever lived. Baby crept out, inch by inch. Once the kid's head was free, I had to hold it up 'cause I feared he might smother. Damned ignorant really, but that's the way it happened. For what seemed like an hour of that particular effort, my arms felt like someone had tied all the muscles into the kind of knots sailors use to hold iron ships to piers.

The distraught husband ran back and forth between the bedroom and the kitchen in an effort to keep me in hot water. Time or two, he just stood at the door, wrung his hands like a wild man, or pulled at his hair like he just might tip over into madness at any second.

Was drenched in dripping sweat myself when, as much to get his mind off what was going on as anything else, I said, "Jonah, go outside. Tell my partner I need him to come in here right now."

Couldn't have been more than a minute later when John Henry showed up. He peeked inside like a kid that'd just been caught trying to sneak a quick glance inside his sister's pantaloons and said, "Looks to me like you've got the situation well in hand there, Tilden."

"Could be," I shot back, "but I'm really tired. Would be greatly appreciated if you'd spell me for a bit."

He grabbed the front of his shirt with one hand like someone else was wearing it and said, "Me? You want me to do what exactly?"

"Come 'round here on my end and take this kid's head in your hands."

He took a couple of tentative steps my direction, stopped, then said, "Take what kid's head . . . whoa, Momma. What the hell's that?"

"It's the baby's head, you ignorant wretch," I said.

He got up close to me and kind of whispered, "Damnation, that sure as hell looks awful, Tilden. You reckon this kid is alive? Mean, sweet, merciful Father, he's all gray like he's been dead for a week. All pruny and wrinkled up like a piece of dried fruit. Just don't look right, you know?"

"Aw, I think that's just the way they all look at first. All wrinkled and off color. 'Pears to be okay to me, just ain't all that anxious to come on out. Can't really blame the little booger much for wantin' to stay where it's safe and quiet, but he's gotta come on out and damned soon, 'cause I ain't sure how much more of this treatment his mama can stand."

With that single statement, the whole situation took a sudden and dramatic change of direction. Mary Two Wolves let out a long, slow sigh and appeared to suddenly relax all over. "There," she barely breathed, "he's ready."

Of a sudden, that kid popped out of that gal's insides like he had a steel spring attached to the bottoms of his tiny feet. Right behind the child, the afterbirth and all the other fetal matter came flopping out.

When the placenta and everything else plopped onto the bed in a gelatinous sacklike pile, John Henry jumped back, snatched his hat off, and yelped, "Shit, almighty. Seen animals do as much, but this is my first experience with a woman. Had no idea it was so close to looking 'bout the same as somethin' that comes out of a cow."

Grabbed the newborn up by the feet and smacked him on the bottom. Didn't get any response. Whacked him again. Kid yelped, then went to bawling. Remember thinking that even if nothing else worked, he had a good strong set of lungs on him.

Jonah Matthews hit the door less than a second after the child first cried out. But he stood outside, twisting his hat with nervous hands, and refused to come in when I motioned for him to do so.

Exasperated, I laid the squalling little boy out on his back, reached over, and slipped John Henry's bowie out of its scabbard. Grabbed a piece of fringe on his leather Texan's shirt, then chopped it off before he could say anything. Tied off the birth cord, sliced the kid away from the afterbirth, then laid him out on his mama's heaving stomach.

Mary Two Wolves wearily raised her sweat-drenched head and gazed at her fryin'-sized papoose. "My God, but he's really beautiful, isn't he? Don't you think he's beautiful, mister?"

"Yes, ma'am. He's gonna be quite a ladies' man someday, I'd suspect."

John Henry slapped me on the back. "Damned fine work, Deputy Tilden. Damned fine. Did a much better job than I could've ever done. Don't mind confessin' my ignorance in such matters one whit. No sirree, Bob. Just gladder'n hell it was you she picked and not me."

Took several more hours to get myself, Mrs. Matthews, and everything else cleaned up. Tried my level best to leave the place spick-and-span. Knew my wife, Elizabeth, would never forgive me if she found out later that I'd left a mess for those poor, emotionally wrung-out folks to deal with.

Held Mary Two Wolves up on her feet long enough for John Henry to change her bedding. Then we stepped outside while her husband helped the exhausted woman get into a clean nightgown. Once they'd finished getting her dressed and into bed again, came back and stared into the room from the doorway. With our hats in our hands, I explained why we'd stopped by their home in the first place. Surprised me no end when they readily agreed to take the Harvey kids in until their nearest kin could be located.

Still clearly unsettled, Jonah Matthews stood next to his wife's bed and held her hand. Wrapped in a piece of clean blanket, the baby rested next to its mother on the side of the bed nearest the wall.

Though obviously still very weak, Mary Two Wolves said, "We'd be more than willing to help out."

"Yes, suh. Yes, suh, we would. We be owin' you genna-mens a deep debt a gratitude fo' yer he'p with our new son, suh," her husband added. "My wife an' me, well, we done be a-feelin' as how takin' dem poor, motherless chil'ren into our home will go a right fer piece to repayment of that debt. 'Sides, dem Harveys was mighty fine people. Dey was de kinda neighbors anyone out here in da wil' places would want to have. We'll be a-missin' 'em, dat fo' sure and certain."

"Well, folks, you have my most heartfelt thanks," I said. Pulled fifty dollars from my wallet and handed the whole sum to Jonah Matthews. He tried to refuse. Not very hard, but the man at least acted like he wasn't going to take the money for a few seconds.

"That should help with the kids until their family can come claim them, Mr. Matthews," I said. "You need any more than that amount, just send word to me in Fort Smith and I'll see you get it."

Stuffed my hat on, pulled at the brim, and nodded my good-bye at those fine folks. Had turned to head for the front door when I heard Jonah Matthews call out, "Wait. Suh. Please wait jus' a minute."

John Henry peered over my shoulder as I stood in the bedroom's doorway and snatched my hat off again. "Is there something else, Mr. Matthews?"

"Well, suh, Mary done tole me as how while you was a helpin' wid dis here chile of our'n, she done had a vision."

"Vision?"

"Yassir. She say a spirit done come down from Heaven an' visit wid her."

"A spirit, you did say a spirit, right?"

"Yassir. Spirit of a departed chile. She say the spirit a blond-haired, blue-eyed little boy. He say as how you his daddy. Tell Mary how he had to go away from dis worl' when he not very ole. Say a terrible sickness took him over to the other side. Say he miss you an' his mama very much."

Couldn't believe my ears. 'Course I'd heard tales of such supernatural events, but nothing to compare with what Jonah Matthews had just implied had ever happened to me before. Not once. Couldn't imagine that my long-dead son, Tommy, had managed to communicate with Mary Two Wolves. But there it was. Couldn't deny it. Tried to speak, but the words wouldn't come out. Held my hat in my hands and twisted at the brim. Stuttered around some more. Felt like my whole body had suddenly been weighted down with iron.

John Henry must have known that Matthews had hit a tender spot with me. He cuffed me on the shoulder, then patted my back as though he understood my distress.

Barely heard her when Mary Two Wolves called out, "Mister, what did you say your name was?"

Stopped long enough to glance back and say, "Tilden, ma'am. Hayden Tilden."

She turned and kissed her baby on the forehead. "Then we'll name our son Hayden. Hayden Thomas Two Wolves Matthews. I hope you approve."

"Thomas? You'll name your child Thomas?"

"Yes. The spirit said that was his name. It's a fine one, I think, and that's what we'll call our son—Thomas."

Truth of an old saying from the Bible hit me in the gut and almost doubled me over. Just no way for us to know God's great plan, or how he'll choose to reveal it to each of us. To my great astonishment, He'd let a bit of divine wonderment come from the mouth of an Indian girl named Mary Two Wolves Matthews who'd just given birth.

John Henry punched me on the arm and grinned.

Have to admit, I was so surprised by the whole amazing experience that, for several seconds, I couldn't think of anything to say. Toed at the floor and kind of shuffled around, then finally said, "You've done me a great honor, ma'am. Know if my son were still alive, he'd be pleased to know that he had a namesake. With God as my witness, Mary, I won't forget what happened here, and I won't forget you."

11

"Sons a Bitches Even Slaughtered the Kids."

JOHN HENRY SLATE and me hit the trail west as if all the horned, red-eyed imps of a sulfurous Hell had boiled up out of the fiery pit like a nest of red ants and were breathing their putrid breath down our sweaty necks. Pushed our animals to their absolute limit for almost three straight days. Fourth day, we began to slow down and run fresh sign along the easily followed trail Carl and Nate had left behind.

Zeke Blackheart had led his growing gang of thugs in a lunatic, zigzagged path that ran west along the Deep Fork of the Canadian, north for a spell, then south. None of their wanderings appeared to make any sense as we plowed across miles of prairie covered with thick, dry grass that grew up to our animals' bellies.

Then, for a spell, we followed those skunks through rugged, deep, canyonlike, red-clay ravines and gullies until the track they'd left behind ran out and emerged amidst more grass-covered emptiness. The meandering trail suddenly veered north for a few miles, then dove south again as if the earth had somehow been propped up on a slant.

John Henry turned out to be a godsend. While I'd never claimed any great talent as a tracker, he had the same unerring ability that Carlton always exhibited when the chips were down. Man could literally follow water spiders across swift-moving rivers, or find the trails of scorpions across mud holes the size of a Texican's sombrero.

Third night of the chase, I think, he surprised me with something totally unexpected. To be truthful, so many years have passed that these days it's not real clear in my cankered mind exactly when it happened, but for some reason the event sticks with me as having occurred that third evening after dinner. We'd camped in a shady grove of weeping willows along the banks of Mad Bear Creek, couldn't a been more'n a hundred yards from where the barely trickling stream joined up with the Canadian River at Seminole Bend.

We'd stretched out our tired, knotted-up, saddle-bruised bodies beside a good fire. I'd almost dozed off after chowin' down on the wild pheasant John Henry had killed earlier that day. Man was a hell of a shot from horseback. Typical of all them Comanche-fighting Texas boys.

Of a sudden, my new partner rolled up on one elbow, stared through the flames of our campfire, and said, "Might remember as how I mentioned I 'uz searchin' for Arvil and Delbert Boston when we first met up."

"Yes. Do seem to recall you sayin' as much."

"Have to confess that the crimes them boys committed down in the Winding Stair Mountains ain't the only reason I'm after 'em."

"That a fact?"

"Yes. Yes it is. Actually came all the way up here from Waco lookin' to see some justice done, Tilden. Joined up with the U.S. Marshals Service 'cause I figured it might be easier to find them boys. And, too, wanted the law on my side when we finally met up."

His unsolicited confession brought my own situation into extremely sharp focus. The grinning ghost of Saginaw Bob Magruder, and the mindless murders of my entire family, flashed to life on the hellish tips of the flames that danced in front of my tired eyes. Parallels with John Henry's experiences amazed me.

Took a deep drag off the panatela I'd lighted up after our meal. Blew a smoke ring the size of a wagon wheel, then said, "Well, I'm absolutely certain you're not the only man carryin' a badge in the Indian country that took on the awesome responsibility we've all shouldered for what he deemed good reasons."

"Aim to send Arvil and Delbert Boston to a burnin' Hell first chance I get, Tilden. Just wanted you to be aware that my plans for those men don't include taking either of them back to Fort Smith for trial, once we catch up with 'em. Bastards rubbed out an entire family of mighty fine folks when they raided a ranch house over near Tascosa."

"You knew the folks they murdered?"

"My brother, Alonso, his wife, Karen. Sons a bitches even slaughtered their three kids. May the Good Lord damn the whole bunch of 'em. Murderin' slugs sure as hell didn't want any witnesses tellin' who'd done the sorry deed."

Felt awful about having to ask the question, but it had to have an answer. "Well, then, why are you so certain the Boston boys are responsible for the killin's?"

"Unfortunately for them boys, one of the children managed to hide out. Stayed alive to identify those murderin' bastards. Seems the Boston boys had worked for Alonso for a few days, left, then come back to take whatever they could. Essie, my youngest niece, hid in the corn crib when the shootin' started. Ten-year-old girl saw the whole, bloody, horrific massacre."

"Well, damn. That's just by-God awful."

"Yeah. Poor child told me them killers turned that place upside down lookin' for her. Just a God-sent miracle they didn't find the girl and that she managed to live to inform the world about their ghastly deeds."

Leaned into my bedroll. Propped my head up by putting one arm between me and my saddle. Stared up at the amazing array of stars that peeked down at me from between the weeping willow leaves that flittered back and forth on a soft breeze. Said, "You sure they're with Zeke Blackheart and his bunch?"

"Followed 'em right up to the Harvey family's front doorstep. Figure they'd been tryin' to find Blackheart for weeks. Once he and his bunch went on a robbery and killin' rip the likes of which no one in the Nations had ever seen, just made their search a bunch easier. Be willin' to bet my Brazos River ranch, just west of Waco, that the Boston boys are riding with Blackheart right this minute."

Man rolled back into his bedding and didn't say another word. No need. He'd let me know where he stood, and I appreciated his frankness. Couldn't blame him much for the way he felt. Hell, I'd harbored the same kinds of feelings myself on a number of occasions, and even acted on them. Couldn't find it in myself to condemn John Henry Slate. Even gave serious thought to adding him to the Brotherhood of Blood. Knew Carlton would've approved. But the more I thought on the thing, the more I figured it best to wait and see how everything played out once we found the Blackheart bunch. Hell, John Henry could very well have changed his mind by then. Or maybe he wasn't the man he appeared. Just never can tell when it comes to people. Not until the chips are down and the fresh, hot blood starts to run as freely as spilled buttermilk.

'Bout noon of the fifth day, we stopped in the tiny hamlet of Vamoose, located in an ancient stand of live oaks five miles or so south of the Canadian. Whole town didn't amount to much more than a set of wagon ruts, decorated on either side with an illegal whiskey-selling operation that figured to be doubling as a whorehouse. Few doors away was a dry goods store owned by some feller named A.J. Overby. 'Cross the street a small blacksmith and stable concern. There were eight or ten other nondescript storefronts here and there, half a dozen or so clapboard houses, twenty-five or thirty canvas tents that people appeared to be living in, and, thank God, an actual grocery and mercantile store. Rugged, frontier community bustled with nervous-looking people who darted back and forth across their one and only thoroughfare like frightened rabbits running from a pack of redbone hounds.

John Henry leaned on his saddle horn and said, "We're in need of bacon, beans, coffee, some sugar, hell, all manner of supplies, Tilden. Gonna have to slow down long enough to stock up 'fore we go any farther, or we're gonna starve to death somewhere out there in the big cold and lonely. Can't depend on me killin' a pheasant or prairie chicken every day."

Grinned and said, "Aw, that ain't no problem for a big shooter like you, John Henry. Figured you'd keep us in game till we got back to Fort Smith."

He chuckled, then said, "Nice of you to say such, but I'd feel a bunch better with some store-bought supplies in our saddlebags as well."

'Course I knew he was right, so we drew our tired animals to a halt out front of a grocery store and mercantile operation that sported a bright yellow sign lettered in cobalt blue that proclaimed it as SIMON GLUCK'S STORE. Threw my reins over the hitch rail out front of the place just in time to hear the thunder of horses' hooves coming up from the south. Glanced across my saddle. Be damned if I didn't spot the murderous bastard we were chasing at the head of a party of at least nine or ten brigands. Band of killers bristled with weapons and were headed our way like grinning death its very own self.

Went to grabbing for my shotgun and rifle. Over my shoulder, I yelled, "That's Zeke Blackheart and his bunch, John Henry. 'Pears he's picked up some more men in his travels. They musta backtracked on Carlton and Nate. Look to have blood in their eyes."

Words hadn't even got out of my mouth good when I saw Blackheart pull a brace of pistols and motion for his men to spread out on either side of him. The pack of murderous animals came into town like a death-dealing scythe cutting through dry wheat. Soon as those killers passed the first tent, they started firing at anything moving. Screaming people went to running in every direction. Wounded horses squealed and fell at the hitch rails.

Cold-eyed, murderin' scum couldn't of been more'n sixty yards away when I pitched both my long guns onto Gluck's low covered porch, jerked the reins loose, and slapped Gunpowder on his muscular rump hard as I could. Big sorrel couldn't wait to get away from all the shooting. Jumped like he'd been fired from a cannon and headed for safety, anywhere it could be found.

I hoofed it for Gluck's front door. Grabbed up my weapons on the way, then dove inside. Landed hard on my belly. Reddish brown dust and splinters boiled up around me in a thick, gagging cloud. Rolled onto one side and laid there for a second or two, and watched John Henry as he heeled it for shelter on the opposite side of the street. Could see that he'd managed to get both the big poppers off his own animal as well.

Right quicklike, he took a spot between a barrel of ax handles and a stack of used saddles in front of a hardware outfit. Only had an instant to think on it, but quickly realized that we'd have Blackheart and all his murderous thugs in a withering cross fire soon as they got to the spot where we'd been standing just a few seconds before.

Shotgun in hand, I got onto my knees about the time the lead-spitting line of killers swept into view right outside Gluck's front entrance. Four of them evil sons of bitches turned toward me, just in time to find themselves looking down the barrels of my ten-gauge Greener.

Before them ole boys could think twice, I cut loose with a thunderous double-barreled blast that knocked three of them off their mounts. Hurt a fourth feller so bad, all he could do was flop around in the saddle like a corn-shuck doll. Two of their horses dropped right in their tracks. A third one let out a hair-raising, agonized squeal and disappeared in front of the roiling cloud of spent gunpowder that spooled out of the barrels of my smoking weapon.

Initial shots from my direction turned the entire party of still-mounted men toward me. Dropped flat on my belly as a storm of pistol fire riddled the fancy, beveled-glass windows on either side of Gluck's entrance. Barrage of gunfire rendered his equally impressive doors to little more than splintered, flying shards of glass that fell on my back like shattered icicles. Pitched the shotgun aside and grabbed up my Winchester.

Bullets ripped holes in the floor that inched my direction. Hot lead gouged splinters out of the rough-cut lumber like the glistening sharp and deadly teeth of an advancing buzz saw. Over all the gunfire, I could still hear the shouting men and screaming women customers of Gluck's behind me. Panicked folks knocked over loaded showcases, chairs, apple crates, and display boxes as they clamored in the direction of the hoped-for safety of a back exit.

About the time I felt my number was sure enough gonna be called by St. Peter, John Henry cut loose from the other side of Vamoose's only thoroughfare. Two more of Blackheart's men dropped out of their saddles and hit the rutted street like burlap bags of seed dropped from the bed of a passing freight wagon. Gunfire became random but unrelenting.

111

After my partner's initial salvo, the dark, gray-black cloud of gunpowder hanging over the street got so thick I could barely make out the remaining horses, much less anyone riding them. Levered a shell and fired when I thought I had a chance of hitting something important. But I swear 'fore Jesus, those ole boys that were still in the saddle were peppering me with a withering storm of lead. Seemed not to even notice that someone behind them was now doing all the real damage.

Then, of a sudden, one of those crazy sons of bitches, a blazing pistol in each hand, took the reins in his teeth and rode his beast right through Gluck's obliterated entryway and into the store, just like the animal belonged there. Dropped the Winchester and grabbed for my own handguns, but it was too late, and then some.

Horse reared up on its hind legs right there in the store. Rider was blasting everything and everybody he could lay an eye on. Knew beyond any doubt that whoever the man on the horse was, he'd spent some time riding with the bushwhackers up in Missouri, Kansas, or maybe Arkansas during the war. Only place a body could've learned to shoot like that from a crazed, bug-eyed, scared-slap-to-death, rearing jughead of a horse.

In a fraction of a second, I noticed that the skunk trying to kill me had four pistols strapped to his waist, a pair of pommel guns, and two more in holsters attached to the skirt of his saddle just behind the rear rigging ring. Christ, I thought, eight pistols. Son of a bitch can fire damn near fifty shots at me without stopping. Figured if I didn't find someplace to hide, I'd sure enough be shaking hands with Heaven's bearded gatekeeper and damned quick.

Only good thing I had going was the ever-growing, dense screen of black powder smoke that had collected between me and imminent death. Ripped off several shots at the rider. Couldn't have been more than ten feet away, but missed him every time. Put at least one in his horse though—

maybe two. Animal let out a pitiable shriek, stumbled, and damn near fell sideways in my direction. Felt bad about killing three horses, maybe four, but, hell, awful shit sometimes happens when you're trying to bring down merciless killers bent on sending you, and everybody else in sight, to meet the Maker.

Turned to try and find something to hide behind. Well, suffice it to say, I was a day late and about twenty dollars short. Heard the gun go off, then felt a burning sensation in my right hip and, in considerably less time than it'd take fresh, shucked corn to go through a goose, realized that my leg wouldn't support me any longer.

Dropped to the floor again. Rolled up under a table right in the middle of the store that was loaded down with all manner of odds and ends that a big-eyed shopper might find to his or her liking. Rider had somehow managed to keep his animal on its feet. Maintained a blistering barrage of gunfire focused in my direction.

Jars of jelly, canned meats, buckets loaded with a variety of recently picked vegetables, wooden boxes filled with fresh cackle berries—brown in one box, white in another—exploded atop the table over my head in a hailstorm of splinters as 255-grain, .45-caliber bullets plowed trenches in everything between me and certain death. Horse whinnied, screeched, slung hot black blood here and yonder, and clomped all over everything between me and the door.

Thought sure I'd seen the end. Had absolutely no place to run. Worst of all, knew the man pursuing me still had plenty of firepower left. Rolled onto my back beneath the table. Bucked myself up to flop from under my cover and make out the best way I could.

Cocked both my pistols, and was just before taking action I figured would surely get me killed, when I heard John Henry yell, "Drop them pistols, you son of a bitch."

Well, the son of a bitch either didn't hear or wasn't listening. Pair of near-deafening shotgun blasts sent shock waves my direction that set up a curling wave of dust from the floor and blew it all toward me in a single gigantic swoosh of sandy grit. Heard a loud thud above me. Even bigger one right at my feet. Jelly jars, meat tins, and eggs went flying in every direction.

Figured I wouldn't move for a second or two. Didn't want John Henry to mistake me for one of the Blackheart bunch and blast me to Kingdom Come as well.

Then I heard my friend yell, "You in there, Tilden? Speak up. Where are you?"

"Here. I'm under the table." Held one pistol-filled hand out and sort of waved.

"Ah. See you now. Come on out. Feller who was afflicting you has gone on to his just re-wards. Don't think he'll be botherin' you anymore. Looks as how, maybe, we've got the whole bunch of 'em subdued."

For several seconds, all I could do was lay there, sucking in air like a man who'd just been rescued from near drowning. Rolled over in the mess caused by blasted groceries with my eyes closed and whispered my sincerest thanks to a gracious and merciful God for letting me live a bit longer.

12

"... Your Thievin' and Murderin' Days Are Over..."

CRAWLED FROM BENEATH my bullet-riddled, blood-sloshed shelter, grabbed the closest thing I could get hold of—edge of a shattered display case that had been home to several large boxes of cut-plug tobacco—and pulled my shot-in-the-ass self erect. First thing I noticed was a feller in the white shirt, black vest, and silk sleeve garters of a grocer. He slowly came to his feet behind the counter right in front of me. Figured he was most probably the stunned owner of the mess we'd just made, Mr. Gluck.

Bug-eyed feller cast a saucer-eyed gaze at the rampant destruction we'd visited upon him and his place of business. Another anxious, stunned-looking gent crept from behind a potbellied iron stove in one of the far corners of the oblong room. The pair of them couldn't do much of anything except shake their heads in disbelief and mutter things like, "My, oh, my." "Damnedest thing I've ever witnessed." And, "Thank you, Lord, for lettin' me live through this mess."

Jackass who'd damn near taken my life lay flat on his back atop the table I'd been under. Surrounded by gobs of strawberry jam, broken eggs, and pickled cauliflower, he was glassy-eyed and bleeding from massive wounds in his chest and neck that pumped gouts of spurting gore. Lake of fresh blood soaked his gunman's duster and dripped into a spreading pool on the floor below. His gore-soaked hands clutched at some of the more prominent holes in his person. Astonished me no end that the bold bastard still lived and was able to breathe—barely.

His wheezing mare had collapsed into a blood-and-froth-spattered heap right at the foot of the table. Appeared that the poor, gut-shot beast's legs had simply gone rubbery slack, and then dropped from numerous wounds right where she stood. River of steaming, life-giving liquid gushed from the animal's nose, and its tortured breathing came in short, snorted bursts and pained, raspy gasps.

John Henry stepped up, shotgun in one hand, pistol in the other. He placed the pistol's barrel against the side of the wounded bangtail's head, and blasted it out of its misery.

Feller I took to be Gluck shot me a confused look, pointed at the freshly dispatched hay burner, and yelped, "Jesus H. Christ on a crutch, what the hell am I supposed to do with a dead horse in the middle of my store? Good God Almighty."

As John Henry edged his way toward me, he said, "Tells me plenty, mister, that you're more concerned 'bout the horse than this shot-to-pieces feller all spread out on your display table like a slab of bacon."

Gluck raised his arms to heaven in disgust. He was damn near yelling when he glared back at Slate and yelped, "Goddammit, I can move the dead man's worthless, sorry ass, but the horse is a totally different, and considerably more problematic, matter. Have to drag the beast outta here most likely. Take a draft animal, maybe two of 'em, to do that. Not even sure there's a draft horse within fifty miles of this godforsaken place."

As John Henry holstered his still smoking pistol, he flashed an embarrassed grin, then said, "Well, don't yell at me. Appears as how Deputy Marshal Tilden here shot the poor creature. All I did was put it out of its obvious misery."

Gluck made some kind of unintelligible noise between a grunt, a groan, and an obscene epithet. He threw up his hands as though sickened by the whole mess and, cursing a blue streak, headed for the street.

Soon as the disgruntled storekeeper was out of sight, I leaned against the table, checked for spent rounds in my strong-side pistol, reloaded, then said, "Well, how'd we make out. Musta been one helluva fight out there in the street. 'Course, I was under this table a good bit of the time and probably missed most of it."

John Henry flashed a toothy grin. "Mighty modest of you there, Tilden. Near as I can tell, you sent at least four of these murderin' bastards on their way to a burnin' Hell all by yourself." He flicked a nod toward the man stretched out amidst Gluck's destroyed display of canned vegetables and such. "You know the feller on the table?"

Hobbled a short, tortured course through all the trash, litter, and broken glass that surrounded the dead horse and the display table. Pulled the brigand's hat away from his face, then said, "Just be damned. This here's Elroy Black Jack Morris." Slapped the corpse across the face with his own hat, then said, "You shot me, Jack. You crazy son of a bitch."

"He wanted?"

"'Course he's wanted. Man's killed a wagonload of innocent folks all over the Nations. We've been tryin' to catch him for over a year. Got a signed warrant for his arrest in my saddlebag."

Slate glanced down at my side and pointed. "That your blood on them pants, Tilden?"

"Yeah. This mangy, murderin' stack of hammered horse-shit put one in my hip. Don't think he did any real serious damage, but I am leakin' some and it does smart a mite." Pressed against the wound. Bit surprised to find that it was leaking a bit more than I'd thought.

John Henry nodded, then motioned me toward Gluck's blasted-to-pieces front entrance. "Well, if you can totter on over thisaway, guess you'd best come on outside and get a good look at the whole story for yourself. You made one hellacious mess all by yourself, Tilden. My tiny contribution didn't amount to much more'n a hill of beans."

Limped out onto the boardwalk and into a scene straight out of the worst nightmares imaginable. Slate held his weapon in one hand and made a kind of all-encompassing, wandlike wave with the shotgun, then said, "Behold the result of your deadly handiwork, Marshal Tilden."

Counted seven men I could see down in the street. They were scattered in all directions. One sat upright in stunned silence. Couple of others groaned and rolled around in the dirt puking all over themselves—just nothing to match a gunshot wound in the right spot to set a man puking. One or two of the obviously dead lay, unmoving, in odd, twisted positions and stared, sightless, at cottonball clouds floating overhead. Single biggest concentration of the fallen had dropped right in front of Gluck's front step. Those three lay sprawled in the street near their gut-twistin' cayuses— not a one of them appeared to have any more pulse than a pitchfork—deader'n a bunch of drowned cats, both men and animals.

John Henry made a second, but somewhat abbreviated, motion with the barrel of his big blaster toward a couple of the gang that I'd put down. "Them two fine-lookin' gents yonder are Arvil and Delbert Boston. You musta dropped 'em with the very first blast from that shoulder cannon of yours. Not sure as who that third feller might be. Somethin' nigh on a cupful of your buckshot hit him in the face. Might be somethin' of a puzzler just identifyin' the poor ugly son of a bitch. 'Less we can get some of these other sons a bitches to identify him."

"What about all them boys over there closer to your side of the street? 'Pears to me we're more or less about even on the overall score."

"Hell, I don't know any of these skunks, 'cept the Boston brothers, Tilden. But think maybe that tall feller, middle of the street, wearin' the felt hat, one sportin' the turkey feathers, might be Blackheart."

Peered through the rising cloud of gun smoke and dust toward the center of the rutted thoroughfare. "Think maybe you'd be right about that. Let's stroll on over and talk to 'im. 'Pears he's alive, sittin' up like that and all?"

"Well, he was still breathin' and complainin' when I disarmed him. But I ain't gonna offer up no guarantees as to how long he'll be that way. Could get the call from Satan just any second now."

John Henry let me use his shotgun as a crutch so I could shamble over to where Zeke Blackheart was sitting. He'd hit the ground just like he'd chosen to take a seat right there in the middle of the thoroughfare. Took some painful doing, but I managed to get myself down to his level. No doubt about it, the man was close on to being blown to pieces. Looked like he'd caught both barrels of heavy-gauge shot from John Henry's big blaster. Amazes me to this very instant that he was still breathing. And, hell, that he could even talk.

Gazed at his pockmarked, grizzled face and growled, "Guess your thievin' and murderin' days are over, Zeke. Way I've got it figured, Ole Scratch is stokin' up the furnaces of Hell 'specially for your arrival on his front doorstep. 'Pears the Devil's playground is your next stop."

Blackheart had both hands clamped over his dripping

guts. Reminded me of the kid we'd found out on the trail—
Milt Glass. Swear 'fore Jesus, the angry skunk glared at
me like he would've ripped my heart out and eaten it raw if
he could've managed it.

Behind me, I heard John Henry say, "No need to worry
yourself, Tilden. I kicked all his weapons away 'fore I came
over to dispatch ole Black Jack and check on you."

"You got tobacco, Tilden?" Blackheart grunted from
between cracked, trembling lips.

Fiddled around in my vest pocket and pulled out a
panatela. "You know who I am, outlaw?"

The twisted-faced half-breed let out an exasperated, liquid groan. "'Course I know who you are. Every badman in
the Nations has heard of you, lawdog. You're the man who
brought Saginaw Bob Magruder, the Crooke brothers, and
a damned lot of others to book."

"Well, at least the parts about Magruder and the Crooke
boys are true."

He moaned as sweat dripped from his chin. "Hear tell
you watched Magruder hang. Feller I met tole me as how
lightning fell from heaven and struck the gallows at the exact moment ole Bob hit the end of Maledon's famous piece
of oiled Kentucky hemp."

"Was quite a scene," I said. Bit the pointy end off the
panatela, then leaned over and shoved it into the wounded
brigand's mouth. "Sure you can smoke?"

Clenched a set of perfect teeth around the cigar, then
groaned, "You light it, I'll smoke it."

He sucked hard on the stogie, then coughed. Kept the
cigar from falling into the dirt with those blindingly white
choppers. And between the two of us, we finally got that
see-gar stoked to life. "Damn. That's mighty fine," he said,
and blew a wheezy, coughing, bluish gray cloud toward
heaven. "Gonna miss a good smoke once I'm cookin' in
Hell's fiery pit."

Ran a hand down my side. Noticed my pants leg was

soaked through with blood that oozed from the wound in my hip. Pressed hard on the hole in my britches where the bullet had entered, then said, "What started you on this path, Zeke? Know you had a few problems here and there. Read reports that told as how you'd been accused of stealing some horses and such. Bit of drunkenness once in a while. Some introducin' here and there. No existing record of any real serious problems with the law till you just seemed to go slap crazy and start killin' folks."

He threw a blank, rubbery, dark-eyed stare my direction and shook his head. Let his gaze ricochet around the street from one body to the next. "You fellers sure 'nuff shot hell outta all my boys, lawdog." He glanced over at John Henry. "'Specially you, you badge-totin' son of a bitch. Kilt some damned good men today. Snuffed Jackson Bowlegs. 'Pears as how you got the Boston boys, Tilden. Hell, they hadn't been with me but about a week."

John Henry hooked a thumb toward the bunch I'd put down. "That Bowlegs over there with the Boston brothers?"

A shudder of life-sapping pain behind beads of hot sweat shot across Blackheart's drenched, glistening face. He jerked his head up and down in a barely perceptible nod. "Yeah, and that'n over yonder way, closest to the spot where you was hid out, is One Cut Petey Mason. Angry little bastard could carve up a human body like no man I've ever known before. Looks like you killed him deader'n a bucket a rocks, mister."

Decided not to let Blackheart slip over to the other side without him hearing a bit of hard-handed truth about his murderous behavior. Said, "You brought the bloody hand of a vengeful God down on them and yourself, Zeke. Every corpse you can see is lying here because of you."

Something in his coal-black eyes flickered back to angry life. Knew beyond any doubt he would've killed me in a heartbeat—if he could've pulled it off.

A spittle-laced trickle of blood ran from the corner of

his mouth and stained the teeth biting at the panatela. "Were all dead men years ago, Tilden. Just markin' time till some white feller, like you, decided to kill us."

"That's total bullshit, Zeke, and you know it. Hell, you're half white yourself."

He nodded, then grimaced as though a foot-long bowie knife had been shoved into his guts. From the side of his mouth not occupied by the cigar, he grunted, "Yeah, and I woulda murdered the white half myself if I coulda figured out how to do the deed and still be alive so's I could send more whites to their particular spot in a festerin' Hell."

Of a sudden, I got real light-headed. Turned just a mite to look over at John Henry. Whole world set to spinning like a kid's top. As if from a great distance, and like he spoke from the bottom of a barrel, I heard him say, "You okay, Tilden?"

Then a flame-rimmed, inky hole seemed to open up in the earth right at my feet. Everything went darker than a barrelful of black cats on a moonless night. I dove into that unfathomable pit headfirst as if my wife, Elizabeth, was waiting for me.

Not exactly sure how long I stayed out. Next time I opened my eyes, Carlton was staring down at me and wiping my forehead with a damp piece of rag. "Well, well, well. Guess ole Black Jack didn't manage to kill you after all, Tilden," he said.

Appeared as how Carl was perched on the edge of a gigantic box, and I'd somehow got down in the bottom of the thing. Reached up and took the rag out of my friend's hand. Ran it around to the back of my sweaty, dirt-encrusted neck. "How long you been here?"

"Me'n Nate rode in right after you passed out. Got here just in time to see ole Blackheart breathe his last."

"Still got bodies all over the street?"

He swept his hat off, wiped his face on the sleeve of his

shirt, and gazed off to a spot I couldn't see. "Naw. We've pretty much got everything tidied up. All the dead 'uns is propped up atop some boards on what's left of the porch in front of Gluck's store. Helluva sight. Got Zeke Blackheart, then Jackson Bowlegs. Next to Bowlegs is One Cut Petey Mason. Then there's ole Black Jack and the Boston brothers. Even got their weapons laid out with 'em. Nate found a feller out on the edge of town who owns a damned fine team of mules. Got him to drag Black Jack Morris's horse out in the street with the rest of the dead animals."

"Well, thank God. Hope that Gluck feller's feelin' a bit better about his situation."

"Yeah, maybe. But you know, Hayden, he bitched and moaned the whole time we was movin' outta his store the animal you went an' shot. Feller with the mules was good enough to agree to drag all the poor dead beasts off later on today. Guess you could say Gluck's makin' the best of a bad situation, though. He's chargin' folks fifty cents just to wander by on the boardwalk and take a look at all the dead men. No fee for lookin' at the animals. He even came up with a big ole box camera from somewheres. If you've got a dollar, you can have your picture took standin' next to them dead fellers."

"How long I been out, Carl?"

"Coupla hours. Nigh on to three actually. Lost a right bit of blood there, amigo. Good thing we got you patched up when we did, or you just mighta bled slap to death."

Glanced around at the box I was lying in and, for some reason, couldn't get my mind around where I'd ended up. "This a coffin? Looks almost like you boys were gettin' me ready to bury."

Carl let out a snorting chuckle. "Aw, hell, we decided not to plant you till you'd been good and dead for at least a day or so. Put you in this here wagon so's you couldn't move around much, and figured as how we'd have you already loaded up to transport your lazy ass back to Fort

Smith. No doc around these parts, but the local vet said you didn't need to be ridin' no horse for a spell."

"Vet take the bullet out?"

Carl shook his head. "Naw. He said it appeared to be in somethin' of a delicate spot. Not exactly sure what he meant by that, but he did mention arteries, veins, stuff like that. Figured it'd be best if we just left it alone."

I fingered around on the patch of bandages, then said, "What all did the vet do?"

Carl leaned over and patted me on the shoulder. "Don't worry. I watched him close while he worked. Cleaned you up real good with carbolic. Sewed the hole up. Said your only problem now is just makin' sure you don't fester. Get a dose of the blood poisonin' or somethin'. Likely we'll have to change the dressing at least once a day, but my money says you'll make it home to Elizabeth okay. Gonna be some uncomfortable by tomorrow mornin', though."

"Where's Nate and John Henry?"

"They're gettin' them boys as you and Slate didn't kill ready for the trip back to Fort Smith."

"How many?"

"There's four."

"Know any of 'em?"

"Well, we've got Jasper Day. Had him in jail once before for stealin' a horse over near Okmulgee. Cherokee feller named Crawford Starr as well. 'Pears this might be Crawford's first, and last, encounter with the law."

"That's only two."

"Then there's Orville Willie. Sent him up to the Detroit Correctional Facility for introducin' liquor to the Indians at least twice. Figure he's the one what knew the best places for this bunch to get their jig juice along the trail. Oh, other'n is a Choctaw kid, Marcus Swan. Cain't be more'n fourteen, fifteen years old, but he's already a killer."

"Any of 'em hurt very bad?"

"Not as bad as you. Swan looks to be the worst off. He

caught a stray rifle slug in the meatier part of one leg. Rest of 'em just got peppered pretty good with shotgun pellets. They're a mite uncomfortable, but won't die till we can hang 'em."

"Guess a dose of shotgun balls is about all it takes to snatch the starch out of most of their kind. Up till they rode into Vamoose, don't think anyone else had even tried to resist their brutish ways."

"Naw. They might not a-done much of the shootin' and killin', but every one of 'em boys was an active party, in one way or another, to the murders the whole bunch committed. Anyway, near as we can tell, all of 'em 'cept Swan can still sit a horse. He might have to ride in the wagon with you."

"Won't bother me any, Carl."

"Well, we all talked it over some and figured to get headed on back toward Fort Smith quick as we can. There's some unrest amongst Vamoose's citizenry. 'Pears as how maybe one or two of the gang mighta got away. Not sure who they was, or even if it's true, but we coulda missed at least one of 'em."

"No point worryin' 'bout that now."

"Nope, but there's more'n a few of the local citizens kinda pissed at the way the whole dance played out, and they're afraid anybody as mighta survived could be comin' back with revenge in their ungrateful hearts. Number of the townies is sayin' you boys handled the situation badly. Scared hell outta some folks. Damn near destroyed a valuable, prominent business establishment."

"Well, they'll just have to suck it up and come to the realization that it couldn't be helped. We didn't start the fight. Deadly dance just kinda happened. Developed on its own because of the gang's tactics when they entered town."

Guess I must've gone unconscious again right after that. Woke up, and the wagon rocked and swayed beneath me. Someone had moved me around so I was lookin' at the driver's back. Couldn't see his face, but knew it was Nate. Wounded feller I took as Marcus Swan sat in the wagon bed up next to the driver's seat. Spent most of his time moaning and crying out for his mother.

Trip from Vamoose to my house out on the Arkansas, near Van Buren, took about three days. Most tortuous three days of my life, as I recall. Honest to Christ, after just a few hours of riding in that wagon, trip got me to thinking I'd never get home.

Made Carl, John Henry, and Nate get me up and out of that contraption as often as possible, but the existing roads in the Nations in them bygone days were usually little more than a set of rough, deep ruts between one town and the other. In most cases, nothing like an actual thoroughfare existed at all. Several times I had to make them pull up and redress the extra hole in my ass. Did that right up until we stopped over for the night in a place the locals called the Devil's Den. You know, sure enough, ole Scratch had his pitchfork out and was waiting for us.

13

"... I'M STABBED. STABBED THROUGH THE HEART."

TO THIS VERY instant, I could not tell anyone who asked how the Devil's Den got its name. Mystery might still be hiding somewhere amongst the cobwebs of my ancient, cankered-up brain, but I can't find it anymore. Doesn't matter, though. It's enough you understand that I never cared for the spot, and seldom stopped there. Not exactly sure why, but it seemed that every time I rode up to the place, the hair on back of my neck prickled. Carl and Nate harbored no such misgivings and overrode my feeble objections. John Henry didn't appear to care one way or the other.

Place is on the Choctaw side of the Canadian's rough banks—a good fifty-to-sixty-mile ride west of Fort Smith. Sheltered bend of the slow-moving river is protected from the weather by a towering set of rough sandstone bluffs that jut out over a series of hidden caves carved eons ago by the flowing water.

Back when I rode for Judge Parker, the riverbank was thick with pin oak, blackjack oak, weeping willow, and cottonwood that grew as thick as chiggers right down to the water's edge. A body could barely make it through the trees along the shallow stream anywhere, except at the Devil's Den. It was a pleasant-enough-looking plot where someone, years before, had cleared the ground and built an almost Edenlike retreat for weary travelers to stop over for the night, rest up, and get renewed.

An abandoned one-room log cabin, and several outbuildings located there, had been used, at one time or another, by nigh on all of Judge Parker's deputy marshals for as many years as any of us could remember. By the time we arrived there, with the living remnants of Blackheart's gang in tow, I'd become somewhat feverish. Didn't even realize that Carl and Nate had moved me from the wagon to a more comfortable spot on the shack's dilapidated front porch. Must've slept right up till John Henry Slate woke me with a cup of fresh-brewed coffee and one of Carl's famous campfire biscuits. He used to stuff those heavenly lumps of doughy ambrosia with a handful of crisp-fried bacon. Aroma made my mouth water like a starving dog's.

John Henry helped me get propped up against the cabin's rude, bark-covered, outside wall. Sat with his back against a porch pillar, then handed me a steaming tin cup of stump juice.

I took a nibbling sip from the hot liquid, then said, "Sun's gonna be goin' down soon. You boys got our prisoners all taken care of?"

Slate ripped a splinter of wood from one of the porch's hand-hewn floorboards. Used it to pick at his teeth. With the sliver dangling from the corner of his mouth, he said, "Nothin' to worry yourself over, Tilden. Them friends of yours know their jobs. They've already chained the wounded feller—name's Swan, I believe—to his dry-gulchin' amigos. If them boys try to run, they'll have to drag that hurt one along like a hundred-and-fifty-pound sodbuster plow. We've got 'em staked to a tree over yonder, next to the river."

"Not gonna leave 'em out there, I hope."

"Carlton says he'll bring 'em up to the cabin for the night. Gonna cuff hisself to one end of the chain. Nate to the other. I'll be inside with 'em as well. That way we should all get a good night's sleep."

Took another sip of John Henry's beaker of belly-wash, then said, "Sounds good, but do me a favor. Try not to sleep any more'n you have to. These boys are headed for the hangman, sure as the knob on Satan's front gate glows from Hell's eternal fires. Nothin' like confronting the distinct probability of messin' your pants danglin' from the end of a rope, in front of a crowd of thousands, to get you motivated. Any one of 'em spots even a half-assed chance, he'll kill all of us deader'n Andy by-God Jackson 'fore we can make our way back to the safety of Fort Smith."

Not sure how much of an impact my little oration had on John Henry. He nodded. Acted like he heard me. I gave the same speech to Carl just before it got real good and dark. Carl did the same head-bobbing routine, then grunted and took another bite out of his biscuit and bacon.

Later on, I watched as Carl locked himself to one end of the chain of prisoners. Nate did the same with the other end. Whole crew marched right past me as they clinked and jingled into the cabin for our night at the Devil's Den.

John Henry was the last man through the door. He carried a kerosene lantern, which he placed on the floor, just inside the doorway, and allowed it to burn. Flickering glow from the lamp danced through the gaping portal, across the plank porch, and down the steps, before it faded into the all-enveloping darkness. At some point during the night, or early hours of the morning, the lamp burned out.

Tried my best to sleep beneath a cover of mosquito netting. Kept a cocked pistol close at hand. Must admit, I felt a strong need to be prepared for anything wayward that might occur. Still not sure why, but there was just something about the Devil's Den that gave me a case of the creeping willies.

Can't even begin to know how long I rolled around in fits of tortured wakefulness. Had some terrible nightmares when I did manage to catch a few winks. Was rudely snatched back to total awareness by the most horrible screaming I'd ever heard in my entire adult life. No doubt in my mind that men were dead, or dying, not ten feet from where I lay.

A washerwoman's rub board of chicken flesh shot up my back and neck. Hair stood up all over my body. Don't care what anyone says, there's just nothing like being snapped awake, in the pitch-dark, with the full knowledge that grinning Death has arrived and is in the process of wreaking havoc only a few feet away.

Sat bolt upright in my rumpled, bloodstained bed. The mosquito netting was draped over me like a widow's veil. Inside the rude cabin, men yelped, screamed, cursed, and called on God for assistance. Swear 'fore Jesus, sounded as though a dozen people were running around and beating on the interior walls with ax handles. Though of fairly sturdy construction, the whole building shook as if in the clutches of a killer Kansas-born cyclone. Then, honest to God, I'd willingly take an oath that draft horses were climbing up and down the walls like monstrous spiders wearing iron boots.

Whatever furniture still existed inside the abandoned house was being rendered into kindling. Couldn't imagine what shattered but, for a second, I would've swore I heard something made of glass break. Then the entire core of the place lit up with thunderous pistol fire.

Enormous, blue-tinted spots flashed before my eyes from a pair of thumping shots fired so close to one another they almost sounded like a single explosion. A second or so later, the acrid odor of spent black powder wafted past my nostrils on a little bit of barely noticeable breeze.

Then the screaming and mayhem got more general. Heard some unfortunate soul yell out, "Oh-h-h-h, goddamn, I'm stabbed. Stabbed through the heart. You've killed me, you stupid son of a bitch. Save me, sweet Jesus."

Ripped the mosquito netting away, grabbed for the porch pillar nearest me. Fumbled around in the blue black darkness for some passage of time before I finally found it. Pistol at the ready, I hoisted myself into a half-standing, crouched position just as someone staggered past me, then drunkenly ricocheted off my support column. Sweet, coppery odor of blood trailed behind the staggering man as he tumbled headfirst off the porch. Poor bastard hit the ground with a dull, moaning thud. Landed in a patch of briars and brambles next to the steps. Swear I heard his neck crack when he hit the ground.

Turned back toward the cabin's open entryway just in time for someone to slip up and grab me by the throat. Sneaky skunk caught me by total surprise. Man had fingers like iron bands. Cut my windpipe off so fast with his thumbs, I quickly came to wondering if I'd ever get the air of life back into my body again. And before I could bring my pistol barrel up against his chest, must admit I got right light-headed. Worst of all, I dropped the hammer on him, and my weapon misfired. Only instance of an 1873 Colt failing me that I can bring to mind.

Drew back with what dwindling energy I had left to swing the weapon like a club. Talonlike fingers suddenly turned me loose. Dropped to my knees like a sack of flour thrown from a grocer's delivery wagon. Could barely make out the shadowy movements of two men as they wrestled back and forth on the porch. They grunted and grappled with each other in the darkness for several seconds. Lot of hissing, spitting, and swearing coming from one feller. Cocked my pistol again. Figured it couldn't possibly betray me a second time but, hell, much as I tried, couldn't figure out who to shoot.

131

Managed to gain a bit of purchase on the cabin's windowsill with my fingertips. Dragged myself erect again, and got braced for a killing. After the passage of what felt like hours, one of the struggling combatants made a gagging, strangled sound, then dropped at my feet.

God as my witness, I didn't have any idea who the man was that had survived. Could barely see my own hand in front of my eyes. Brought the pistol to bear on the only one left standing.

Survivor leaned against the wall next to the door and gasped, "You all right, Tilden?"

Lowered my weapon, fumbled around till I found his arm, then said, "Where's your lantern, John Henry? Hell's bells, it's so damned dark out here, if a feller lit a match, he'd probably have to light a second one to see if the first one was actually burning."

"Don't know where the lantern ended up, Tilden. Mighta got busted. Damned sure fizzled out on me, though. Thought I had enough fuel to last all night. Musta miscalculated, or maybe the wick burnt up."

Still couldn't see much of anything, but knew by his movement that John Henry had turned and stepped back through the cabin's open doorway.

Noise from the fight inside had fallen away to little more than some sporadic groaning. Then I heard Carlton say, "Move over, you son of a bitch. Either of you bastards make another effort at escapin' and I'm gonna save Maledon the trouble of a-hangin' ya. Kill the hell outta you belly-slinkin' bastards, gut ya, then string up the pieces on the bushes 'round this place myself."

Heard the chains rattle and clink and, of a sudden, my best friend stood at my side. He grabbed me by the arm and said, "Damnation, Hayden, are you okay?"

Groped in the shadowy gloom till I found his shoulder. Patted him and said, "Still with you, Carl. Still with you. Where's Nate?"

Several seconds passed before Carl said, "Shit. Tell the truth, I didn't even think to check."

About then, as if by magic, John Henry's lamp came back to life. I leaned on Carl, and he helped me hobble over to the cabin's threshold. My God, but that place looked like somebody had painted the walls with blood. Soft, flickering, reddish orange glow from the kerosene-fueled flame simply enhanced an eerie scene of butchery and carnage.

Nate Swords sat with his back nestled in one corner. He had both pistols trained on the remaining pair of terrified criminals.

"You hurt, Nate?" I called out.

Watched as the man struggled to his feet. He holstered both weapons, then carefully picked at a spot on his right side. A jagged slit in the chambray material of his bib-front shirt oozed with a splash of fresh blood. "Well," he said, "one a them sneaky sons a bitches tried to put an end to me, but 'pears as how he missed anything of real importance. Didn't manage to do much but put something of an insignificant nick in my hide. From the look of the thing, doubt it'll take much to repair the damage." He glanced up at me and grinned, then pulled tobacco and makin's and set to rolling himself a smoke with blood-crusted fingers.

Took us nigh on to an hour, but we finally sorted the whole mess out—leastways, we figured out the deadly development of those events as best we could. Came to the conclusion that, somehow, Crawford Starr had slipped his cuffs, then helped Orville Willie get loose as well. Both of them had secreted folding pocketknives on their persons and went to hacking at anything available in the darkness.

Unfortunately for Jasper Day, who was the goober chained closest to Nate Swords, Willie must've mistaken his friend for Nate and stabbed the poor man near half a dozen times. Got him in the neck, belly, and chest. Couple of the wounds pierced the unfortunate man's heart. He bled out right there on the cabin's dirty floor alongside a fireplace built of pale brown, water-smoothed stones from the sandy bed of the nearby Canadian.

As a bloodred sun peeked over the towering sandstone bluffs, John Henry pointed at the body lying in the patch of briars next to the front steps. "Starr caught both the slugs I put in the air. 'Pears he stumbled out here, fell off the porch, and died right where he's layin'. Willie came out right behind him, grabbed you by the throat, and that's when I stepped in."

Porch pillar helped hold me up. Ran a shaking hand through my hair, then reached over and patted my savior on the shoulder. "Can't thank you enough," I said. "Way things were goin', not sure I woulda made it if you hadn't shown up when you did. Willie's grip on my throat felt like the man could've easily crushed walnuts with his bare hands."

Last thing I heard was somebody saying, "Maybe you oughta sit back down, Tilden."

14

"...CAUGHT LITTLE MISS HOLLY IN
BED WITH A GAMBLIN' FELLER..."

WHEN I FINALLY came back to something akin
to reasonable lucidity, Elizabeth stood over me and mopped
at my brow with a cool, damp rag. An absolutely radiant
smile played across her beautiful face when she said, "Thank
God you're still with us." She leaned over and kissed me on
the forehead. "Had begun to worry, my dearest."

Tried my best to sit up. Got my head far enough off the
pillow to realize that I'd somehow managed to end up in
my own bed. Open-curtained window, just a few steps
away, revealed one of my favorite sights in all the world.
Could see the rolling, green, tree-covered hills on the north
side of the Arkansas where the river made a sharp turn on
its run toward Little Rock and thence to join up with the
mighty Mississippi.

Flopped back into the comfort of my feather mattress
and down-stuffed pillow. Gazed into Elizabeth's eyes.
Those usually clear, near-crystal orbs were streaked with a

webwork of weepy red. Surprised me how thin my voice sounded when I took her hand and said, "No need to worry, darlin'. I'm doin' fine. You know me. Be raring to go in just a few days. Promise."

She shook her head, then pulled away. Dipped the rag in a basin of water on the bedside table, squeezed it out, then laid the damp cloth across my feverish head once more. "No. No, you won't. Doc Bryles tells me you need to take it easy for some time to come. Maybe as much as a month to six weeks. Longer, if I have anything to say about it."

'Course I tried to minimize the damage. "Aw, now I can't be that bad off. Just a nick in my hip. 'Sides, can't begin to imagine how I'd ever live it down with Carlton if I should die of such a wound. God Almighty, the rawhidin' and hoorahin' would never stop."

Look of stern determination flashed across her face. "You were badly injured, Hayden. Lost a lot of blood through that hole in your hip during the wagon ride back from the Nations. Took the doctor almost two hours to get the slug out and patch up the damage. And he maintains that a fragment of lead is still in there and can't be removed. Said it's a wonder you didn't bleed to death. Suppose if it hadn't been for Carlton, Nate, and John Henry Slate you probably would've. Feels like an icy hand around my heart every time I think on how you could very well have been alone, and died out there somewhere in the Nations, and no one would've ever known where to find you."

Of a sudden, she collapsed onto the bed beside me and sobbed. Sound came from deep inside her heaving chest. Racked her body as though an unseen hand had reached out from an unknown place and slapped her on the back. Couldn't remember hearing anything to match it since our son Tommy died. And sweet Jesus, I'll readily admit, such a display from the strongest woman I'd ever known scared the hell out of me.

Placed a trembling hand on her straw-colored hair and

stroked it in the same way I did with my infant son when he seemed afraid. Said, "Aw, darlin', no need to let yourself go and get so upset. 'S all over now. I'm safe at home. You're here with me. Figure young Billy's probably in his bedroom takin' a nap. Near as I can tell, the sky's as clear and blue as your eyes. Life's mighty good, don't you think?"

She sat up, and wiped tears away from both cheeks. Appeared pained when she finally looked me in the eye again. "We're the wealthiest people in Fort Smith, perhaps in all of Sebastian County, Hayden. Papa's Elk Horn Bank makes money for us—hand over fist. More now than when he was alive. Our grocery and mercantile is the busiest in town. Lately, my wedding arrangement business takes so much of my time I barely have a minute in the day to hurry by and visit the bank or the store. Our sawmill and lumber concern goes from daylight to dark. Subsidizes all the construction we're involved in."

Tried to lighten the mood a bit when I stopped her by sayin', "Might help if you'd stop buyin' up everything in town that somebody sticks a for sale sign on."

A fleeting smile flickered across her lips. She pulled a tiny, lace-edged hanky from somewhere. Dabbed at dripping eyes, then rubbed an inflamed nose. Her gaze darted up to a painting hanging over the head of our bed. Depiction of an angel guiding a pair of beautiful children across a stone bridge in deep woods. Then she stared at nervous fingers that twisted the tiny square of lacy material into a tight knot.

"I'm not handling this situation well, Hayden," she said. "You've been hurt before, but never as bad as this. I truly feared for a time you might die."

Patted her on the arm, then gave it a squeeze. "Oh, come on now, darlin', doubt I was ever that far gone."

She sniffed and wiped at her nose again. "You could work in the bank, the store, the sawmill. Manage any of our commercial concerns, or all of them, if you wanted. Take over any of our firms, whenever you'd like. Well, maybe not the wedding business, but any of the others." She stopped, locked me in a scrunch-faced gaze, then said, "I'd be happy to step aside just to keep you out of danger."

Took her tremulous hand in mine. Tenderly as I could, placed it over my heart, then caressed her cheek. "I'm not a clerk, Elizabeth. Just ain't in me. Chain me to a desk, I'd go slap crazy. Couldn't stand bein' behind a counter shufflin' groceries back and forth all day long. Countin' beans, sellin' dry goods, and such down at your store isn't the life for me, and you know it. Not even sure I could put up with bein' tied to an outfit as freewheeling as a sawmill. Restrictions of a clerk's life might well drive me to self-destruction."

She turned her tortured gaze out the window, then stared down at her twitching hands again. Shook her head. Let a trembling, rueful smile play across her lips.

Pulled on the sleeve of her dress in an effort to bring her attention back my direction. "The law's my life," I said. "All I've ever done, since the day you first outfitted me in your father's store. Same day I started on my quest to bring Saginaw Bob Magruder in for punishment in Judge Parker's court for murderin' my entire family."

"I remember. You were quite handsome in your new duds," she sniffed.

"Life of the lawdog's all I know. Not sure I'll ever be able to walk away from the work. Can't truthfully say I can foresee a time when I'll want to leave the profession. You've known all that for as long as we've been acquainted. Known there's always been the possibility I might be injured. And, unfortunately, good men die every day doin' this work."

She pulled her sleeve from my fingers, reached out, and patted the spot over my heart, but continued to stare out the window. "Yes. You're right. I know. Just thought I'd see if you might be ready to give the whole dangerous dance a rest."

Watched as she stood and started for the door. As her hand touched the knob, I said, "What I do for a livin' is important, Elizabeth. Personally, I can't think of a more worthy way to serve mankind. Perhaps even more significantly, not many men can do what I do—not even a handful in the entirety of the U.S. Marshals Service. Need you along with me for the ride 'cause I'm not sure I could stand to keep up the quest without you."

She leaned her head against the door facing for a second, quickly snapped upright again, then, as she disappeared into the hallway, said, "I know. I know. But I had to try." Near as I can remember, she never mentioned the subject again. Not even right up to her last moments on this earth, during the great flu epidemic of 1918.

My recovery turned out as slow a process as Doc Bryles and Elizabeth had forecast. Took nigh on to a week before I was even able to clamber out of bed, then hobble my way to the covered veranda that surrounded all four sides of our home and sit in my favorite, cane-bottom rocking chair. The hill the house occupied gave me a downright magnificent view for miles in any direction. Fort Smith's smoking presence lay mere miles to the south. God, but I loved that place.

People make fun of folks who get shot in the ass, but let me tell you, I can't imagine much that could be any worse. Such a wound makes life difficult in a number of ways that are just too ghastly to describe. Had to carry a big ole fringe-trimmed pillow Elizabeth got in New York City around with me so I could get myself comfortable once I'd finally decided on a spot to land. Cushion had a picture of a big ole bridge on it with the legend WELCOME TO NEW YORK stitched across a cloud-filled sky overhead.

Best thing to come out of that entire mess was how often Carl, Nate, John Henry, and other friends stopped over for a visit. Seemed as though hardly a day went by that someone didn't show up on my porch carrying a covered dish, a deck of cards, a fresh copy of the *Fort Smith Elevator*, or, in John Henry's case, a checkerboard.

Slate loved his checkers. Do believe he enjoyed winning about as much as anybody I've ever run across. He'd take my last man, throw his head back, and cackle like a thing insane. Stomp his feet and, sometimes, jump up and do a victory jig the likes of which bordered on the outright comical. Resembled a demented chicken trying to dance. Got to a point where I'd let him win just to see the chicken dance. Chuckle for hours afterward when I happened to bring his latest caper to mind again.

Once I got to feeling pretty good, John Henry slipped by a time or two, rousted me out of bed, helped me into our single-seated carriage, and drove me down to a creek on our property for a bit of fishing. Swear 'fore Jesus, the man was worse than a little kid about catching fish. Let him hook a hand-sized bream, big-mouthed bass, or a slab-sided crappie, and he'd hoot and holler like a twelve-year-old. Had a smile on his face for two days after he landed a catfish that weighed nigh on thirteen pounds.

Remember as how, more than once, we sat on the porch of a late afternoon and watched as the sun began to nestle itself behind the thick, green forest of trees on the Arkansas's rolling, western bank. Seemed right wistful when, of a sudden, he said, "'S a beautiful spot you and Elizabeth have here, Tilden. 'Course, I still prefer Texas. Whole different kind of geography and all, but I still favor the area around Waco. Can't wait to get back there. It's home, of course. And no matter what anybody says, there just ain't nothin' quite like home and family."

"Figurin' on goin' back to Texas anytime soon, John Henry?" I said.

"No plans right now, but you've been around long enough to know how life is. Anything can happen, and usually does. A man moves from place to place in an effort just to get by. Often wish I could light on a single spot the way you have. Find me a good woman like Elizabeth. Maybe have some kids of my own. Ranch a bit, raise a few blooded horses, that kind of thing. But, hell, right now it's nothin' but a dream."

More'n once he showed up carrying a bucket of cold beer from a saloon he favored, named Tilly's, down on the north end of Towson Avenue. By then, I'd taken up a cane and could get around reasonably well. We'd sit out on the porch of an afternoon, in a nice shady spot, talk about politics, horses, women, religion, and such. Drink beer and watch my son Billy crawl around on the pallet his nanny laid out at my feet.

John Henry Slate was right fine company on a slow-moving day when you might want a friend over just for a bit of idle chitchat and an icy brew. He commented, time and again, on how he envied me the relationship with my wife and the smiling, gurgling, thumb-sucking child he often bounced on his knee. Number of times I remember him muttering, "Lucky man, Tilden. Might be the luckiest man I've ever met." 'Course, he was right. And on more than one occasion he spoke wistfully of his home place near Waco and an aged father who now there lived alone.

Noon would come around and sometimes, if we asked just the right way, John Henry would stay over to eat with Elizabeth and me. Could tell she was right taken with the man. Wasn't the first time I'd noted him as one of those fellers women see something in that none of us other hairy-legged types can seem to understand. Not for a single instant did I ever envision the tragedy unfolding behind the man's friendly, open manner and twinkling eyes. Hurts and burns like sulfurous Hell to even bring what eventually happened to mind these days, but it's still there. Can't ever be erased.

See, one morning, about five or six weeks into my

convalescence, I'd hobbled out to my favorite spot on the porch and eased into the most comfortable chair—the one whose wicker seat had worn down and begun to collapse a bit. Remember throwing my pillow onto the chair and thinking at the time that maybe my good friend John Henry might still be in town. That he'd stroll on by for a game of checkers, a beaker of cold beer, and an afternoon of friendly fellowship and discussion.

Had just lit me up a nickel cheroot. Glanced up the road that led south into Fort Smith and saw a rider coming. Knew without even thinking twice it was Carlton. Could identify my old amigo from a mile away just by the way he sat his horse. Soon as he rode up into the yard, I knew from the slope of his shoulders something had gone amiss.

Climbed off his hay burner and jingled up the steps. Snatched off his hat like a man who wanted to apologize for some hidden sin. Flopped into a chair facing me across the table where I like to sit my coffee cup. He nodded and said, "Got some bad news, Hayden. Real bad."

Rolled the cane back and forth between my feet. "Kinda figured as much, Carl. Watched you ride up. Looks almost like you're carryin' the weight of the whole world. Helluva burden for a man."

Slapped his hat onto the toe of one boot, pinched the bridge of his nose. Squinted hard at me, then shook his head. "Sure as hell feels exactly as you've so aptly described, Hayden. Been thinkin' 'bout it. Worried over how I'd tell the tale all the way up here from the marshal's office. Still ain't real sure how to go about the thing."

"Just spit it out. No point beatin' 'round the bush." Of a sudden, I had the darkest kind of feeling rush over me. Felt as though pale Death, his very own bony-fingered self, had slipped up behind me and stealthily slapped a skeletal hand on my shoulder.

Said, "This don't have anything to do with Elizabeth, does it, Carl? Stood right over there by the steps, not more'n three hours ago, and watched her ride off to the office. Said she'd be at the bank all day. Ain't nothin' happened to my wife, has it?"

Stricken, apologetic look swept over his careworn countenance. He sat up straight and waved my agitated concern away. "Oh, no. No. Assure you my visit ain't got nothin' to do with Elizabeth. Nothin' a'tall."

"Then, what? What's the problem?"

As though still under considerable duress, he finally blurted out, "John Henry Slate ever say anything to you 'bout a lady friend a his by the name of Holly Bankhead?"

Considered his question for several seconds, then shook my head. "No. Near as I've been able to tell, he has a number of *lady* friends. Man appears to draw women like honey draws bees."

"Well, sure 'nuff looks like he had one in particular he favored. Gal he met who worked a spell down at the Double Eagle Saloon. Seems she quit her job some weeks back. Moved in with John Henry 'bout two minutes after the pair of 'em got together for the first time. You might not know it, but he rented a house out on the east end of Rogers Avenue. Gal was livin' with 'im."

"So? 'S all news to me. Never even heard him mention Holly Bankhead, or the house. You keep talkin' in the past tense. Like somethin' awful's happened. Go on and get to it, Carl. Gonna get gray-headed, croak of old age, at the rate you're goin'."

He leaned forward, rested his patched elbows on the table. Locked me in a stern gaze and said, "Sometime after midnight, last night, John Henry came in from a quick run down to Poteau to pick up a prisoner. Near as anybody can tell right now, he dropped his man off at the courthouse jail, went straight home, and caught little Miss Holly in bed with a gamblin' feller name of Grantland Betts who worked at the Double Eagle."

"Jesus."

"Sure 'nuff. Caught 'em in the act. In flagrante delicto, as Handsome Harry Tate used to say. Kilt 'em both. Shot hell out of 'em right there in the bed. Pair of 'em was nekkid as jaybirds. John Henry emptied a Colt pistol on 'em. Made a helluva mess."

Stared into Carl's troubled eyes. Knew he still hadn't told me the whole story. "That it? That the whole weasel— teeth, hair, eyeballs, and all?"

He slumped back into the chair and steepled knotty fingers under his stubble-covered chin. "No. Unfortunately, that ain't the worst of the whole doo-dah, not by a long damned shot."

"Knew it. Got the impression from the way you're actin' there was something even worse than a double killin' comin'."

Carl dropped his hands into his lap and blurted out, "In spite of the late hour, word of the murders got around town pretty damned quick. Within an hour of the shootin's, the Fort Smith city police department came to the U.S. marshal's office lookin' for help. One of the few men on the scene at the time was DuVall Petrie. He hoofed it outta the courthouse like his feet was on fire. Caught John Henry somewheres down near the river tryin' to hire a boat to ferry him across to the Nations."

"You don't mean . . . ?"

"Yep. Killed DuVall in a pistol fight next to one of the wharfs, then disappeared. Ain't nobody seen hide nor hair of 'im since. Way we've got it figured, he either swam that hammerhead of his over to the Nations, or managed to pay somebody to ferry him across. Hell, you know as well as me, all you gotta do is flash a little money at the right person and they'll do damn nigh anything. Throw more'n ten dollars at mosta the snaky bastards workin' the river, and they'll eat a raw alligator gar, stem to stern, and let you watch."

Couldn't believe my ears. Felt like the bones in my neck

went soft. Closed aching eyes. Let my hundred-pound head loll onto the back of the chair. Sharp, piercing pain shot across a scrunched forehead. "Damnation, Carl. You're certain about all this? He killed a fellow deputy U.S. marshal?"

"Spent most of the night and this mornin' checkin' it all out 'fore I came up here to tell you. Way I've got it figured, Judge Parker's bailiff is gonna contact you sometime today. Set you loose to run John Henry down."

For almost a minute, I felt as though my entire life had drained right into the soles of my boots. The thought of having to go out after a man I'd grown to genuinely like, and even admire, repelled my ever-present sense of justice and fair play. But I knew Carl had hit the bloody nail right on its square-cut head. My special arrangement, as the judge's secretly appointed assassin, would most likely require that I take the despicable job. The ugly thought flashed across my mind that a vengeful God had finally called payment for all the blood I'd spilled in the past. Made me sick to my stomach. Thought for several seconds I was just about to puke my guts up.

Coughed, rubbed a hand across my flushed forehead, then cleared my throat. Even then, I found it hard to speak. "Marshal already got men out after 'im?"

"Damned gang of 'em. You know how the judge feels 'bout them as would murder his deputies. And, God help the boy, what he done is worse—one deputy marshal killin' another. Sweet weepin' Jesus, Hayden, I ain't never even heard of such a thing. Never even imagined it could happen. Bad enough we have to worry 'bout bein' rubbed out by them out in the Nations as have joined forces with the Devil. Can't imagine bein' kilt by a fellow deputy marshal. Beyond the pale—just by-God beyond the pale."

Turned away from my friend and gazed out over the river. Couldn't get my mind around the problem. Shook my head like a dog with a tick in its ear. Muttered, "He won't come back, Carl. No matter who the judge sends, John

Henry won't come back to Fort Smith alive. Soon as Du-Vall Petrie's dead body hit the ground, he had to have known his fate was sealed."

Carl shook his head, groaned, and stared at his hands.

"With a slick-talkin' Texas lawyer, he might have a chance of gettin' sent up for life, times two, on them other killin's. And Judge Parker could very well let it happen. But he won't give an inch, or let Deputy Marshal Petrie's murder pass—gonna have to have payment in blood for that one. Shit almighty. John Henry's a dead man and just don't realize it yet."

"I know. But I been thinkin', Hayden. Cursed thought, but I figure it's better if'n you and me go out after 'im than have folks as don't even know the man track 'im down and bring 'im to book."

"He won't come back for us either, Carl. Gonna be a fight to the death when we finally run the man to ground."

Of a sudden, I got tired. Tired right to the bone, and some deeper. Felt as though I couldn't have stood, even if I'd wanted to. Sky and earth whirled around my chair in a jumbled spasm of cosmic grief and disbelief. Leaned over, rested my head in my hands, and came damn near to weeping. Wanted to upchuck my spurs, but couldn't. Seemed as though the good Lord had put too much on me at one time, and the burden came nigh on to breaking my heart.

As if from a great distance, like the bottom of a deep well, I heard Carl say, "Just surpasses all understanding how a woman could be the root of such tragedy. Can't begin to imagine why a man'd let one get under his skin enough to lead him into three killin's. Just baffles hell outta me, Hayden. You understand it?"

Seemed to be talking to the unlimited depths of Heaven when I said, "No. I can't comprehend this mess either. But you know, Carl, I fear there's a demon inside all us men. A demon that's hot and deadly, who could easily lead any one of us to commit heinous acts equally as unfathomable, should we ever be confronted with a similar set of circumstances."

"You know, I've met them as say they already know exactly how they'd react in any given set of conditions. Say they'd never be driven to unsavory acts by a particular state of affairs."

"They're lyin' sons a bitches, Carl. Either that or they're so full of themselves they can barely stand to be in this world with other people."

"Well, I can feel the call a-comin'. We'll be the ones what have to bring John Henry to book. Whole situation's got me so down in the mouth I could eat oatmeal out of a churn. Ain't gonna be easy, no, sir, this 'un ain't gonna be easy, Hayden." Carl shook his head, stared off into the distance as though distracted, then added, "Have to kill John Henry. My, oh, my. What's our world a-comin' to?"

15

"I'm Being Sent Out To Kill the Man?"

COULD HAVE EASILY waited for an official summons from Judge Parker's special private bailiff, George Wilton, to meet with him in his office for a discussion about the terrible situation concerning John Henry. Knew beyond any doubt he'd call on me sooner or later. Decided against lingering on tenterhooks of dread. Had Carl help me get loaded into my cabriolet and drive me into town.

Wilton's graying pork-chop whiskers twitched with expectation when he glanced up from piles of legal papers stacked atop a highly polished mahogany desk. Spotted me standing in the doorway of his paneled office. Waved me inside. He placed a pen, freshly loaded with ink, into its rest. Leaned back in a tack-decorated, Moroccan leather chair, and motioned me to a near identical seat across from him.

"Please sit, Marshal Tilden. In truth, I was just about to send for you. Appears you've become something of a mind reader, amongst your other rather astonishing talents."

Lowered myself into the welcoming comfort of the overstuffed chair he'd proffered. Watched the elegant gent run a nervous palm from a sweaty forehead to the back of a hairless pate. Then he placed one elbow on his chair's well-worn arm and rested a whiskered chin against his clenched fist. Man appeared tired. Careworn. Concerned and, in my considered estimation, completely wrung out.

Dropped my hat on the floor, pulled a pair of nickel cheroots from an inside jacket pocket, and leaned forward in an effort to tender him one. He waved my offering aside, reached for a cedar-lined humidor on his desk, and flipped the top open. The polished, gold-trimmed, ebony box overflowed with apple-scented, maduro panatelas.

"Have one of mine, Marshal Tilden," he said, and flashed a tight smile. "'Specially rolled for me in Cuba. Had them shipped here from New Orleans. Mighty fine smoke. Can't raise tobacco like this in the United States. Won't find a bite in a single one of 'em. All milder'n a bunch of fifteen-year-old lapdogs."

Within minutes, a thick cloud of the world's finest, most aromatic cigar smoke filled Wilton's office, wrapped around shelves crammed with thick legal tomes, and gathered in a dense, fragrant layer next to the ceiling. After several deep, clearly satisfying puffs on his rootlike stogie, he rose, strode to the open door, and gently pushed it closed. Holding the cigar in front of him, as though it were a treasured jewel to be taken out and admired only on special occasions, he made his way back to the desk and roosted on the only uncovered corner. Knew his simple act of studied familiarity was the man's premeditated way of putting me at my ease.

"I assume you've heard the terrible news about Deputy Marshal John Henry Slate?" he said.

"Unfortunately, yes. Yes, I have, sir."

He let a thin trail of smoke curl around his face and head, sniffed at the pungent aroma occasionally, and took another puff before saying, "As you well know, Judge Parker views the killing of one of his deputy marshals with the utmost sadness. To have one dispatched by a fellow badge carrier has sent the man into a state of sorrow and depression unlike any I've witnessed in all my years of working with him. And while he's equally distressed by the two murders that precipitated DuVall Petrie's unfortunate passing, it is the death of one of our own that is of utmost concern to him."

"Can well imagine, sir."

He turned, and quickly moved to the heavily draped window behind his desk. Using a single finger, he pushed one panel of the thick, plush curtains aside. Knew from previous visits that his office overlooked the shallow hollow on the south side of the courthouse where Judge Parker's twelve-man gallows stood. Wondered if he could see the gaunt-faced ghosts of men who'd died there.

He stared down toward hangman George Maledon's Gates of Hell and said, "You know, Marshal Tilden, it is a betrayal of trust unlike any other for a man to take the same sacred oath of office that you, and more than two hundred others, have sworn, then brutally murder one of his fellows."

Knew such an admonishment was forthcoming, but still felt as though I'd been sledgehammered in my gut when he said it. Could do nothing but concur with his rather pointed assessment. "Indeed, sir. I'm bound to agree completely. Deputy Slate's actions can only be deemed unforgivable."

He glanced at me from the corner of one dark, hooded eye, nursed his smoke a bit more, then swiveled his attention back to whatever he could observe from the window's elevated vantage point. "We do not expect John Henry Slate to return for trial, Marshal Tilden. His reappearance in Fort Smith, after having committed such a heinous crime, would be intolerable. Is my meaning quite clear, sir?"

Squirmed in my seat, both hands glued to my knees. Wilton noticed the pause before my response and turned to face me. Threw him an anxious nod, then said, "This is very difficult for me, sir. As you may be well aware, John Henry and I have, of late, become friends. The man has unflinchingly stepped into imminent danger and saved my life. Not once, but twice. Weren't for him I'd be dead—times two. Very likely buried in an unmarked grave somewhere out in the Nations. I like the man, sir, and must admit that I am deeply conflicted about being sent out on this particular mission."

A look of concentrated concern etched its way across Wilton's near ebony face. He swept from his station at the window, stopped near my elbow, and patted me on the shoulder. Then he whirled about and resumed his creaking, leather-covered seat behind the desk. "While I do sympathize with your position, Marshal Tilden, I must remind you of your pledge to Judge Parker when he first approached you with the conditions of your special place in the hierarchy of men under his command. You, and you alone, enjoy his blessing in matters that require the application of death-dealing force."

"Oh, trust me, I remember his words as though he spoke them mere minutes ago, sir. He said, 'I want you to take on the job of finding the worst of the worst, and bringing them back or killing them on the spot. I don't care which.'"

As though wielding a broadsword, Wilton sliced the air with an emphatic wave of his smoldering cigar and hissed, "In this particular instance, His Honor does not want Slate brought back for trial." The bluntness of his reply felt like a duelist's challenging glove slapped across my face.

"Please do not misinterpret my insistence, sir, but I want to be crystal-clear on this issue. I'm being sent out to kill John Henry Slate?"

No pause, delay, emotion, or hitch in his voice when he replied, "Yes."

"No doubt?"

"None."

Fingered an inch of ash from my smoke onto the palm of one hand, then carefully deposited it into a glass bowl on the edge of Wilton's desk. Leaned forward and locked eyes with the man. "I've never questioned any of the judge's assignments in the past. Dragged Saginaw Bob Magruder back and watched him hang. Brought Smilin' Jack Paine to book for all his foul and unnatural acts. Ran Martin Luther Big Eagle to ground and sent him to Jesus. Killed the Crooke brothers and a score of others who deserved what they got and then some."

"True, Marshal Tilden, all quite true. Please believe me when I tell you that Judge Parker and I are well aware of, and thankful for, your devotion to the execution of all our past assignments."

"Well, that's good to know, Mr. Wilton. But it is also true that in service of the acts just mentioned, that I've witnessed the deaths of two of my closest friends—Handsome Harry Tate and Billy Bird. More important to the question at hand, though, it is my considered opinion that John Henry Slate's an entirely different kinda cat from any of the other villains I've chased down or killed. I've not yet reconciled my friendship with his acts of deadly violence."

My thoughts were running wild. Hesitated for a second before I finally stammered, "Reckon I could, well, you know, somehow . . . manage to bring him back . . . wouldn't that be enough?"

Wilton wagged his hairless head from side to side. "To be blunt, Marshal Tilden, no. Despite all your misgivings on the subject, we expect the man to pay the ultimate price in the exact same manner he used to take the life of Deputy Marshal Petrie and, I might add, the other two people whose lives the man so casually and brutally ended in the same manner. No other man in our cadre of deputy marshals enjoys the kind of reputation with a gun as do you, Marshal Tilden. We require your best effort in this matter, and when you find John Henry Slate, make no mistake, we want you to kill him. Are my words unambiguous enough?"

He left me with not a single iota of wiggle room in the matter. Knew beyond a doubt that any further protestations would be met with ever toughening responses. The decision had been made and, for all intents and purposes, might as well have been carved in a block of Italian marble. John Henry Slate's continuance among those of this earth was a question that had already been taken out of my hands. His life was over, and I would be the instrument of his passage to God for judgment. For a second, I knew what Judas must have felt like, but the die was cast, and by my hand John Henry would cease breathing the sweet air of life.

Then, for the briefest of moments, a ray of hope shot through my confused mind. "Isn't there someone else you can send? My recovery and convalescence, from being recently shot while in performance of my duties, continues. Must confess, I am not certain that I can fully function at my best in my present condition."

Wilton's gaze narrowed. "As you are well aware, there is no one else for this particular kind of job. Your special station in Judge Parker's cadre of deputy marshals is unlike any other. The task is yours and yours alone. Standing aside, in the hope that someone else will take on an unsavory job in your stead, is not an option." He stood, and motioned toward the door. "For your convenience, a package complete with letters of introduction and assignment, transportation vouchers, warrants, and such awaits you on my secretary's desk." His conversation-ending words had the power of Heaven's golden gates being slammed in my face with resounding finality.

Took some effort, but I grabbed up my hat and struggled to shaky legs. "May take me a day or two, but I'll be after him as soon as possible." Turned on my heel, and headed for the outer office.

Snatched the portal open, then paused long enough to barely hear Wilton when he said, "Please believe me, Hayden, this decision did not come down to you lightly. We completely understand your situation at present. You should be fully aware that we do sympathize, but cannot waver in this matter. Judge Parker and I both have full faith that you will carry out your assignment to its final conclusion with the same devotion to duty as you have done with all those in the past."

Perhaps an edge of sarcasm tainted my reply when, over my shoulder, I spat, "I'll do my best, sir."

As I limped through his secretary's office, Wilton called out through the open doorway, "Take anyone you like along for the trip. No questions will be forthcoming about expenses and such."

Snatched up the envelope stuffed with documents and papers offered by his harried assistant, then headed for the street. Needed a lung full of fresh air somethin' dreadful.

Making my way down the stone steps of the courthouse's covered portico when Carl hopped up from his seat in the cabriolet. He took the granite steps two at a time to meet me. Look of innocent, puppy-dog inquisitiveness on his face when he said, "Well, what'd he say?"

Could tell he harbored hopes that someone, anyone else but us, would take care of the gnarly hair ball of a problem. He scuttled along beside me like a clumsy turtle trying to keep up by moving sidewise.

I said, "Appears we're going after John Henry, Carl, soon as we can get our shit together."

His demeanor changed, but so little as to be barely noticeable. Doubt anyone else could have even detected the minute alteration in my friend's bearing. But we'd been together for so long a time that I could easily tell he felt the same way I did. Perhaps even more deeply, for Carl's passions rested nearer the top of his heart.

Neither of us spoke a word on the way back to my

house that fateful day. After I'd clambered down from the carriage, and Carl had climbed aboard his own animal for the trip back to town, I held his mount's bridle and said, "Find Nate Swords. Tell him to meet us at the Missouri, Kansas & Texas Railroad depot tomorrow mornin'. I'll pay the freight for the three of us for tickets on the day coach. We'll put our animals in a boxcar the way you, Billy, and I did when we went out after the Crooke boys."

"Where we goin'?" he asked.

"Waco."

"Waco? Why Waco?"

"'Cause that's where John Henry's headed. Could be he'll stop off in Fort Worth. If he does, we might be able to get to Waco before he can make it back home."

"Where's home?"

"Family ranch a few miles outside town."

"You sure?"

"Yeah. Sure as it's possible to be right now. Way I've got it figured, once we get to rollin' on the rails, just might be able to beat him there. And if our luck holds, there's an outside chance that maybe we can talk him into comin' on back with us."

Carl squirmed in his saddle. Stared at passing clouds for a second, then leaned over on the narrow, silver-capped saddle horn. "But you said he wouldn't come back. Said he'd fight, probably die, 'fore he'd let us bring him back alive for a hangin'. And I got the distinct impression on the courthouse steps not long ago that, just like the Crooke boys, them folks behind the big desks don't want us a-bringin' him back."

Gazed up into my friend's troubled eyes and knew when it came out of my mouth that I was just wishing. Said, "Well, you're right about all of that, my friend. But for now, we'll just play this task by ear. Leastways, until we've had a chance to confront John Henry. Gotta admit, Carl, while my heart tells me this dance probably ain't gonna turn out the way we'd like, I'm gonna hope over hope that he'll see the light. Maybe come on back with us and face the music for what he did."

Carl whirled his mount around in a tight circle. Heard him say, "Shit," as he kicked back for town.

Elizabeth came home from the bank and found me dragging my gear around in preparation for the trip. No doubt at all what was going on. Had an arsenal of weapons laid out. She hit the ceiling when I told her I'd be leaving at the earliest possible instant, and that the object of my trip was to bring John Henry to justice.

Gal whirled on me like a cornered wildcat, snatched at my sleeve, and as hot, salty tears gathered in blinking eyes, said, "Oh, Hayden. You just can't. He's your friend. For the sweet love of God, if it weren't for John Henry, I would have attended your funeral by now. You've got to pass this obligation on to someone else."

Ran an oiled cloth down the barrel of my Winchester hunting rifle. "There isn't anyone else, darlin'. Trust me, I've already tried that particular dodge. Didn't come anywhere close to workin'. Got told in no uncertain terms as how it's me and no one else for this dance."

Trembling hands darted to her temples. She tugged at her hair and leaned against our dining table. "Lord God, this is madness. Judge Parker can't possibly expect you to hunt down the man who saved your life, saw to your wounds, brought you home, visited almost every day while you recuperated. Entertained you. My God, I think I'm losing my mind."

Laid the weapon aside, reached out, and took her hand. "All that and you're well aware of what else he's done. No way you've spent the day in town and not heard why this trip is necessary."

"Of course I heard the story. You can't walk through the

bank, buy necessities at the store, or even stroll along Rogers Avenue for more than half a block without hearing people talking about it. A triple murder involving one of Fort Smith's shade-tree-covered neighborhoods doesn't go unnoticed."

"Well, then, you must understand why I'm the one who has to go after him."

"No. No, I don't."

With no place left to run, I dropped back into the dining room chair, reached out, took her hand again, and drew her to my side. "Who better, darlin'? Wouldn't you rather I went than someone with no connection to the man? Someone not inclined to even try and talk him in? Wouldn't surprise me a bit if someone from the families of the dead didn't post a reward for him. There's troops of violent men who'd jump at a chance to collect money on his lifeless body. A chance to kill him and assume the mantle of the heroic figure who avenged the murders of three innocent people."

She brought her free hand up to my face, then ran caressing fingers through my hair. Bent over at the waist and raised my face toward her lips. She placed a lovingly tender kiss on my forehead. "I'll never understand any of this insanity, Hayden, but I'll pray for both of you."

For years after that touching scene, I felt like the lowest skunk living. There I sat, lyin' like a yeller dog. Doing everything I could to justify the unjustifiable to the woman I loved more than life itself. And at the same time knowing full well that, once John Henry and I finally met again, one of us would not survive the encounter.

Took a bit longer than I'd expected for Carl and me to get out on the track. Thought we'd just pack up and leave. But Nate proved a bit harder than usual to rustle up. Seems he'd taken a trip down to White Oak Mountain to visit with distant relatives. Carl finally ran him to ground the morning of the second day after my discussion with Mr. Wilton. They fogged it back to Fort Smith quick as they could. Still and all, we'd been delayed almost an extra day. By then, I'd developed a less than anxious attitude about leaving on the trip in the first place.

Morning we finally headed out, I kissed Elizabeth goodbye on the steps of our house. In the past, she had always accompanied me to the station in those instances where I left town aboard a train. That day, she refused to see me off.

Remember how she leaned her trembling body against mine, placed her head in the hollow of my shoulder, and sobbed. And when my departure could be delayed no longer, she clung to my arm and whispered, "Oh, please be careful, my dearest. I've had terrible nightmares ever since you told me about the trip. Harbor awful feelings about this entire dance."

Tried to think of something to say that would reassure her. Not a single thing came to mind. Could do nothing but kiss her cheek, climb onto Gunpowder's back, and kick away from the raw emotion of the moment.

Now, nearly sixty years later, still can't imagine how I would have justified the dark secret of vengeance, punishment, and death I carried on my shoulders to that wonderful woman. A secret that I could not ever allow her to know. Such personal failures of character torment me to this very moment. And, when a cold moon is just right in the sky, God sometimes comes to my side to remind me of all my painful shortcomings. Many's the night I've hit bony knees, bowed my head in supplication, only to find that the words necessary for forgiveness just won't come. Such is the curse I carry wrapped around the heart of a tortured soul. Not sure what Hell's really like, but over the years I think I've already served some time there.

16

"JUDGE PARKER MIGHT HANG SIX AT A POP..."

BACK IN THEM days, our raids were usually peppered with more than a healthy dollop of good-natured, nervous, grab-assedness and joshing around. Kind of thing men tend to do to take their minds off the enormity of the human problems and desperate situations that may soon confront them. Not on that trip. Not by a long damned shot.

Three of us caught a short run of the Kansas and Arkansas Valley Railroad over to Muskogee. Then each of us took an empty, well-worn seat on the M.K. & T. line's day coach for ourselves and our individual mountains of gear. M.K. & T. went south like a snapped chalk line right to Fort Worth, and from there on to Waco. We hardly spoke during the entire first leg of the trip.

Could detect in myself, and my friends, the distinctly understandable emotions of men who appeared on their way to attend the funeral of a dearly departed member of a close-knit family. Person who seemed most affected by the news of John Henry's fall was Carlton. Man's gloomy demeanor more than attested to his disillusionment with the situation.

Shudder came up through the floor as the M.K. & T.'s Baldwin ten-wheeler belched to life amidst a hissing cloud of steam. The massive iron wheels slipped, slid, then grabbed onto the twin ribbons of steel beneath our feet. Passenger, freight, and stock cars jerked and snapped into forward motion. The locomotive chugged as though in labor, slowly rumbled away from Muskogee's soot-stained, red-brick depot, then slowly snaked out of town.

Friends, relatives, and casual onlookers all along the rail line's advancing course waved and gandered in wonder as we flew by. Their faces glowed with awe as though witnessing the passage of some kind of enormous, prehistoric, smoke-belching beast bent on destroying anything unlucky enough to cross its fiery path. Took a spell, but we finally built up considerable speed and plummeted south through the Indian country like an anvil dropped in a well.

Spent most of my time gazing absentmindedly out the window, my fevered brain a bewildered knot of seething turmoil and upheaval. Locomotive rattled, clattered, and thundered over vast stretches of rolling, green, tree-covered hills and endless prairies dotted with dusty former buffalo wallows. We skirted the edges of the rocky-peaked Brushy, San Bois, Jack Fork, and Kiamichi Mountains. Roared across the Red River, shrouded beneath a curtain of burned post oak that drifted away from us like the melded spirits of lost souls.

Above the horizon to the west, as far as the eye could see, a roiling, anvil-shaped bank of slate-colored clouds churned and seethed our direction. Their diaphanous, knifelike, misty kin fled before them like escaping animals running ahead of a murderous predator. The jagged shelf of bad weather followed us all the way from Arkansas to Fort Worth. So, bushed from riding the rails, we decided to lay over at the El Paso Hotel for a night.

'Bout the time we disembarked at the Texas & Pacific depot, down on the south end of Houston Street, the heavens opened and dumped enough water on us, as Nate observed, "to match Noah's flood." Combination of the trip and the cool, wet weather stove me up to the point where I could barely walk.

Rained like a son of a bitch all that night. El Paso Hotel's sturdy building vibrated like a picked banjo string as winds from New Mexico howled through Tejas on their way to Louisiana. Bright blue pitchfork lightning fell from the tips of God's fingers. Earth-shattering claps of thunder followed on the heels of each near-blinding bolt that dropped from inky heavens. The thick, saturated Texas air crackled with electricity.

Now and again, the entire earth seemed to heave and shake as though the good Lord himself had leaned down from His golden throne and smacked the ground with one enormous open palm. Carlton observed as how the lengthy abuse of the earth was enough to scare hell out of any poor soul who might find himself stuck out on the Llano Estacado with nothing but a horse and a hat for shelter.

Nate stood at the window of our room and muttered, "Damned ominous, don't you think, fellers? Almost like the Deity's a-tryin' to tell us somethin'."

Carlton, who'd claimed one of only two beds in our room, pushed his hat up off his face with one finger, then said, "Swear 'fore Jesus, Swords, you're worse'n an ole spinster woman. Always lookin' for signs and portents. Remind me of my poor, long-dead, snaggle-toothed granny. Worryin' over this. Worryin' over that. Worryin' over what might or might not happen."

Nate puffed up like an angry bullfrog. "While I might legitimately be concerned with the weather, Marshal Cecil, sure as hell ain't nothin' akin to your poor ole granny."

Carl grinned, then said, "Why don't you lay your tired, railroad-abused ass down on the pallet them hotel fellers made for you and get to sleep. We've got a long day ahead of us when we reach Waco tomorrow." He pushed the hat back down over his face and, in a matter of minutes, sounded like the biggest blade at a local sawmill chewing through solid oak logs.

Don't believe any of us really rested well that noisy night. Next morning, think everyone woke up feeling like men who'd slept on the floor of a saloon where a bunch of waddies had played tenpens all night long. Then, beneath a stark, cloudless, crystalline blue, typically Texas sky, we loaded our red-eyed, groggy selves back onto another M.K. & T. coach, and chugged on down to Waco.

Claimed our animals at the depot. Led them off the boxcar, got saddled and loaded up in the middle of one of the busiest rail yards I'd ever seen. People, animals, freight wagons of every size, shape, and description surged back and forth like ocean waves lapping at sandy beaches during a hurricane.

"How many railroad lines they got comin' into this yard?" Nate wondered aloud as he threw a California-style saddle on his animal's back.

Jerked my cinch strap up tight, then said, "Think there's three of 'em, Nate. Waco and Northwestern, M.K. & T., and the St. Louis and Southwestern. Hear tell the town's one of the busiest shipping hubs in Texas. Got nigh on twelve thousand people living here these days. Can brag of the biggest red-light district south of Hell's Half Acre—place called the Reservation. So many saloons and gamblin' houses that locals and cowboys passin' through from the south often refer to the town as Six Shooter Junction."

Carl climbed aboard his horse and got settled. Came near having to yell when he said, "Busier'n hell on a Saturday afternoon all right. Where we gonna start, Hayden?"

Took some effort, but I was barely able to get myself

aboard Gunpowder. My ass still pained me considerable. Felt most like somebody was jabbin' me in the rump with a sharpened knitting needle. Hadn't been in the saddle more'n a minute when I got to wishing I'd brought Elizabeth's fringe-trimmed New York pillow along.

Said, "Let's just follow the rest of the traffic into town. Keep an eye peeled for the local constabulary's office. Gotta be a sheriff, marshal, or chief of police around here someplace. Keep in mind, boys, that there are times when these local Texican law enforcement types are just as helpful as they can be, and other times they're just obstinate as a half-witted, one-eyed Missouri mule. Let's not make any enemies first jump outta the box 'less it just can't be avoided."

Directed my comments at Carl mostly. He just pitched me a rueful grin, shook his head, and mumbled, "Ain't no problem for me, by God. You know how I feel 'bout hard-heads and horse's asses, Hayden. I can get along with Satan, long as he's reasonably civil."

"Well, that's just exactly the problem. Seen you get right brusque a time or two when a native lawman, for whatever reason, just didn't want to cooperate with us."

He stared at his hands. Studied crusty fingernails as if they were the most important thing in his life at that moment. "Ain't no good excuse for any kind of rude behavior, by Godfrey. 'Specially when we're looking for a man wanted in a triple murder."

"True, but I'd rather not set a fire under any of these folks until we can figure out just exactly what kind of esteem the locals have for John Henry and his family. Understand?"

Carl twisted his head to one side as though to say, "Horseshit," then nodded.

"No problem for me," Nate offered, "long as none of 'em wanna try'n take a dump in my hat. Stuff has a tendency to make my hair all stinky."

Nate led the way. Carlton laid back and rode next to me.

Could tell he was concerned and wanted to make sure I didn't overtax myself. On at least one occasion, he leaned over in the saddle and said, "Other than bein' concerned about my manners, or lack thereof, you doin' all right, Hayden?" 'Course I wouldn't have told him how bad I was hurtin' on a bet.

All too typical of most Texas towns of the time, Waco appeared to have grown up in the most slapdash way. Wagon yards, dance halls, parlor houses, saloons, liquor stores, lines of crib shacks, and various other types of sporting establishments that appealed exclusively to those of the hairy-legged persuasion were scattered at odd, unpredictable intervals along the bustling city's main thoroughfare.

A number of the two- and three-story structures I saw did not appear to have been in place for more than a few weeks at the very most. Their coarse, unfinished exteriors still seeped streams of sticky, aromatic sap. In stark contrast, here and there, a busy cantina or false-fronted mercantile, grocery, bank, law office, or other establishment with some age on it wore a garish, near blinding coat of yellow, pink, green, or turquoise blue paint.

We trailed an unbroken stream of wagon-and-people traffic from the rail yards along a wide, dusty, rutted thoroughfare into town. Busy city seethed with people that skittered about from every conceivable direction, like they were angry bees that had boiled out of a tree-bound hive after some honey-hungry bear had pawed around in their nest. Throng got so confused and knotted in places, it proved right difficult to keep moving at times.

Sat in one spot for nigh on five minutes while a couple of irate bull-whackin' teamsters pounded each other bloody for the amusement of all those who couldn't get around them. Never did figure out what the fight was all about. Didn't matter anyhow. Between the gambling, shouting, and sympathetic drinking inspired by the fisticuffs, the rowdy crowd thoroughly enjoyed the impromptu entertainment.

Constantly shifting tide of people and animals had stirred up a powdery cloud of dust that rose from the ground like a curtain and floated all the way up past the roofs of two-story buildings. Dense, gritty veil drifted back and forth, carried from one side of the street to the other, depending on where the greatest concentration of human activity was centered at the time.

Every other business available to the human eye was a saloon, bar, tavern, gambling house, liquor outlet, or parlor house. Drunks wallowed in the doorways and on the boardwalks, or stumbled about in the unrelenting traffic. Saw one feller covered in bluebottle flies and appeared dead, laid out between a horse trough and the boardwalk. Swarms of hard-eyed soiled doves called out from the open windows of buildings, alleyways, and covered porticos that fronted most of the gambling joints and booze halls.

Outside one place, named the Continental Bar and Saloon, caskets filled to overflowing with ice displayed three bullet-riddled corpses. Sign tacked to the wall above the dead men admonished the inquisitive passersby that such a fate awaited all those of LOW CHARACTER AND WEAK MORAL FIBER.

Feller with a box camera on a tripod cut loose with his flash powder as we eased by. Photograph he took was of several duded-up inebriates who stood in front of the dead men, smiled, and held up rifles and pistols as if they'd killed the poor pasty-faced bastards in the coffins. Puff of flash powder set my mount to crawfishing in an effort to get away from the light and noise.

Carl glanced over at me and said, "'Pears as how the law's a bit on the loose side 'round these parts. You'd never witness such a sight in Fort Smith. Judge Parker might hang six at a pop, but he'd never allow a display like this 'un here."

"Don't call this place Six Shooter Junction for nothing, from the look of it," I said.

Of a sudden, Nate waved, then pointed off to our left. He'd spotted the sign we were looking for. Reined our animals to a set of hitch rails outside a whitewashed storefront building with a sign over the door that designated it as the city marshal's office. Heavily barred windows distinguished the spot as a jail.

No farther than we'd traveled from the depot, thought I was gonna pass out when I tried to raise my leg in an effort to step down from Gunpowder's back. Stabbing pains shot from my knee all the way to my waist like Satan himself was poking at my tender behind with a rusty pitchfork. Carlton hopped off his animal and hustled over to help me, but stepped aside, gritted his teeth, and frowned when I pushed him away.

Hobbled up to the open entrance of the marshal's office. Bright red, six-inch letters on the wooden sign nailed to the doorframe admonished those who entered to WIPE YOUR FEET ON THE MAT BEFORE YOU COME INSIDE.

Took my time. Made sure I'd cleaned up before stepping into the office's well-swept entryway. Carl and Nate stomped their boots, then trailed me inside.

Shiny desk on the right, just a few steps past the open door, had not a single thing atop it—except a brass plate mounted on a piece of wood with the name HORACE SPENSER engraved into it. Well-stocked rack of rifles, shotguns, and other weapons hung on the wall behind the desk. All the firearms I could see appeared freshly cleaned and oiled. Entire interior space looked and smelled as if recently painted. Iron-barred gate leading to the cell block sparkled. Could hear men incarcerated behind the gate yelling back and forth from one of the cells to another.

Morose-looking feller, sporting the bleary-eyed, red-nosed countenance of a practicing drunk, pushed a broom around a table and set of chairs in the far corner. Several surly-looking men who wore star-shaped badges lounged there. They eyed us like we smelled bad or something. Broom pusher stopped, leaned on the handle of his man-powered dirt mover, and stared at us as though shocked that we'd had nerve enough to invade his just swept, personal, and restricted space.

A pinch-faced, hook-nosed popcorn fart loaded down with pistols was seated behind the desk. He glanced up, then frowned. His nostrils crinkled around the edges as though I'd just limped up and thrown a steaming, fresh pile of horse manure into his lap. Slouched back in his chair, he eyeballed us like we'd interrupted the conduct of passing the plate during worship services.

Tried my utmost to sound gracious when I said, "After-noon, sir. Are you Marshal Spenser by chance?"

Sullen jackass pushed back in the chair till it bumped against the wall. He chewed a splinter of wood from one corner of his twisted mouth to the other. Glowered at me as though a tumblebug had just rolled into his private king-dom and left a sticky trail from the door's threshold right up onto his immaculate desk.

"Marshal Spenser's outta town at the moment, gents." Word "gents" came out sounding as though he'd just de-tected something irritating stuck back between his tonsils and was forced to hock it up. "Left me in charge durin' his absence. I'm the chief by-God deputy here'bouts. You can tell me whatever'n the hell you thought you needed to dis-cuss with him. Just what kinda goddamn business you jay-birds got with the marshal?"

Knew as soon as he stopped yammering that the stupid son of a bitch might as well have got up out of his chair, walked around me, stood on tiptoe, and slapped hell out of Carlton, then pissed on his feet.

From behind me, and as friendly as he could have man-aged it, my friend snapped, "You gotta name, Mr. Chief by-God Deputy? Or do I have to come around that desk, snatch you outta your chair, then beat it outta your insolent ass?"

Inaudible groan rumbled around in my chest. While I agreed with him, I wanted to turn around, snatch his hat off, and smack Carl on the back of head like a smart-mouthed kid.

Mr. Chief Deputy's eyes glazed over, then damn near crossed. A rush of hot blood climbed from beneath his shirt collar, crept up a chicken-fleshed neck, and reddened his stubble-covered cheeks. Took about two seconds for him to look as though Carl had slapped him so hard his long-dead grandpa could feel the handprint.

Rustle of movement at the table in the corner went quiet, and damned quicklike. Sound of pistols being drawn and cylinders rolling to a hot charge when fully cocked tickled my ears. Knew without even bothering to glance over my shoulder that Nate had taken care of whatever problem he perceived as coming from the other deputies.

Insolent Mr. Chief by-God Deputy clawed the wood splinter out of his mouth, then flipped it across the room toward the cell house door. The jittery floor sweeper rushed over and snatched it up.

"Just who'n the hell you jaspers think you are?" the evil pipsqueak snapped. "Gotta lot of hard bark growing on your sorry asses to come strollin' in my office, all bold as brass, talkin' the kinda shit that can get a man kilt, and pullin' pistols on my assistants."

Eased our bona fides from my jacket pocket. Slid them across the desk. "Name's Hayden Tilden—Deputy U.S. Marshal Hayden Tilden. Gentleman holding pistols on your 'assistants' is Deputy U.S. Marshal Nathan W. Swords. Outspoken gent on my right, and behind me, is Deputy U.S. Marshal Carlton J. Cecil. We serve at the pleasure of Judge Isaac C. Parker, who's in charge of the Federal Court for the Western District of Arkansas."

Mr. Chief by-God Deputy leaned over. Pushed the leather

pouch of papers back my direction without so much as looking at them. Then he slumped backward, squirmed in his chair, made a gargling sound like he wanted to spit, and said, "Well, I don't particular give a good god—"

Carl snorted, "Hold on there, bud. My good-natured friend, Marshal Tilden, a gentleman and a scholar, was kind enough to answer your questions. Think it's time you told us just who'n the hell you are. Get started on another smart-mouthed rip, I'll be forced to stroll over there and kick your bony ass till your nose bleeds."

Arrogant city deputy almost went apoplectic. Thought the man's eyeballs would pop out and bounce around atop his spotlessly clean desk. As though being strangled, he finally gasped, "Name's Tater, by God. Deputy City Marshal Dudley Tater."

Nate Swords let a muffled snicker escape.

Tater hopped out of his seat—pretty good trick for a man his size, being as how he was loaded down with a Colt Cavalry-model hip pistol, equally massive Smith & Wesson cross-draw weapon, and a short-barreled sheriff's gun mounted at his back. Man had enough iron on him that we could've used him for a boat anchor. Went to shaking his finger in Nate's direction.

"Ain't funny, by God. Ain't nothin' funny 'bout my name. Been Taters in Texas ever since the very beginning."

Of a sudden, I noticed a barely discernible hint of derisive guffaws coming from the group of other deputies. Somebody mumbled, "Ain't that the God's truth."

Someone else whispered, "Damned lotta taters 'round these parts, for sure."

Thought Tater would have a stroke. He glared over my shoulder at the men in the corner, then yelped, "You sons a bitches best watch yerselves. I'm in charge here, by God. Marshal Spenser gets back, yer dumb asses'll be in a sling fer certain sure. Put you on my list, by God."

Heard someone else say, "Aw, shit, Dud. Please don't

put nobody on yer goddamned list. Fer the love a God, just ask the man what'n the blue-eyed hell he wants, then let these federal boys git on their way."

Tater glared at me as though he'd like to snatch my nose off and jam it up my behind. "'Cause evertime any a these federal boys show their faces, it ain't nothin' but a pain in the ass. Got our hands full right now. Busier'n a buncha chickens drinkin' water out'n a pie tin. We cain't help you bastards, no matter what you want."

Carl snapped, "Yeah, we saw three examples of how hard you boys are working just down the street. Looked to me like them poor bastards, all iced down in caskets a-gettin' their pictures took, mighta got themselves rudely lynched. Would tend to make a man wonder just exactly where you local lawdogs were when the sorry event occurred."

"Them boys tried to rob one of our banks. Did a damned poor job. Shot a clerk to death in the process. Waco Vigilance Committee stepped in. Took care of that particular problem. Caught 'em fellers over on the Brazos when they tried to get away. Strung 'em up yestiddy."

Shook my head, then said, "Look, Deputy, I don't care one way or the other what happened with the dead men on display in Waco's main thoroughfare. If you could just point us to the family of a man named John Henry Slate, we'll be on our way and outta your hair."

Tater didn't miss a beat. He tapped a nervous finger against the buckle of his pistol belt. "Don't know nobody named John Henry Slate."

Behind me I heard, "I do."

Turned to see a chubby, red-faced boy, who sported a moustache the size of a full-grown weasel, holding his finger up like a kid in school. He wagged the finger back and forth. "Old feller name of Slate lives out on the Brazos few miles north and west of town. Used to raise some horses. Think he got hurt 'bout five years back. Don't do much these days 'cept sit on his porch in a rocker. Seems like I remember someone a-sayin' as how he had a son named John Henry, but I don't think anybody's seen the son in nigh on a year."

"Ranch fairly easy to find?" Carl said.

Fat Boy nodded. "Can't miss it. Just follow the street outside goin' north. It'll turn into a single-rut country road that runs right along the river. Slate place is a couple a hundred yards off the road, 'bout six or seven miles up. Cain't miss it. Ole man'll be sittin' on the porch."

Snatched up the sheaf of documents and stuffed them back into my jacket pocket. Tipped my hat and said, "Appreciate the help, gents. Hope we didn't cause too much of an interruption in your busy day." Motioned Carl toward the door. We waited on the boardwalk until Nate had backed out and holstered his weapons.

Big grin creaked across Nate's face when he said, "Them boys came nigh on messin' their pants when I pulled down on 'em. Not sure they've ever dealt with anything quite like us, Hayden."

"Probably not," I said.

Carl stepped off the boardwalk, leaned against the hitch rail, then fished makin's from his vest pocket and started himself a cigarette. "What we gonna do now?" he said.

Snatched Gunpowder's reins off the wooden rack. "Gonna ride out to the Slate ranch. That's what we're gonna do."

Struggled to get mounted again. Eventually had to give up. Let my friends help me into the saddle. As we eased away from the Waco city marshal's office, remember thinking that I hoped to God John Henry wouldn't be at his father's place when we arrived. Killing him was one thing, but killing him in front of his father was something else altogether. Made my heart hurt just thinking about it.

17

"Sons a Bitches Feared John Henry . . ."

WHILE DUD TATER had showed himself a purebred horse's ass when it came to cooperating with fellow law enforcement officers, his friendlier cohort gave good directions. We pushed our animals out of town along Waco's double-crowded main thoroughfare and, in no time at all, found ourselves riding beneath a thick canopy of trees that grew in wild profusion along the west bank of the Brazos.

Nigh on exactly six miles up that primitive, rutted pathway, we stopped atop a rocky hillock where the road gently curved to the east. Off to the west, the trees thinned out, almost like a picture frame, and exposed grassy, wide-open spaces that appeared to go on forever.

Few hundred yards from the road, dead center of a plot of about ten acres of sun-blasted, knee-high grass, sat a ramshackle, dog-run house. Exterior board-and-batten siding of the dwelling had weathered to a misty silver gray color. Six-foot-deep covered veranda shaded a sprung-out sofa that sprouted its innards like growing flowers. Broken-down couch sat on the side of the porch farthest from that portion of the house used as a kitchen.

Number of windswept, paint-blistered outbuildings located in the fields around and behind the Slate family's home leaned from west to east as though on the verge of falling down. A worse-for-wear barn that had once sported a coat of bright red paint was now faded to rust. Several empty rail corrals flanked the main house on three sides. Except for the reclining figure of an ancient, white-haired man seated on one end of the porch, seemed to me that passing travelers might think the place vacant, deserted, perhaps even haunted by the ghosts of those no longer amongst the living.

Barely heard him when Carl muttered, "Looks like these folks had a right active horse operation here at some point. Shame to see it in such a state of disrepair." His comments sounded almost like he was thinking out loud.

Nate hooked one leg over the saddle horn, then put flame to a fresh-rolled smoke. He picked a stray sprig of tobacco from the tip of his tongue before saying, "Kinda eerie, ain't it? Ole man's a-sittin' right there on the porch just like the fat boy back in town said. Reckon he's dead, wind-dried, and folks have been ridin' by for years a-wavin' at a corpse?"

Slapped my leg with my hat, then stuffed it back on my drenched head. "One way to find out," I said.

Tapped Gunpowder's sides with both spurs and eased onto the overgrown trail that led from the road up to the house. Nate and Carl followed. Three of us rode right up to the rickety porch.

Tall, antique gentleman, wearing a sweat-stained tan Stetson and frayed woolen pants held up with red-striped suspenders over his patched long johns, clambered from the comfort of a run-down rocker. Sunbaked face behind a ragged, white beard blessed him with the kind of physical appearance you'd expect most Texans had in mind when they hit their knees at night and spoke with God. Had a Winchester propped against the wall next to his chair.

Old feller left a pile of wood shavings at his feet from the pine picket in his hand, and strode to the edge of the decrepit veranda. Mexican rowels of the silver spurs attached to his battered stovepipe boots jingled and chinked. He pitched the picket into the yard, then leaned a bony shoulder against one wobbly porch pillar. Light breeze played with the snowy hair that trickled from under his well-worn hat and onto his shoulders.

Yeller dog, size of a small pony, hopped off his end of the couch. Gigantic skillet licker eased up beside the old man, grunted out a less than enthusiastic growl, then flopped down at the gent's feet as though he'd been poleaxed. Biscuit eater lolled his massive head off the edge of the porch and stared at us sidewise as though hardly interested in the fresh smells his twitching nose detected.

Tipped my hat and said, "Afternoon, sir."

Godlike figure flashed a cautious, toothy grin from behind a droopy, pure-white moustache and shot me a curt nod. Deep, rhythmic voice that added to the divine image rolled up from his chest when he said, "You boys lost or somethin'?" Man even sounded like he might have just stepped down from the Pearly Gates for a brief, earthly visit.

Carl crossed his reins, laid them over his mount's neck. Went to rummaging around in a vest pocket for tobacco and papers. "We ain't lost, but you might help us out a bit. Your name Slate, by any chance?" he said.

Old gent ceremoniously folded a glistening barlow knife and slipped it into the top of one boot. Jammed both hands into his pants' pockets, then kinda hiked his britches up. "'S right, mister. I'm Josiah Slate. Exactly what is it I can do for you young fellers?"

Rummaged through my sheaf of papers and found Judge Parker's letter of introduction. Leaned over as far as I could and tried to hand him the document. "We're deputy U.S. marshals working out of the federal court in Fort Smith, Arkansas, Mr. Slate. My name's Hayden Tilden. These fellers are my colleagues in arms, Carlton Cecil and Nate Swords. We're here on official business."

One of the hidden hands came out of his pocket and waved the letter away. "Cain't read for spit, sonny. Least-ways, not well 'nuff to understand what you're tryin' to give me. Eyesight just ain't what it used to be, you know. You say it's so, I'll believe you. O-fficial business, huh? Seems to me as how you boys are jus' about a hoot and a holler and a right far piece down the road from Arkansas. What kinda o-fficial business you got with Josiah Slate all the way out here on the Brazos?"

Put my fancy authorizations away again and gazed into sky-blue eyes. "Hate to be the one to tell you this, Mr. Slate, but we're lookin' for your son, John Henry."

No trace of surprise in the man's creased, weathered face or eyes. "What's he done now?"

"He done murder, sir. Three times," Carl said. "One of 'em was a deputy U.S. marshal, just like us."

Slate grunted, stared at the toes of his used-up boots for a second, then kicked at a rusted nail peeking from the board beneath his feet. "Cain't say as how I'm all that sur-prised. John Henry's always been a wild 'un."

Came as something of a surprise. "That a fact," I said.

"Yep. Lost any ability to control the boy when he was still just a nubbin. Ran off 'bout a week after he turned fifteen. Only came back to visit a time or two over the years. Hell on wheels with the local law. Real problem from beginning to end. Some say he'd done a killin' or two afore now. Sent his mother to an early grave. Woman died of sad-ness and worry. Thought a time or two I might have to take care of him myself. But, you know, in spite of his rowdy, wicked ways, he growed up and turned into the kinda feller women love and men admire."

Nate grinned and said, "Sounds like John Henry all right."

The old man flashed a sad grin. " 'Course, he seemed to go downhill mighty quick after them Boston boys went and kilt his brother. Think maybe Alonso was the only person John Henry ever really cared anything about a'tall. Only one he ever bothered to listen to. Sure's hell didn't pay me no never mind."

I said, "Your son told me about the circumstances of his brother's unfortunate demise."

Corners of Josiah Slate's eyes crinkled. "That a fact. Well, he musta liked you a bunch, young feller. Don't think I can call to mind anyone else he ever confided in about the murder of my oldest boy and his family. Really find it somewhat odd that he unburdened his heart to a stranger on that particular subject. Never even bothered to talk to me about Alonso's passing. Leastways, not till he decided to go on his killin' quest."

Nate pushed his hat off his head and let it dangle down his back on a leather thong. He pulled a bandanna and wiped a river of salty liquid from his drenched hair. "Say he got kinda wild after leavin' home at such an early age, Mr. Slate?"

"Well, took a few years for him to grow into it but, yeah, he finally got big enough to start drinkin', gamblin', carousin' with loose women, gunfightin', and such. Hung 'round with some mighty bad company down in Waco. Came close to a stretch at Huntsville time or two."

"He favor any Waco spot in particular?" I said.

"Can't say for certain sure, but I heard from those as knew that John Henry spent wholesale lots of his life over the past few years in a joint called Pinky's Ten Spot Saloon. Evidently, the boy has a way with cards—or so the story goes. Seems he and that snake Pinky Falcone got to be good friends. And another tale that got back to me was all 'bout how he took a shine to a woman of questionable virtue what worked at Pinky's, name of Laticia Gallagher. Some have said the gal mighta been the cause of a rift 'tween him and Falcone."

"You sure 'bout all that, sir?" Carl said.

"Well, to be absolutely truthful, wouldn't wanna put my hand on the Bible, testify in court to the truth of it. Never had an opportunity to meet the gal, but I heard plenty a stories 'bout her and him and ole Pinky. Seems that gal got John Henry in plenty of trouble over the years. Then, oh, musta been almost a year ago, he came by late one afternoon. Said he'd prayed on it a mite. Made up his mind to kill the men who'd murdered Alonso. Said he might not come back. Then he just disappeared. Ain't seen the boy since. Your visit today is the first I've even heard from 'im since he left. 'Course ain't nothin' unusual 'bout that. Didn't see him a helluva lot 'fore he left."

After several seconds of awkward silence, Carlton said, "Wouldn't mind if we kinda took a look around, would you, sir?"

The elder Slate's leather-brown face crinkled into a pained, sardonic grin. "Hell, no. Go on an' look all you want. Won't find nothin' 'round here 'cept unused, rotted-down buildin's, barn full of field mice, empty corrals, and me. 'Course, if'n you do run upon John Henry, best be fast."

Carl stepped off his animal, threw the reins over a wobbly hitch rail, then slapped Nate on the leg and motioned for him to follow. They pulled short-barreled shotguns and, like men on a Sunday morning stroll to church, headed around back of the house toward the barn and other outbuildings.

Called out after them, "I'll stay here till you boys finish up." For almost a minute, I could hear them talking back and forth to each other, and one time Nate cut loose with a hearty laugh.

Our host motioned toward an empty rocker near his favorite nesting spot on the porch and said, "Might as well climb down and sit a spell, Marshal Tilden. Lotta corners, crannies, and holes to look into for anyone what might be a-hidin' back there. Figure your friends'll be a spell 'fore they get done."

Took considerable, pain-drenched effort, but I managed to scramble off Gunpowder and limp up onto the man's decaying porch. Got seated, swept my hat off, leaned back, and came nigh on to drifting off to sleep. Fact is, I must've napped a second or two. Compared to a saddle, the worn-to-fuzz cane-strip seat of that old rocker felt mighty good on my achin' behind.

Not sure how long we sat there. Felt a tug at my sleeve. Glanced over at Josiah. He held a dented tin cup my direction and nodded. "Buttermilk," he said. "Get it from a widder lady what lives on up the river a piece. Tall, stringy, long-legged gal. Nigh on seventy year old, but still has hair the color of hay. Eyes like chunks of turquoise. Think maybe she took a cotton to me some years back. 'Round the time John Henry's momma passed away, as I remember."

Took a sip from the cup. Wonderful stuff. "It's cold," I said.

He nipped at his own beaker, nodded, then grinned. "Yeah. Keep a big ole earthen jug of the stuff on a rope down in my well. Built this house around the well. Figured as how that way I wouldn't have to go outside for water. Made sense back in the days when we was still fightin' them murderous Comanches. And, a course, made life a bit easier in the winter, too."

"Guess you haven't seen any wild Indians 'round these parts in quite a spell."

"No. They're all gone now. But I'll tell you, Marshal, back in the days when 'em red devils used to raid all the ranches 'round here, that boy a mine was the damnedest Indian fighter ever lived. Sons a bitches feared John Henry from the time he got any size a'tall to 'im. Not sure where he learned shootin' and killin' way he did. Know I didn't teach it to 'im. Boy's been dangerous since his tenth birthday. Takin' him into custody ain't gonna be no Sunday afternoon picnic for you lawdogs. He ain't gonna go easy. Maybe not a'tall. You know that, don't you?"

"Oh, I've seen your son at work in a gunfight. No doubt in my mind we'll have a tough time with 'im. Just hopin' when we do find 'im, he'll decide to give it up and lay down his weapons." The lie on my lips burned so much, I had to take another swig from the cup to put out the fire.

The old man sipped at his mug again, then wiped frothy lips on a dirty sleeve. "Well, you just keep on a-hopin' there, Marshal Tilden. 'Course if'n you want my advice, I'd say once he finds out you boys is here, you'd best be lookin' for him to send some of his Reservation friends out to try and *reason* with you 'fore he does any face-to-face talkin'—if'n you get my drift."

"Reservation friends?"

"Oh, yeah. He's got lots of 'em. And they ain't the kind of folks you're gonna like dealin' with neither. Rougher'n petrified corncobs, ever one of 'em. And Pinky Falcone's the worst of the bunch."

About then, Carlton and Nate came back from their raid on the chicken coops and barn. Carl made a beeline for his horse. Slid the shotgun back into its bindings. "Nothing to see, Hayden. Might as well get on back to town. Maybe we can have a talk with that Pinky feller. Could be he's seen John Henry."

Sat my cup on the porch beside the chair. Mr. Slate stood when I did. Watched me hobble down the steps and struggle onto Gunpowder. Tipped my hat, and was about to pull away when the old man said, "You ain't come right out and said as much, Marshal Tilden. But I get the impression you boys ain't here just because of the Boston boys. Whatever happened didn't really involve them, did it?"

Rested my hands on the saddle horn and stared at my fingernails. Finally looked up again. Found myself locked into Josiah Slate's powerful, crystalline gaze. "Truth is, I killed the Boston boys. John Henry just happened to be there when it happened. No, we're here for the murder of a young woman John Henry kept company with, her lover, and a deputy U.S. marshal who died when he tried to stop your son as he ran from the scene."

Slate's chin fell to his chest as though I'd slapped him. Barely heard it when he said, "Good Lord in Heaven. Always felt as how the boy'd come to a bad end, but never believed anyone woulda had the need to tell me a tale like that 'un. Kilt a woman, you say? Damnation."

Pulled at Gunpowder's reins, started away from Slate's porch. He brought a hand up and motioned for me to hold my place. Lifted his hat and scratched. Socked the battered felt back onto his head, then said, "Bit of advice before you leave. Best be careful around Pinky Falcone, Marshal Tilden. Man's a cold-eyed killer. Cut your throat for the buttons on your vest. Carries a big ole bone-handled bowie in a scabbard at his waist. That 'un's just for show. Watch out for the piece of steel he hides in his boot. Longer, thinner, and sharper. Know for certain he's deadly with that blade. Hear tell, he favors gettin' up close to a man. Likes to watch the light of life go out in an opponent's eyes once he's done his deadly business."

"Damned good thing to know," Carlton said.

Tipped my hat and put the spur to Gunpowder's sides again. Cannot recall a time when I felt as awful as I did the afternoon we rode away from Josiah Slate's rambling, wobbly front porch. Couldn't help but like the old man. Had traits that reminded me of my own father. Liked his son about as much as any man I'd ever known. But the die was cast. Nothing I could do to change the future. And the future, so far as I knew it, was already written in blood. Only question open for me to puzzle over at the time was whose blood would end up being spilled. Made my head hurt just thinking about how the deadly dance would all turn out.

18

"... Gonna Blast 'Im Right Where He Stands."

COULDN'T HAVE TAKEN more than ten minutes to find Pinky's Ten Spot Saloon once we got back to Waco. Joint was one of the biggest combinations of gambling hall, billiards parlor, dance hall, and booze dispensary on the busy town's most hectic thoroughfare. Falcone's substantial building took up three stories. Appeared every bit of thirty feet across the front. Enormous set of curtainless windows flanked bloodred batwing doors on the ground level. Massive chunks of cleaned and polished glass offered passersby an inviting glimpse at the liquor, gambling of every conceivable type, and female glories to be had by simply entering.

Cowboys, whiskey drummers, gamblers, traveling salesmen of every stripe, along with painted women who hung on any available man's willing neck, flowed in and out of the tavern in a seemingly endless parade of people. Level of riotous noise from all the whooping, hollering, music from a three-piece band, pushing, shoving, fighting, and general tumult going on inside the place simply added to the hubbub and uproar already happening out on the busy street.

Had to look a spell to find someplace to hitch our animals. Ended up several doors down from the Ten Spot out front of a watering hole named the Texas Club. Huge sign, which covered the entire front of that particular building above its colonial-style veranda, declared the rough-hewn spot as WACO'S HEADQUARTERS FOR FULLY MATURED REIMPORTED STRAIGHT WHISKEY. A second posting, nailed above the establishment's door facing, declared that they sold ICE COLD BEER ON DRAUGHT.

Sun hung low in the sky by that point. Didn't feel all that good about leaving our heavily loaded mounts on a street filled with every kind of reprobate I'd ever seen. So we left Nate to watch over our animals and goods. Could see Carl's mouth water as we stepped up onto the boardwalk, passed the Texas Club's entrance, and headed for the Ten Spot.

Had to walk past the Gem Lunch Counter, Red Onion Saloon, the Eldorado, the Alhambra, and Buster Smeed's Arcade and Billiards Hall to get back to Pinky Falcone's gambling and whiskey-slinging establishment. Didn't appear to me that any of the booze halls, eating joints, or places that very obviously catered to a man's more carnal needs suffered from anything even vaguely resembling lack of business.

Felt like we'd stepped into a volcanic flow of sweaty humanity when we pushed the Ten Spot's café doors aside and elbowed our way to a polished mahogany bar that was every inch of fifty feet long. Must've been nigh on twenty drink servers working like field hands behind that marble-topped counter.

Smartly dressed, overly friendly bartender, who sported a shock of hair that looked like he'd put a beaver on his head and parted it down the middle with a broken wagon wheel, hustled over as soon as our boots hit the brass foot rail. Grinning bar dog wore a royal blue cravat decorated with a thumb-sized gold nugget as a stickpin, and had a greased handlebar moustache as big as a mule's front leg.

Feller rubbed a spot in front of me with a wet rag. He couldn't have been much more than two feet away. Didn't matter. I had trouble hearing him when he flashed a twinkling gold tooth that appeared the twin of his stickpin and yelled, "What can I do you for, gents?"

Yelled back, "Cold beer for me and my friend." Waited till he brought the suds, then dropped the money in his palm and yelled, "You tell me where we can find a feller named Pinky Falcone?"

He used the hand with the money in it to point toward the farthest table of the seething, rectangular-shaped room. "If you can get through the crowd, he should be takin' up space in that corner yonder. Does most of his business back there while he plays poker. Has an office upstairs, but he only uses that for special stuff."

Carlton and I swung our attention in the direction the barman had pointed, put the marble counter against our backs, and sipped at the icy mugs of beer. Big smile washed over my friend's face. He said, "God almighty, this is good stuff. Bet it beats the hell outta that buttermilk you were sippin' back there on ole man Slate's porch."

Wiped a foamy moustache off my lip and nodded. "Looks like we might need an ax to chop our way to the other side of this joint. People are jammed in here like cordwood piled on a railroad flatcar."

Threw the contents of my mug down in one gulp, slid the beaker back onto the bar, then wiped my mouth on my sleeve again. "Well," I said, "ain't gonna get there by just standin' here rooted to the floor like a couple of trees."

We pushed off the bar. Picked our way through the constantly surging throng. Squeezed between several card tables, each surrounded by a crowd of yelling, drunken spectators. Passed a faro operation, fanciest roulette wheel I'd ever seen, and a gaudy, colorful seven-foot-tall wheel of fortune that clicked loudly as it spun around to the delight of at least a dozen eager bettors.

Carl pulled at my shoulder and yelled into my ear, "Be willin' to bet there's more thieves in this place right now than the Texas Rangers got locked in all the cells down in Huntsville."

Easily spotted Pinky Falcone before we got to his table. Crammed as far into the corner as he could get, but there was no way to miss the man. He bore a striking resemblance to a gigantic, shaved pig whose stinkweed-farming owner had jammed him into a custom-made, three-piece suit with a ruff-fronted white shirt and black string tie. Horn-handled bowie with a foot-long blade lay across his tub-sized belly—right next to a Colt double-action Lightning revolver jammed behind a red silk sash.

On the little finger of the brute's left hand, a diamond as big as a pigeon egg grabbed all available light and threw impressive, flashing sparkles around the room. Man's completely bald head and hairless face glowed like a polished cue ball on a snooker table. Expensive-looking, gray-striped suit the size of a circus tent strained to keep all of him inside. Whole package had more than a passing similarity to a grinning, bullet-headed, heavily armed stuffed sausage.

Carl grabbed me again. "Tub a lard ain't been pushin' hisself away from too many dinner plates in sight, has he? Son of a bitch must weigh nigh on three hundred pounds."

Caught Falcone just as he gave us a quick, beady-eyed once-over when we stepped up to one side of the crowded table. As if by some kind of secret mind-reading act, or sheer magic, a stringy haired, hard-eyed, albino thug, who leaned against the wall near Falcone's elbow, came to his full, menacing height. Professional pistoleer and bodyguard brought both twitchy hands around and placed them on either side of the fancy, silver-and-gold-inlaid, oval-shaped buckle on his gun belt. Rabbit-pink eyes skimmed over me, then Carlton, and back again. Gunman wore his bone-gripped, silver-mounted weapons high on the hip, but reversed in their holsters similar to the way I'd seen in a famous tintype picture that purported to have been of Wild Bill Hickok. No doubt he was a dangerous man. One who'd kill without compunction or remorse.

Carl leaned up so close his lips almost touched my ear. Could feel his breath when he whispered, "Sweet merciful Father, Hayden, these bastards would kill the both of us for a plug nickel. You put the brace on Falcone. I'll take care of the gunny. Pasty-faced son of a bitch moves the wrong way, I'm gonna blast 'im out of his boots right where he stands." I nodded, smiled like he'd just told me something funny.

Falcone flipped the last pasteboard over in a game of seven-card stud. Ace of hearts had barely hit the felt when he ran a beefy arm forward, like a fat snake, and started raking in a mountainous pile of multicolored poker chips. All the other players at the table groaned, then reared their chairs up and away from the action. Several stood, kicked their seats back, snatched up anything they were lucky enough to have left, and stomped away grumbling.

Calm as the bottom of a fresh-dug posthole, and without actually looking at us again, the beefy gambler insolently stacked his chips and said, "Federal lawdogs, huh? Do somethin' for you badge-wearin' boys? Always stand ready to help the law whenever possible. Just the kinda upstandin', culturally responsible fella I am." Soon as that venomous lie oozed from Falcone's lips, he glanced at me and flashed a frozen, counterfeit smile.

Loud enough to be heard by everyone within fifteen or twenty feet, I said, "My partner and I do hope you can excuse the inconvenience, Mr. Falcone, but it would be most helpful if we could have a word with you in private."

The biggest toad in the puddle gritted his teeth, flicked another reptilian glance my direction, then went back to his money-stacking routine. He forced a wet, brown-stained grin around the ax-handle-sized cigar stuffed into one corner of his cruel-lipped mouth and grunted. "Well," he said, " 'pears I've pretty much cleaned these amateur card benders out. Think I could use a break. Maybe a glass of somethin' refreshin'. Hell, yes. I've got time for you gents. Be more'n happy to accommodate you."

The Ten Spot's owner placed both puffy-fingered hands atop the table, then pushed himself out of the cane-bottom chair he'd been punishing. He turned to the gunny. Said something I'd of needed ears like a south Texas bat to hear. As his bodyguard snatched a fancy-crimped, silver-belly Stetson off, and went to scraping his employer's chips from the table into the felt bucket, the big man shot each of us another furtive glance.

Carlton leaned over and whispered, "Cook that boy up and you could feed the Peruvian Army."

Falcone eased from behind the table and moved our direction with all the grace of an elephant that someone had attempted, but failed, to teach to dance on its toes. As he passed, he waved the gigantic cigar toward a carpeted staircase that led to the second floor. For the first time, I noticed the enormous man wore a pair of glistening, patent leather boots. To me those gleaming feet appeared almost tiny attached to a person of such colossal size.

We trailed along behind as our semigraceful host lumbered his way heavenward. Seemed as though any agility the man might have possessed on a board floor vanished like spit on a hot stove when he mounted that staircase. He trudged from one step to the next highest as though it took every ounce of effort he could muster from a sorely abused body.

Falcone's private office, while not overly large, could best be described as dark, richly appointed, and in an odd, cheap way, downright sumptuous. Thick Persian carpets, along with heavy Oriental tapestries draped from ceiling to floor on every wall—except the windowed one behind the desk—went a long way toward deadening all the commotion in the rest of his energetic business. Number of impressive cut-crystal oil lamps gave off the only available light in the room.

By the time our host, who had to sit down in shifts, finally got himself situated behind an imposing, oversized mahogany desk, Carlton and I'd already taken the seats in the guest chairs he'd proffered. Our bony rumps had just hit the plush and elegant feel of Moroccan leather when the albino barged in, strolled over, and dumped his boss's pile of chips onto the desktop.

Falcone slid the cigar from his mouth, glanced up at his ghostly-looking toady, then said, "Much appreciate your assistance, Philo." He raked the chips into a rough pile, then glanced over at Carlton and me. "Do excuse my uncommonly rude behavior, gentlemen. Money has a way of making me forget my manners. Please say hello to my assistant, Philo Burch. You gents might've heard of him. He's well known in these parts for his skill with revolvers. Deadly accuracte, and lacks the willingness to step aside for any man alive."

Threw Burch a less than friendly glance as he backed into his assigned spot near Falcone's right elbow. Cadaverous stack of human scum slouched with his arms crossed over his chest. Stance allowed him to tap the butts of each of his weapons with a nervous finger. Appeared to me as likely being the way he preferred to set up, just before jerking the big Smith & Wesson Schofield .45's on his hips. Tension between him and Carlton sent sparks back and forth across the room from the second the pair locked eyes on each other.

Didn't waste much of my time studying Burch, because I knew all I had to do was make the right motion with one finger and Carlton would immediately have the man dead in his boots. But a near nose-to-nose gunfight inside Falcone's tiny office held not one whit of appeal for me. Right quicklike, I made up my mind to avoid confrontation if at all possible.

Swung my attention back to the man who looked like he'd just eaten his brother and said, "We're in need of your help, sir."

Falcone grinned—same way the snake must've grinned at Eve in the garden. He pushed back in a grossly overburdened chair to the point where he'd almost laid down, then said, "Oh, hell, boys, Pinky Falcone's always ready to assist our gallant law enforcement officers. 'Specially you federal boys. Just what is it I can do for you? You name it. Pretty sure I can do whatever you ask."

Couldn't figure any reason to beat around the bush. "We've come to your fair city to arrest a friend of yours, Mr. Falcone."

Piggish eyes narrowed ever so slightly. "Friend of mine? Do tell. Don't sound good, now does it? And which of my many *friends* might you have your sights on."

"John Henry Slate," I said.

Knew instantly I'd hit a raw nerve. Falcone shifted in his chair as though he'd suddenly discovered a cocklebur in his balbriggans that was rubbing against something important. He tried to cover the barely discernible movement with a feigned cough to the back of the hand holding his cigar. He sat bolt upright, then leaned forward onto the top of the desk with both burly elbows and coughed again. For several seconds, he glared around as though looking for something, then ponderously leaned back again.

All the cumbersome movement and coughing set Burch off. He shifted from foot to foot. Shot a sneaky glance his boss's direction, as though nervously expectant of something in the way of guidance. When none came, he went back to flicking his cold-blooded gaze from Carlton to me, like a western diamondback rattler hemmed up in a tight corner. Whole dance gave me the sensation of sitting in a bathtub full of snakes as Falcone dumped more in on top of me and grinned like a thing insane.

Finally, Falcone cleared his throat, then hissed, "Well, damnation. That's a startler for sure and certain. Truth is, gents, ain't seen John Henry in more'n a year. Don't think he's anywhere around these part presently."

Carlton just couldn't resist. His anger over having to come gunning for John Henry had been steadily building ever since we stepped onto the train in Fort Smith. Could tell he was itching for a fight and, at that precise moment, the pair of brigands across the desk from us were just his cup of tea. Way down in the bottom of my soul, didn't know if I could stop him once he got started down the path of blowing holes in people.

My best friend twisted in his seat, leaned forward, and took a somewhat more threatening posture. "Well, if Slate ain't here now, he will be soon," he snapped. "We know for a damned certain fact this is where he's headed. 'Pears as how we just happened to beat him home. Might consider our visit today a courtesy call to let you know we're in town and that your old amigo is a wanted and desperate man."

"Wanted for what?" Falcone shot back.

Reached over and placed a calming hand on Carl's arm. "John Henry murdered three people up in Fort Smith. One of them was a deputy U.S. marshal. Western District Court of Arkansas takes a right dim view of those who'd kill a man in the U.S. Marshals Service. We're here at the behest of Judge Isaac C. Parker to see that he's taken into custody for trial, or killed should he resist."

The tension in the room suddenly shot up like a July Fourth whizbang. For several seconds, nothing in the room moved. No one spoke. The air around us began to feel as if a blistering storm of lightning was about to blow up. Seemed to me as though Falcone and his wraithlike gunman both stopped breathing.

The monstrous man across the desk from me eventually let out a sigh, then gasped, "Assure you, sir, no one here has had any contact with John Henry for some time past. Sure you'll find those as will tell you, John Henry and I parted company quite a long while back."

"I see. Well, then can you introduce me to a woman who works here? Old friend of John Henry's, I'm told, named Laticia Gallagher. Like to talk with the lady for a few minutes, if that's possible."

Response from both men proved immediate. Burch grunted like I'd hit him in the gut, and gritted his teeth. Falcone snorted, "Bitch don't work here anymore. As a matter of pure fact, she hasn't been an employee of mine since right after John Henry pulled his picket pin and went to driftin'."

Carl's lip peeled away from his teeth in a sneer when he said, "Well, where can we find her?"

Burch flinched and fidgeted.

Falcone raised a hand in an effort to still his henchman. "She has her own parlor house now. Musta passed it on the way into town, if you boys came up from the south. Can't miss the place. Painted yellow, with blue shutters, like some kinda damned Easter egg. White picket fence all 'round. She calls the place the Yellow Rose. Just ask anybody you meet on the street. Sure someone will be more'n willin' to point the way."

Sliced a quick glance back at Burch. Man vibrated like the plucked string on a Smoky Mountain hoedown fiddler's favorite instrument. Beneath my hand, Carlton's arm went cold as marble. Knew with absolute certainty that if I didn't get us outside and damned quick, gun smoke and blood would shortly be the order of the day.

Stood, snatched at my friend's sleeve, and tipped my hat. "Pleased to take your word on the matter of John

Henry's absence from the scene, Mr. Falcone. However, should he contact you, or even try to make contact with you, or anyone you know, we'd appreciate it if you'd get word to us as soon as possible."

Falcone's lip curled. "Now, that might prove kinda hard to do, bein' as how I don't have the slightest idea how I'd go about gettin' in touch with you boys."

Held onto Carlton and kinda pulled him toward the door. "Noticed a hotel back up the street not far from here—Beverly House, if memory serves. Can get a message to us there, or at the city marshal's office. One way or the other, we'll be easy to find. Probably be back around here to talk with you again 'fore this square dance has its last do-si-do called."

Falcone rolled his head around as though we'd finally got on his last nerve. "Beverly House's only a few doors from Laticia's place."

"Ah, glad to hear it," I said. Tipped my hat one more time, then moved in front of Carlton and whispered, "Let's get the hell outta here. Better we don't engage this crazed son of a bitch in a lead-pitchin' contest just yet."

With that, I pushed Carlton out the office door, then muscled him down the Ten Spot's staircase, and eventually back out onto the boardwalk. He breathed like a winded horse. Patted him on the shoulder, brushed his back off, then said, "Well, draggin' you outta harm's way damn near wore me out."

He snatched his hat off and slapped it against his leg. Rush of blood had colored his neck and face. Even in the waning afternoon light, his hair looked redder than usual. "Shoulda let me kill Burch, Hayden. Gonna have to do it sooner or later, I'd bet."

Patted my friend on the shoulder again. Tried to ease him back down the street toward the spot where we'd left Nate. "He can wait, Carl. He can wait. We've got other fish to fry right now. 'Sides, given that Marshal Spenser's out of pocket, I'd rather not have to deal with an idiot like Deputy Marshal Dudley Tater."

Lot of water's passed under the proverbial bridge since that dangerous evening. Many is the time I've wondered just what the outcome would've been had I turned Carlton loose and let him have his way there in Pinky Falcone's office. Often as not, I've even wished I'd gone ahead and let him gun both of those evil skunks. With the gift of time and total hindsight, can say without any doubt that I now know, for certain sure, I'd feel considerable better about the way that particular raid finally shook out if I had done exactly that. God Almighty, but I could've slept better, felt better, and been more at peace with myself for the passage of nigh on fifty years.

And maybe, just maybe, there wouldn't have been so much blood when the last scene of our tragedy finally played to its ugly and surprising end.

19

"... IF YOU DON'T KILL HIM, PINKY FALCONE WILL."

NEVER WOULD HAVE expected such consideration from a man so ill-tempered, but an oily-faced, irritable desk clerk at Waco's Beverly House Hotel treated us pretty good when we walked into his earthly realm and all but insisted on a room. Got so snooty at one point, before coming around, that I had to whip out Judge Parker's sheaf of bona fides and all but beat him about the head and shoulders with them. Could tell it really got his goat, but he finally admitted that he did, in fact, have one room left large enough for the three of us, and that if we'd leave him the hell alone he'd let us have the place.

Could tell we'd about pushed the man to his outer limits when he whacked the bell on his marble-topped counter and motioned for an old guy seated in the corner to come on over.

Ancient feller hobbled up, snatched his Confederate trooper's cap off, and bobbled his head. Clerk sneered, then snipped, "Mr. Beaudry will see you *gentlemen* to your room." He handed a key to the geezer and, as he flitted through a doorway at the far end of the counter, said, "Two twenty-two, Tobias."

Scarred and missing an ear, the codger tried to lift some of our gear, but when it appeared he just couldn't be of any help, Nate eased him aside with, " 'S okay, Pops. We'll take care of this stuff. You just lead us to the place where we can bed down."

While not much use as a porter, Beaudry proved a godsend. Man motioned for us to follow. Started talking as he mounted the hotel's staircase, and I'm not sure he stopped during the entire time we were in town.

He parked himself in front of our room's door, flashed a snaggle-toothed grin, waved the key, and said, "Mr. Smoot's somethin' of a pain in the rump at times, but he done give you fellers a damned fine room. One of our nicest, I think. Right spacious. Comfortable for all three of you boys." He unlocked the door and flung it open. "Only drawback's that it faces the street and, Sweet Jesus, it can get damned rowdy out there at times."

Turned out Beaudry couldn't have been more accurate with his assessment. While the room was large, airy, and well appointed, the noise level coming up to us from the board-walk below had the potential for making sleep nigh on impossible. Racket did finally die down around two in the morning. If memory serves, we all managed to get in a good nap before there was a knock at our door not long after the sun came up.

Nate stumbled to the knob. We were somewhat surprised to have the old soldier stand in the hallway, wave his cap, then say, "You fellers ain't up yet?"

A group groan let him know exactly how we felt about his question, but that didn't stop him. He strolled on in and pushed the door closed. "Thought you boys might need a good breakfast. Looked kinda wrung out when I brung you up last night. Nice place just down the street. Be happy to introduce y'all fellers to the owner if'n you'd stand me to a plate a eggs or somethin'."

Carlton lifted the pillow off his bleary-eyed face and said, "'S the name of this place, Toby?"

Beaudry grinned, then took another step into the room. Said, "Bessie's. Cain't get a better plate a groceries in Waco, gents. Ain't no other eatin' joint even compares."

Well, we let Tobias usher us on down to Bessie's Place a bit later that morning. Think he spoke to just about every other person on the street. Appeared the entire population of Waco knew him. Soon as we hit the door of the eatery, he introduced us to a loud, jolly, red-faced lady wearing an apron the size of a revivalist's tent. Guess she must've liked ole Beaudry 'cause a mountain of food ended up on our table. Stacks of pancakes the size of wagon wheels, whole slab of fried bacon, nigh on two dozen eggs, and enough coffee to wake up the whole of central Texas. Gal fed us so much we could barely climb out of our chairs once Carl had finally sopped up the last of his sunny-side up eggs.

We stood on the boardwalk outside Bessie's that first morning, rolled ourselves a satisfying after-breakfast smoke, and jawed around about what to do and how to go about our task. Carlton and Nate took turns supplying Beaudry with smoking materials, but refused to roll them for the old bum.

Put our heads together and decided Nate should watch Pinky Falcone's place. I told him not to do anything if he spotted John Henry, but to hustle back and find me and Carl soon as he could.

Second or third day out, Nate discovered as how Pinky had people following Carlton and me. Didn't much care for having shadows, but figured there wasn't much I could do about it. At the same time, Tobias led us all over town so we could talk with those he felt might be of some help in our search.

We spent long hours with bartenders, dance hall girls, shopkeepers, and local waddies who worked the cattle yards. Once, we even ran into a couple of the deputies who'd witnessed our encounter with Dud Tater. They laughed and told us how much they appreciated us putting the haughty, squirrel-headed bastard in his place. No doubt in my mind that everything we did or said to anyone got back to Falcone, one way or the other.

Week or so after we arrived, Carl stood in the street, shook his head, toed in the dirt, and muttered, "You know, Hayden, this here mess would be a whole bunch easier if we could find just one person willin' to bad-mouth John Henry. Just one. Sure you've already figured it out, but this case is beginning to depress the hell outta me."

Said, "You're right, Carl. No sense continuin' the way we're goin'. Wanted to get the lay of the land 'fore we bothered the lady, but I think it's time we spoke with Laticia Gallagher."

Early next morning, we headed for the Yellow Rose. Thought maybe our old soldier, Tobias, would drop out and find something else to do, being as how we'd about walked him slap to death that week. But he was waiting at the door as usual. And as soon as the Yellow Rose was mentioned, he lit up like a Christmas tree with a scented candle mounted on the tip of every branch.

"Jes' foller me," he said, and limped off down the boardwalk like a crippled tour guide parading ignorant Easterners around for a viewing of all the wildest spots you could see in a den of iniquity like Waco. Really didn't need his guidance, since we'd already passed the place at least a dozen times that week. But the old man appeared to be having such a fine time, neither of us could bring ourselves to run him off.

The Gallagher woman's parlor house looked exactly the way Pinky Falcone had described it. Coat of paint so bright in the morning sun you had to shade your eyes and squint just to look at the place. Tiny bell on the white picket fence jingled when we opened the gate and strode up to a fine, deep, shaded veranda littered with at least two dozen cane-bottom rockers.

Beaudry grabbed himself a seat near the house's entrance, and rocked back like a pig who'd just been put on payroll to do nothing but wallow in cool mud. "Cowboys what cain't get in the parlor on real hectic nights sit out here," he said. "Ofttimes I sneak down. Take a spot just to sit 'round and visit. Most of them horny brush poppers bring a jug along so's to build up their courage. Nerves make 'em right free with their liquor, too. And, best of all, you can see everthang on the street from here. Finest view in town, I think."

Carl pulled his pocket watch and snapped the cover open. He glanced at the silver-plated, two-dollar, fist-sized railroad ticker, then looked at me. "Little after nine o'clock, Hayden. Reckon anybody in there's even up this time of the mornin'?"

I pulled the screen open and tapped on the door. "Oh, oughta be someone stirrin' by now. Know these girls have a rough way. Lot of 'em sleep late. Even so, I'd bet the owner's already prowling around checking on 'em just to make sure last night's business went well."

Second time I tapped on the door, it popped open just enough for us to see inside. Attractive blond gal in a lace-trimmed camisole she hadn't bothered to close stood at the opening. 'Course, we snatched our hats off and tried to act like gentlemen. Not sure our efforts at false civility worked, as bug-eyed as Carl got.

Less-than-dressed gal put a hand on the doorframe and leaned her head against it in a most fetching way. Said, "Well, you boys are handsome devils. Ain't no doubt about it." She reached out and fiddled with Carl's vest buttons. "Tall, stalwart, and, oh, my God, you're both wearing badges. But, truth is, much as I'd like to take care of you, we won't be opened till 'bout five. Fellers are gonna have to come back then."

She made to close the door, but Carl stepped up and gently leaned his shoulder against it. "Not here for a good time, darlin'. Need to see the lady in charge. Laticia Gallagher, I think."

A confused look washed across the girl's angular, once pretty face. Then she shrugged. "Oh, well, guess you can come on in." She stepped aside and waved us into the parlor, then lifted one arm, which further exposed her near-complete state of undress. "Just down the hallway, other side of the landing. Mrs. Gallagher's office is the third door on the left. Knock 'fore you go in, though. She sometimes gets right testy if'n you don't."

Place was as quiet as a grave. But the hardwood floor, scarred and abused by thousands of pairs of Mexican rowels, creaked and groaned under the girl's diminutive weight as she disappeared from view. Left to our own devices, we made our way down the narrow hall and past the stairs. Tried to be quiet, but the springy boards went miles toward giving our approach away as surely as if we'd danced over while beating on an empty washtub.

Carl surprised me when he kind of swayed at the portal as though confused about how to approach the problem of getting inside. He finally gifted the door with several barely audible taps, then stepped away as though fearful the room might explode in his face. He needn't have been concerned.

A delicate, very pleasant female voice called out, "Do come in, gentlemen."

Stepped into one of the finest offices I'd ever seen. Airy and open. All the furniture and trappings were of the most tasteful and expensive that could be had at the time. A number of landscape paintings, of what appeared to be colorful Texas locations, hung on virtually every available bit of free wall space. Seemed as how most of them included rolling hillsides covered with the image of a particular, small, purple flower.

A huge, lifelike rendition of a rough-looking cowhand who'd just roped an angry longhorn graced the wall behind the lady of the house's fine European-style desk. Wall on the opposite side of the room from the entry was comprised of three six-over-six glass-paned windows surrounded by heavy drapes. Altogether, Laticia Gallagher's brilliantly lit nest appeared the exact opposite of Pinky Falcone's.

Handsome, Spanish-looking, Laticia Gallagher did not rise. She was tall, dark-complexioned, ruby-lipped, and ramrod stiff, and her eyes sported the same hue as the flowers in her paintings. The ruffled white collar of a modest, wine-colored dress tickled her chin. With the casual wave of one imperial hand, she invited us to come inside and directed us to chairs opposite her throne.

I suddenly felt as though we'd somehow intruded on the regal lady's privacy. Carl must've sensed the same thing, 'cause he came damn nigh on to tiptoeing from the doorway to the empty chairs reserved for guests. Man held his hat in both hands. Slid it around between anxious fingers. Can't imagine where it all came from, but my antsy friend got to acting like a fat chicken at a coyote convention.

The amazing woman flashed a quick, but somehow insincere, smile our direction, then said, "Jingle bobs on your spurs and all that iron you're carrying announced your approach as surely as if you'd both blown a trumpet all the way from the front door."

Soon as we got settled, she moved forward a bit so as to perch on the edge of her own seat. Leaned onto the desktop as though seeking reassurance from its weight and strength. Got the impression the lady also used the move to demonstrate that she'd given us her full attention. She opened a brass-hinged box, then held it out to offer us one of the machine-made cigarettes within.

Carl glanced into the fancy little chest, but crinkled his nose and declined by saying, "Thank you, ma'am, but no. We swore off smokin' anything lavender-colored some months ago."

An amused grin curled one side of our hostess's crimson lips. She fired her own smoke, took a deep drag, and said, "Well, then, what can I do for you today, gentlemen?"

Took less than two minutes for all the back-and-forth introductions and explanation of our mission. Longer I talked, the more agitated she appeared to become. By the time I finished with the ugly tale of John Henry's fall, Laticia Gallagher had literally pushed herself into the padded refuge of her overstuffed leather chair as though seeking shelter from something awful she wished not to confront. She stared into her lap, puffed on the lavender cigarette, and clicked a thumbnail against the nail of the middle finger of her left hand.

Surprised me a bit when she sputtered, "Are you sure he's coming back to Waco?"

Nodded and said, "Well, ma'am, this is where John Henry's remaining family and all his friends reside. Seems only logical to us that, once he started his run from the law, he'd come to the place most likely to provide him with aid and comfort."

Without looking at either of us, she growled, "Please don't call me ma'am, Marshal Tilden. You can call me Laticia, or Miss Gallagher, but don't call me ma'am, or missus, or granny—and don't make me remind you."

Carl went totally speechless. Took on the aspect of a man intimidated to the point of shocked lack of awareness.

Forced a smile of my own, and said, "As you command, Miss Gallagher. Please be mindful, though, that I meant no offense."

Of a sudden, she bolted from the chair, strode to the sun-filled window, stood, and stared out at the treeless landscape that rolled away to the west. She continued to puff away on the cigarette and blow smoke toward the ceiling. After some seconds, Carlton glanced at me and shrugged as though to ask, "What the hell's she doin'?"

'Bout then, she stomped back to her chair, stubbed the cigarette out in a smoky, glass ashtray shaped like a shriveled apple with the top cut off, then steepled her fingers under her chin. "You cannot imagine the danger to his well-being if he comes back here."

Carlton suddenly revived. "Oh, but we can, ma'am. Should he resist, we'll be forced to take the most violent and drastic kind of action. We hope to talk him into putting his weapons aside and accompanying us back to Fort Smith."

She shook her head. Not a single hair moved. "It'll never happen. Besides, if you don't kill him, Pinky Falcone's assassin most likely will."

Leaned forward in my chair. "We'd assumed Falcone and Slate were friends."

Her violet eyes seemed to sparkle. "Well, you assumed incorrectly, Marshal Tilden. Let me assure you, they hate each other. In my considered estimation, if John Henry does resurface here in Waco, it's because he's determined that one more killing won't matter much."

Studied on all she'd said for about five seconds, then said, "What's at the root of their animosity?"

"Me. And that's all I'll say about the situation, except to add that I no longer work for Pinky Falcone because our relationship had deteriorated to the point of intolerance." Then, as though spitting out a six-inch hair she'd found in her food, she added, "The man's a walking abomination. Don't trust anything he says and only half of what you can see that he's doing." With that she stood, motioned toward the door, and said, "This discussion is over, gentlemen. I have nothing further to add."

Back out on the veranda we had to shake Tobias awake. He dragged himself out of the rocker and followed us onto the street. Ten steps or so along the boardwalk, just out front of a billiards hall that was under construction, a curtain of gunfire fell around us like someone had pushed a brick wall over in our direction.

Hot lead chinked rough-cut, pine wallboards that seeped rivers of fragrant sap. Blue whistlers scorched trenches in the wooden planks beneath our feet. Cayuses, tied at hitch rails two doors in every direction, squealed, pulled their reins loose, and ran for safety.

I dove for cover between a horse trough in the street and the pool hall's yet-to-be-finished front porch. Carlton thudded down beside me. Scrunched up next to my back. The horse trough shuddered and shook as though it was being whacked with an ax handle.

Half a dozen bullets perforated the massive front window of the fragmentary pool hall. Sheet of beveled glass snapped at the bottom and the rest spilled out onto the porch just above our heads and behind us. Flew all to pieces in a shower of shards that sprayed out in all directions. Rolled in the dirt trying to get at our weapons, but before we could get ourselves armed, the dance came to an abrupt end. Roar of gunfire stopped as suddenly as it had begun and, in less than a few passing seconds, was nothing more than a fleeting memory.

Wild-eyed, missing his hat, and looking like he'd just seen Satan himself, Tobias hobbled up, leaned over, and said, "You boys still alive?"

Carlton rolled onto his back, ignored the old soldier, and stared at the sky for several seconds. "Well, that was semi-interesting," he muttered.

Joined my friend in his examination of passing clouds. Lay there with hands crossed atop our chests like a pair of corpses in a funeral home waiting for the loved ones to show up and talk about what fine fellers we once were. "Who do we know that might be behind such promiscuous gunfire?" I wondered aloud.

No hesitation when Carl said, "My money's on our dear

friend, and freight wagon unto himself, Mr. Pinky by-God Falcone."

"Think it's time we paid the man a more-than-serious visit," I said.

"Damn right," Carl growled, then hopped up and went to checking the loads in his pistols.

20

"You Done Went and Killed Three People..."

WE STOPPED AT the hotel long enough to grab up our shotguns and a pocketful of shells apiece. Damn near ran to the Ten Spot. On the boardwalk outside Pinky's place, we took a few seconds to breech our weapons, make sure nothing was amiss. Loud metallic clicks when we snapped them shut.

Grim-faced, with a snarl on his lips, Carl nodded at me, then pushed through the batwings. Followed him inside. Stepped off to his right. Splash of sunlight trailed and painted a bright yellow spot on the floor at our feet. We'd gone through the same deadly process so many times in the past, felt certain my partner and I shared thoughts in some mystic way beyond our understanding.

Took about five seconds for my eyes to adjust to the subdued inner lighting of the saloon. For some reason, the joint's usual crowd hadn't appeared that day. Place was damn near empty. Few gamblers here and there, along with

one or two scantily dressed women prancing about. But
Falcone's corner poker table was jammed full of men who
weren't there for the game. Whole damnable bunch glanced
over at us soon as we started moving their direction, then
scrambled to their feet. Men and women scattered in front
of us. By the time we came to a halt less than ten feet from
ole Pinky's clutch of thugs, Falcone, Burch, and four others
had lined up against the back wall like a pack of cornered
rats. Entire joint suddenly went so quiet you could hear
your own hair grow.

The fat man stationed himself slightly behind Burch and
in the middle of the group. Soon as my spurs stopped ringing, he fidgeted a bit, then waved his monstrous cigar at me
and barked, "And just what'n the hell's this all about?"

Carlton snapped, "Don't play the innocent, you fat
bucket of pus. You know exactly why we're here. Won't be
no more ambushin' deputy U.S. marshals in the streets after we leave here today."

A stupid, surprised grin creaked across Falcone's flabby
face. "What ambushing in the streets? Thought I heard
shots earlier, but none of us had anything to do with that."

Brought my big popper to bear on the group. Leveled it
up so as to cut between Burch and his lard-assed boss with
one barrel, and still be able to easily move to the others with
my second shot. Knew Carlton would do the same. He'd
take care of anybody I didn't put down.

"Not more'n five minutes ago," I said, "somebody peppered us with lead just outside Laticia Gallagher's Yellow
Rose."

Burch, red-faced and twitching like a man with a belly
full of bedsprings, shook his finger at us. "Well, just like
Mr. Falcone said, none of us knows the first thing about
any of that, you badge-totin' son of a bitch. So why don't
the two of ya haul yer sorry law-bringin' asses outta here
'fore I have to kill one or both of ya."

Falcone brought one hand up, as though to calm his

angry gunny, but he'd waited too long. Burch opened the ball when he let a hand drift too close to one of his pistols and, before you could spit, fate reared its ugly head.

I dropped the hammer on a single barrel of buckshot. Thunderous explosion sent a wad of heavy-gauge lead that hit Burch dead center of the chest. Mass of pellets picked the man up like a rag doll. Threw him backward into the wall. Blew the poor son of a bitch completely out of one boot. Blood, pieces of rendered cloth, and flesh decorated the wall as he slid to the floor in a bug-eyed, surprised heap.

Falcone squealed like a stuck pig, then went for his hideout pistol. Hell, seemed like all of them bastards went for their weapons at the same time. That's when Carlton cut loose. Blasted two of those ole boys to Kingdom Come at the same instant. Nailed them both to the wall right beside their fallen comrade, like the thieves on Golgotha.

My second blast caught Falcone in his ample guts. Near deafening discharge drove that big ole belt knife he carried into his belly like a hot railroad spike. Man screeched like a wildcat, then wobbled around the room grabbing at his belly in a futile effort to keep his innards from spilling out at his feet. Sorry son of a bitch screamed till my eyes watered; then he went down like a felled cottonwood. Floor shook when he hit. Worthless skunk rolled onto his back. Gushed blood and viscera for three feet around.

As Carlton blasted a third gunman down, I took two quick steps to my right, dropped to one knee, and reloaded fast as I could. Knew Carl was probably doing the exact same thing, but the cloud of spent black powder settled so thick I couldn't see him for almost five seconds.

Once the acrid, roiling haze finally abated a mite, watched Falcone's last henchman throw himself to the floor, clasp trembling hands together over his head, as if in prayer, and go to crying like a little girl. "Sweet Jesus, don't shoot no more," he moaned. "Ain't done nothing fer you boys to kill me like some kinda yeller dog. Swear it on the sainted Mother of the crucified Christ."

Carl moved in and went to kicking pistols here and there. Guess we'd been making sure those fellers were all disarmed for a couple of minutes when Dud Tater and several of Waco's other deputies came sneaking in. Whole bunch of them were wide-eyed. More than amazed at the devastation we'd wrought. Told Tater I'd write up a report on the event soon as I had a chance. Not sure the man even heard me. Swear 'fore Jesus, the poor bastard acted like he'd been put into some kind of hypnotic trance. Just went around the room shaking his head at the carnage.

One of his cohorts pulled at my sleeve and said, "Wouldn't worry 'bout no report, Marshal Tilden. Vigilance Committee, City Council, Marshal Spenser, town folk, hell, all 'em gonna be tickled slap silly when they find out what you just done."

Said, "Well, that's something of a relief. Wouldn't want Waco's local lawmen after me for this mess."

He dismissed my concerns with a shake of the head, then said, "Bet you can't find a single person within a hundred miles who won't congratulate you and say thanks. In fact, let me be the first." He shook my hand, pointed toward the door, then added, "We'll take care of this mess. Scrape what's left of these skunks up. See to their buryin'. Probably best you fellers get on outta here while the gettin's good."

Well, we headed for the boardwalk. Had just stepped into the street when Nate reined his animal up beside us. We were still in the clutches of anxiety, mind-altering tension, and bloodlust when he said, "What the hell happened?"

Carl propped his shotgun on one shoulder, then grunted, "Not much. Just some unfinished business in Pinky Falcone's joint. Don't think he'll be any problem for us from now on."

Nate stared at the crowd milling around the Ten Spot's front entrance. "Well," he said, "I 'uz just comin' to get you boys."

Leaned against his mount and pulled a piece of unfinished panatela from my vest pocket. "Why, what's up?" I asked around the stogie as I put fire to the tobacco.

"I 'uz sittin' over yonder watchin' Falcone's place like you told me to do, when I seen John Henry Slate ride up 'bout an hour or so ago. He got all the way up to the saloon's door, but musta seen somethin' over the batwings he didn't like. Retreated right quick. Climbed back on a bay gelding and headed north. Followed him out to his pap's place. Just now got back to town."

Raced Carl to the stable. Got our hammerheads out and got mounted quick as we could. Kicked out of town as if all the demons of a sulfurous Hell chased us. Scorched leaves off the trees. Left grass smoking along the ditches on either side of the dirt roadway. In less time than it'd take to sing a couple of Baptist hymns on Sunday, we drew up out front of Josiah Slate's homestead.

Old man and the dog didn't appear to have moved since our last visit. Climbed down, pulled all the heavy artillery, and eased our way toward the porch. Guess the three of us couldn't have been more than ten, fifteen feet away when John Henry stepped out of the kitchen and moved to the center of the rickety veranda. Had some difficulty recognizing him at first. Man looked like he'd been jerked through a knothole backward. Appeared completely run ragged to me—dirty, unshaven, and wild-eyed. Had a Colt pistol in each hand. Unexpected development stopped us dead in our tracks.

Gazed up into my former friend's tired but still smiling face. Said, "Got here pretty quick, John Henry. Must've been a helluva ride."

"Damn near wore three horses right down to the nub,

Tilden. Almost killed one of 'em. Got blisters on my back-side big as onions."

"Hate to hear that. Sure you'll heal up just fine in the cell in Fort Smith we've got waitin' for you."

His gaze darted from Nate to Carl; then he threw me a quizzical look. No nerves in his voice at all when he said, "Thought sure you'd give this crusade up after them associates of mine pitched a bit of lead in you boys' direction, Tilden. Told 'em not to hurt any of you—'less it just couldn't be avoided. Only wanted to put some of the old fear of shakin' hands with Jesus in you if possible. But, with men like you fellers, guess I shoulda known better."

Glanced over at Carl from the corner of one eye. Could tell he was trying to puzzle it all out. Hint of irritation in his voice when he said, "You're the one who sent people to dry-gulch us?"

John Henry's grin got toothier. "Well, not dry-gulch. That's a bit harsh, Carl. Just shoot at you some. Had hopes such an action would send you boys a-hotfootin' it on back to Fort Smith. Wanted you to get to figurin' as how maybe you'd done bit off more'n you could chew. 'Sides, we're friends. Didn't really want anybody to get hurt."

Could tell Carlton was getting hotter by the second when he said, "No point talkin' 'bout this. Our friendship came to an end on the banks of the Arkansas when you kilt DuVall Petrie. Gotta come on back to Fort Smith with us."

John Henry shook his shaggy, unkempt head. A sharp edge crept into his voice. "Ain't gonna happen, boys. Might as well make up your minds to it. Y'all made the trip down here to Texas for nothin'. Ain't goin' back to sit in the dungeon under Fort Smith's courthouse, then get my neck snapped by one of Maledon's pieces of oiled Kentucky hemp."

"You done went and killed three people," Nate said. "One of 'em a deputy marshal. You gotta go back."

Could see the tension growing in John Henry's neck and arms when he said, "Now, you know the one thing I do regret about all this is having to shoot that poor feller what caught me down by the river. Just doin' his job and all, I realize that."

"Put your weapons aside, John, and come along with us," I said. "God as my witness, I'll personally go to Judge Parker and plead for your life. All of us will. Guarantee it."

Tinge of deadly finality in his voice when our previous friend said, "Not today, Tilden."

Of a sudden, silent as death himself, Josiah Slate came out of his rocking chair, rifle in hand, then thumbed the hammer back. "Put them pistols down, son," he said. "Been enough blood by your hand already. Cain't have the deaths of these boys on my head as well."

John Henry coughed up a sneering snicker, but didn't even bother to cast the most fleeting glance in his father's direction. "What in the hell's gone and got into you, old man? Sit your narrow ass back down in that chair. I'll take care of this business."

"Think you've done took care of way more'n enough over the years, son. Time to pay the piper for all your evil ways. Done got away with plenty up till today. But this is where your sinful road ends—right here, right now. Cain't go an' kill three more people, right on my doorstep, and figure to get away with such an act. God won't allow it. Neither will I."

And then, sweet Jesus, he fired a single shot that hit his wayward son in the left temple and came out the right. The .44-40 slug pushed hair, bone, and brains through an exit wound the size of a child's fist. Seemed as though God jerked all the bones out of John Henry's body at the exact same instant. Vaporous spray of crimson still hung in the air when his lifeless corpse dropped, face-first, onto the rotting steps of his father's ghost-filled house.

Act stunned all of us to the point of immobility. Shocked me right down to the soles of my boots. Glanced over at

Carl. He'd dropped the shotgun to his side. Started talking to himself as though he'd lost his mind or something.

Sound of that blast was still hanging in the air when old Mr. Slate carefully propped his rifle back against the wall, then moved to his son's still warm body. As though so tired he could barely keep moving, he flopped into a sitting position on the steps next to the corpse. Patted John Henry's shoulder. Went to talking to him like he was still a small child. "'S all my fault," he mumbled. "Should'na let you leave home the way you done, boy. Headstrong on your part, weak-willed on mine."

Made to take a step his direction, but the emotion of the scene overtook me. I couldn't move.

Man started to weep. Tears rolled down his cheeks and dropped onto his son's back. "Shoulda been a better father. Wished a thousand times over I'd a gone to Waco. Dragged you back home. But that's all in the past. Just couldn't be havin' you murder fine young men like these right here on my very doorstep. No, sir, world's done had enough. Just cain't be a-havin' no more of your evil doin's."

Don't think the astonishment had yet hit me, even when we set to digging John Henry's grave. Buried him next to his mother in a family plot on a hill not far from the house. Iron fence circled nigh on a dozen graves. Josiah must've spent a lot of time there. Not a single blade of grass grew on those graves. Carl said something about me reading over the man, but, hell, I could not think of a single thing that fit the circumstances.

Had just got the body covered up when Josiah stared at the fresh mound of dirt and muttered, "Sometimes it's damned hard to be a father."

Watched as the old fellow stumbled back toward the house and resumed his seat on the porch—totally, and forever, alone. Knew when we rode away, bony-fingered death would come for him as well, and it wouldn't be long before that sad event occurred.

EPILOGUE

I'VE WORKED REAL hard over nearly sixty years trying not to think about the sad and singular events surrounding John Henry Slate's unfortunate passing. Had even fooled myself into believing that I'd managed to erase the whole ugly mess from an aged mind. Then, just be damned, Royce Turberville showed up at Rolling Hills with a face on him that brought it all back to me in a tidal wave of confusion and guilt.

'Course, I fully realize as how I'd sent more than my share of men to Satan prior to watching my friend die on his father's front steps. Dispatched a damned gang of those evil sons of bitches with no more thought than if I'd casually squashed a cadre of dung beetles under my boot heel. And, yes, I personally ushered a bunch more to the other side afterward.

Thing that really gets my goat, all these years later, Lord God help me, is that I went down to Texas with every intention of killing John Henry myself. That's what Judge Parker paid me to do, and I was good at the work. But you know, good intentions don't mean spit when you're standing there with the living man in front of you . . . knowing you're about to jerk the light of life out of someone you like. The doubtful quality of that life-changing predicament still nags at me. To this very minute, just not sure I could've killed the man.

Even now, sitting here in my barren room, staring out at the moonlit surface of the Arkansas, not entirely dead certain I could even answer that particular question if God showed up right at the foot of my bed and asked it of me His very own self. 'Course I still feel, as a matter of personally held belief, that no one of conscience knows for sure what he'll do in a life-or-death situation—not until confronted by it.

And, since I've veered onto the subject, might as well admit as how it still rubs my soul the wrong way that John Henry was the direct force behind Carlton and me killing a bunch of innocent fellers in the Ten Spot. Evil as he might have been, Pinky Falcone and his boys went down for something they didn't do. In an effort to salve my own sense of right and wrong, I've laid those deaths at the foot of John Henry's grave ever since the day he passed over. But, you know, there are times when I feel a profound shame for making a hasty, death-dealing decision that ended with gouts of innocent blood dripping from my hands.

Perhaps worse than everything else, when I finally got back home, I lied to Elizabeth. Hell, she didn't see the report I wrote up for Mr. Wilton and Judge Parker. Swore Carlton and Nate to secrecy, so wasn't any chance of her finding out what actually happened from them. Told her I couldn't find the man.

With my arm around her shoulders and a smile on my face, claimed as how, for all I knew, John Henry was still out riding the wide-open spaces of Texas. Free as the wind.

Chasing willing women down in Mexico. Playing checkers with friends. Drowning worms in the Nueces or the Rio Grande. At the time, that black-hearted deceit seemed the right thing to do. Today, I'm not so sure. 'Cause, you know, I fear that when God's call finally comes, I'll get to Heaven's gate and discover it's probably the greatest of sins to lie like that to your soul mate.

Well, damn, I'm tired. Tired right to the bone. Thinking about the past all the time just wears me the hell out these days. About ready to get my ancient old bones into bed. Need to catch a few minutes' sleep. The real ghosts are gonna start showing up shortly.

Trust me on this one, friends. Don't believe all them ignorant jackasses as want to tell you how getting old is about as much fun as chasing armadillos. In my humble opinion, advanced age ain't worth a damn. You end up with nothing but memories and, sometimes, those memories hurt way more than you ever thought possible.